KARMA

Karma Series Book One

Donna Augustine

Line edit by
Devilinthedetailsediting.blogspot.com

Copy edit by Expresseditingsolutions.com

For Lori…

Chapter One

People say karma's a bitch.

Personally, I really don't think I'm that bad, as long as you haven't done anything wrong that is. Seriously, it's not like I asked for this job. I wasn't even in my right mind when I agreed to the position. I thought it would mean I could stay on Earth. I did, just not how I'd hoped.

Like all contracts, it's the fine print that screws you, not the big fat text that offers you all the good stuff. As a lawyer, I'd spent years warning people about the fine print and now look at me. Stuck.

If I could just go back to that day, the moment when I made my first mistake and agreed. Unfortunately, of all the things I can do, time travel isn't one of them.

After I'm done here and my trial period has run its course, I'll go back into the system and get reborn. They say I won't have any memory of this, but I can't imagine forgetting the day I died.

I couldn't look away from my body, lying lifeless and dirty, blonde hair fanned out around the face. My face. I wasn't moving, not even a smidgen.

In contrast, the chest of the body I was in

felt like a broken accordion with a leak, flailing to get enough air in.

I fought through the fog, which clung to my thoughts, trying to piece the scene together from fragmented memories. I'd wanted a couple of days alone after my fight with Charlie, my fiancé, so I decided to visit a friend from law school who lived in Virginia. The last thing I remembered was looking out the window at the expanse of forest rolling by as the train sped along. We'd crossed into South Carolina a while ago and I knew I'd be home within the hour.

No, there was something else I remembered. A screeching sound, right before I flew from my seat, and then the sounds of screams around me. And not just raised voices, but the kind that are formed only from pure terror. They don't sound human, and there isn't an actor or actress alive who could fake them. These are the type, if you're unlucky enough, you only hear in real life and in situations that are usually deadly. It's the kind of sound that leaves a permanent bookmark in your mind.

I looked down at my hands, the ones that belonged to the body I occupied, not the mangled ones on the ground, covered in a mixture of dirt and blood. They looked solid enough but somehow different, and there was my body on the grass, my blue dress torn and shredded, my pink polished fingernails, chipped and ragged. I knelt down and pushed the few strands of hair away from my...its eyes. My black shoe lay about ten feet away. I must have lost it during the fall.

I looked down at my feet. Where did these tan sandals come from? And these pants? These weren't my things. Nothing was right. Maybe that wasn't my body?

I moved my fingers to its chin and turned it toward me, revealing my full face, then yanked back quickly. I stumbled in my effort to put some distance between us, even though I couldn't seem to look away.

I heard sirens in the distance, a lot of them, all combining to form the sound of dread. One siren could be anything. This many always meant something bad.

But I'd already known that.

I forced myself to look up and take in the scene. I'd been thrown thirty or so feet from the wreck. The streamlined train now resembled a shape closer to a discarded straw wrapper. There were more bodies laid out around its perimeter and a few people, dazed and limping around, not far from the wreck.

"Hello?" I screamed but no one turned toward me. Maybe they were in shock?

"They can't hear you."

I was startled by the nasally male voice coming from right beside me. I heard him clear his throat before he spoke again.

"Your human body is dead, Camilla. We

don't have much time and there are decisions to be made." His pen tapped, tapped, tapped on the clip board he was holding and I clenched my hands to stop myself from ripping the makeshift drum from his fidgeting hands so I could think clearly. I felt agitated and raw.

"Am I having a psychotic break from reality?" I asked as I turned to look at him. He was small of stature and wore Coke-bottle black framed glasses. He looked down at his digital watch and then back at me, with barely restrained impatience. I knew the expression well; I was usually the one wearing it.

"I'm sorry, but I'm going to have to give you the short version. You seem to be routed for express, so there simply isn't enough time to get into all the nitty gritty contract details—"

"I'm dead?"

"That body is, yes. You can choose to move on or—"

"Move on?" What was this strange little man speaking of? He was as odd as the situation, with bright red hair jutting this way and that from untamed cowlicks.

Maybe I was already in the hospital and under heavy medication.

"Yes, heaven, hell, perhaps somewhere in between. It isn't my department so I'm not privy to those details, or what happens after this point, just that there is something. So, you can stay on here or move on."

I reached out a hand and grabbed his arm. Solid. He looked down at where I touched him with unconcealed distaste at the contact but didn't comment. I didn't let go, just squeezed tighter. He felt like he was really here.

"Who are you? Are you an angel or something?" Maybe I was really dead. This isn't what I'd expected though. Where were the bright lights and people to welcome me? And his delivery needed some work.

"I told you, I have nothing to do with that. I'm not an angel. I'm Harold."

"If you aren't an angel, *what* are you?"

"I run the agency Unknown Forces of the Universe."

"And why would I want to remain here, as a ghost, working for you, whatever it is you are?" This was too bizarre to be real. No pearly gates or Grandma and Grandpa welcoming me, just a strange little red haired man? I had to be lying in a coma somewhere, drugged to the gills. I was hoping I was, because if this was death, a lot of people, including me, were going to be seriously disappointed.

He clucked his tongue as if having to explain all this was a bother. "No, not as a ghost. With a normal body. Why? Because I'm going to offer you a chance to make this world a better place. To fix the wrongs of the universe. This is quite a huge opportunity. I only recruit once or twice a decade and I can't remember the last time a human got the opportunity."

"I don't like this dream. This is why I didn't take the pain pills when I got hurt last summer. They gave me the worst nightmares ever."

"This is *not* a dream."

"How do I know that?" I probably shouldn't argue with him, but it was my nature. This was a dream. I should just change it. Couldn't I do that? If I was making this up, I was in control.

"Look at that." He motioned to my body like I hadn't noticed it or been staring already. "That is your dead human form."

"No, that's just a double of me made up by my mind." *It had to be.*

"Do you remember the pain?"

I shuddered as I thought of it. When the train screeched to a halt and I went flying through the air, right before everything went black, there had been a moment of pure agony, the kind that made you forget your name, your life, just made you wish for death, nothingness.

"If it was a dream, you would have woken. The human mind can't handle the idea of its own death, even in a dream. Do you understand me? You would've woken. Technically, you are dead. At least your mortal frame is."

He was right. If I were dreaming, I should've woken. I couldn't escape the logic.

I was dead.

I dropped to the ground, losing the strength in my new legs.

Dead?

"Now, will you work for me?"

"I don't want to be dead. I don't want to fix anything."

I just wanted to crawl back into my body and go on with my life. I wanted to get married next week, instead of being put in the ground. I wanted Charlie to wrap his arms around me as I told him how sorry I was. He needed to know I hadn't meant any of it. He'd been acting strange lately and I'd lost patience with him. I wanted to go to court on Monday and dazzle the jury with the defense I'd been working on for the last month.

I didn't want to move on. I wasn't finished!

"Before you choose, it also means possibly finding your murderer."

"Murderer?"

"The train was tampered with."

I'd loved my life, my family, Charles, everything. I was twenty-seven years old with a brilliant career ahead of me and someone had just stolen what would've been the best times of my life. I'd never be a judge or have kids. I didn't have any siblings. Who would take care of my parents as they aged?

Anger churned and welled up inside of me, growing into something I'd never experienced before. Pure rage.

Then rage answered the question. For the first time in my life, I let anger control me. And if I were to be honest, desperation as well. It wasn't my time, not yet, not now, and if I had to claw my way back in, I would.

"Yes, I will."

"Would you like some more details?" Harold asked, pushing up the glasses that had started to slide down his long thin nose.

"You said I'd have a body? I won't be a ghost, right?"

"Correct."

"Just tell me where I sign."

He held out his clipboard with an x marking the spot. "We need to leave now. Your current form is already in the process of becoming corporeal and this isn't a good place for the transition."

I watched as the lights of the police cars and fire engines started to glow in the distance, and I was sure that seeing my body bagged was something that would haunt me.

"I've got some details to handle first." I didn't know what I was going to do. How was I going to explain this to Charlie? I felt at my pockets for my car keys and then I remembered they were on my *other* body.

"No." Harold's thin hand manacled my wrist, as I made a move toward it. "We need to leave now."

"I need to get my things." I tried to yank my wrist free and realized he was deceptively strong.

"They aren't your things. They belong to the mortal crust lying there." His eyes shifted to where the crumpled lifeless form lay and then back to me.

I nodded. It didn't matter as I remembered my car was miles from here. I had a spare set at home anyway and I didn't want to touch that body again if I didn't have to.

I walked along behind him as the numbness set in. I felt as if I were mentally drowning and nothing made sense. I followed, not from any real desire to but because it was the easiest path while I tried to get a handle on everything. I was fairly certain if I were still alive, this would have been diagnosed as clinical shock.

We walked through the wooded area until we reached a road where a stretch Mercedes waited. A man got out of the driver's seat to hold the door open for me and, like a zombie, I moved my leaden legs forward and crawled inside.

I leaned back against the leather and thought, *what am I doing*?

"You're going to feel strangely for a few days while your soul gets acclimated to losing its mortal wrapping."

My hands, that didn't look like mine, started to shake. "I'm really dead."

"You aren't dead."

"The body lying in the field would prove you wrong."

"Your former body is dead, not you. Well, not exactly. It's sort of a gray area." He let out an audible sigh as he shook his head. "This is going to take some work."

"Where are we going?" I needed to get to Charlie. I needed my parents. I had to tell them I was okay before the police scared them. The idea of them having to ID my body...No, I'd get to them first.

"You can't speak to them."

"How do you know what I want to do?" I swung back to the little man I was disliking more every moment.

Harold looked at me, stone faced. "The reports on you said you had a fairly high intellect. Must I really explain this to you?" He looked at me for more than a few seconds and then rolled his eyes. "What else could you possibly need to do? I always forget how troublesome the transition is. Even if you could talk to them, they wouldn't understand."

"I'll make them understand." My voice didn't leave room for debate. There was nothing he could say that was going to stop me. Annoying little man.

"Can't say I didn't try." He went back to looking through his folder. I ignored his curious response to look at the landscape. I needed to get my bearings.

"Where are we going?"

"I thought it best to take you to your new

residence first."

"I don't need a new home. I have one with Charlie."

"The body that died had one. You can't use it anymore." He spoke slowly, with great emphasis on each word.

"Where is this new place?"

"Texas."

"No. I'm not leaving South Carolina." Or not for long. Even if he forced the issue, I'd walk back if I had to.

Again I heard him sigh and then he mumble something about transfers before he finally said, "Fine." He leaned forward slightly and yelled to the driver who he called Hank. "Looks like it's to be Murrell's Inlet."

The driver nodded his head.

"You're fortunate I believe in having options. Going to have to file more paperwork now." He shuffled through the small stack on his lap.

I didn't care. I'd be right where I needed to be. Beyond that, nothing mattered. I'd figure out the rest after I got to Charlie and my parents.

Harold settled back and then reached into a briefcase I hadn't noticed before.

"Here." He shoved a cell phone with a charger into my hand along with a key. "This is to your new apartment and a work phone. I'm already programmed in, as well as some of the other contacts you'll need."

I took the key, not bothering to tell him I didn't need a place to stay again. It didn't matter what he said. I was going home.

Before I even started strategizing about how I was going to get away from Harold, we were pulling into a driveway and I was getting kicked out of the car.

"Go in and lock the door. I'll send somebody by in an hour, if you're still there." The door slammed in my face and the tires squealed, leaving dark tracks.

I had been officially dead for almost an hour and, in all the times I'd contemplated what happened in the afterlife, there'd never been a bossy little redhead who abandoned me in the middle of a beachfront condo parking lot.

Chapter Two

The second the car was out of sight, I dialed Charlie's number. It hadn't even been a choice. He was the most likely to believe the story. If I could convince him, then he could help me explain it to my parents before they had to go and identify my body. The very idea of my mother and father standing over my body, as it lay there on a steel table...

I wouldn't think about it because I wasn't going to let it happen.

I used the work phone Harold had conveniently provided to call Charlie. He didn't pick up until the third ring.

"Hello?"

"Charlie, it's me. You aren't going to believe what just happened."

No greeting, no frantic "what's wrong," just dead air.

"Charlie?"

Silence.

I looked down at the phone to see "Call Failed" on the screen. No service? Shit! I walked around the parking lot with my arm outstretched until I saw some bars show up again and redialed.

It rang once and stopped.

"Hello?" I looked down at the screen. The call had failed. Again.

"No, no, no!" I hit the send button again. This time I didn't get a single solitary ring.

I kept redialing anyway, tripping on a dip in the pavement and losing a layer of skin in the process. I looked down at my knee briefly, just long enough to register that this new body could bleed, before I held the phone out and moved around the parking lot trying to pick up a signal again.

The possibility that I was having a psychotic break seemed more and more likely. Maybe there hadn't even been a train accident.

My head felt funny. Frantic, almost.

I turned around, taking in the small building in front of me. It looked to have about twenty units, all with their own entrances. I could see the sand dunes on the other side. I looked at the key in my hand. A three was hand written on the tag attached.

I knew this area well. It was just a town over from where I'd grown up and still lived. More importantly, Charlie's practice wasn't far from here. It was early afternoon. He'd be seeing patients right now.

A car pulling in startled me as they leaned on their horn, signaling I was in their way.

I moved onto the sidewalk, knowing for a certainty whatever I was, humans could see me. Harold had said I wouldn't be a ghost but if my human body was dead, how could they? Another check for the "psychotic break" column.

I could walk to Charlie's office. If I couldn't get the phone to work, I'd get there in person. If these people could see me, so would Charlie.

If I hurried, I could maybe get there before he heard from anyone else. This whole situation was crazy but he'd understand. Charlie always understood. Always listened to everyone. That's who he was. He'd help me figure this out and then he could call my parents.

If I was having a delusional break from reality, he was a doctor. He would know what to do. I just needed to get to Charlie. He'd make this better.

I broke into a run and realized I could move faster than I used to. That might qualify as a check in the "I'm really dead" column, but I decided to chalk that one up to adrenaline, since I didn't like that side of the list.

My sandals kept sliding off until I abandoned them on the sidewalk and proceeded barefoot.

His office was only a few miles away from here. I pushed my legs until I felt them burn and I then I pushed even harder. If I was dead, I didn't know how long I'd have before they identified the body and started informing the next of kin. And if I was crazy, at least I was getting some air before they locked me up in a padded room.

I was dripping sweat by time I saw his

building in the distance. My eyes frantically scanned the lot for his Audi. I was on the verge of crying when I noticed it tucked behind a huge SUV. Almost there, only five hundred feet left and Charlie would help me.

I was running across the street when I saw him walk out the door and head towards his car, phone gripped in one hand, keys clenched in the other. His face was a worried scowl. He'd gotten the call.

I tried to scream to him but nothing came out.

He was going to get into his car before I could get to him. I was going to miss him.

With a last push and everything I had left, I ran into the middle of the driveway exit with my hands up in the air, waving. He'd have to run me over if he wanted to get out.

His breaks skidded to a stop in front of me. But at least he saw me.

He rolled down the window. "Miss, please move. I've got an emergency."

He didn't recognize me. I'd already feared that might be the case. I didn't know what my face looked like but if my hands were any indication, it would be different as well. How could I explain that one away? A definite check for the "I'm really dead" column.

I ran around to his door. Before I could touch the handle, I tripped and skidded to the ground.

I looked up to see Charlie's face torn by indecision. I knew he wanted to leave but that's not who he was. He'd get out and make sure I was okay, a stranger fallen on the street.

I'd hoped he'd recognize me. That some part of him would feel the connection there, even if I was different. How could he not sense me on some level? Just a hint of recognition, like when you pass a stranger on the street who you think you know but can't put a name to. But when I looked into his warm eyes, there was nothing, not the tiniest shred of recognition.

Would I have known him if the situation had been reversed? I thought I would – hoped I would – but maybe not.

Just as I expected, he got out and knelt next to me, scanning me in a clinical way for injuries.

"You're okay. Just a couple of scrapes. I've really got to go."

The second he put a hand to me to help me up thunder clapped loud in the sky. And then a dark shadowing fell over him.

And I knew right then and there, without a doubt, that if I did manage to communicate to him who I was, he would cease to exist as well. It wasn't a knowledge I could explain or put in to words, but the moment he touched me, I felt the impending threat to his life. The moment we touched, it was as if death had laid its cloak upon my shoulders. I would be Charlie's demise. It didn't matter what my past was or my future might be, in this moment, I would act as his reaper.

I nodded and got to my feet, scrambling to put distance between the only person I thought might have been able to help me. With each inch, the feeling of death receded. Charlie would be safe as long as I stayed away from him.

Without another glance at me, he got back into his car and pulled out of the driveway. I couldn't move.

He was gone. My family, friends, career – all of them – just gone. In a single moment, my entire existence had ceased, except for one thing. Me. I was still here.

I'd never touch him again. Never speak to him. He was my best friend and I'd never be able to call him up and tell him about my bad day or share good news.

Correction, he *had* been my best friend.

"Get in," Harold said from behind me. "I'll have Hank drive you back."

I turned to see the Mercedes that had pulled up while I'd been otherwise distracted.

"Are you the reason I couldn't speak? Behind the feeling of overwhelming death?"

He shook his head and I saw a hint of weariness in his eyes I didn't think he meant to reveal. "You give me too much credit. Get in the car. I'll explain."

But I couldn't move. It was too much. Everything was too much. I felt like the world was spinning around me and I couldn't seem to breathe. My brain wanted to explode but couldn't burst through the bony confine of my skull.

I was losing my mind. My anchors to life were being torn from me and there didn't seem to be a thing I could do about it.

"No, you tricked me." I stepped away from the Mercedes but I didn't know where to turn. I wanted to run but had nowhere to go.

The door on the other side of the car opened and a man emerged. Dark clothing, dark hair, even his skin was tanned. It fit him. There was a severity to his presence that wouldn't have looked natural in white.

He didn't shut the door after he got out. I might have to add paranoia to the mental break column. All I could think of was he was leaving it open so he could drag me into the car with him more easily.

He had sunglasses on so I couldn't see his eyes, but I still felt the lethal intensity of his stare. I'd met men like this as a lawyer. I knew his type well and could spot it quickly. He wasn't the kind who needed a public defender like me; he was the type pulling the strings behind the scenes. I was used to defending the lackeys of men like this.

If I was no longer human, what did that

make him? Was he the source of the feeling of death before?

"Was it you?" I didn't expand on my question. Didn't think I needed to and he quickly confirmed my assumption.

"No. Death isn't my department." He rested his forearms on the roof of the car between us as he took my measure, just leaning there all too still. "I know you aren't thinking clearly right now but you need to come with me."

No movement. Did he think I'd be lulled closer by his false stillness?

"No. I don't."

I watched as he moved around the car, step by step he inched closer in my direction and I moved backward at the same pace, suppressing my urge to take off in a run. Afraid it might spur an instinct in him to chase.

"You need to come with me," he said, his hands reaching toward me slowly.

"I'm not going anywhere with you." Especially not you.

"You are going into what we call soul shock. It happens with human recruits."

He stopped approaching, stood still, and even put his hands in his pants pockets. I wanted to scream at him that I'd studied body language my entire life. His artificially relaxed stance wasn't doing him a bit of good. In fact, it made me positive he was about to pounce.

"Soul shock?" I'd sate my curiosity while I

played his game and figure out my next move.

"Yes. It's what happens as your mind adjusts to the transition." He was a study in calmness. Every line of his body, every muscle he possessed, was relaxed. He was good at this game of pretend. I was better.

He walked away a couple of steps, only to circle back and edge in a step closer.

"Not going to happen."

"You have to come."

"Harold dropped me off. Why do I have to come now?" This just can't be happening. I've been drugged and this is an illusion.

"Because this is what the new ones always do. We've given up trying to fight it. It's just easier to get it out of the way. But now you've got to come with us. You're starting to slip. I can't leave you here."

"I'm fine."

"You're hands are trembling. Soon, your entire body will be. That's the beginning. You aren't thinking clearly. That too will get worse. There is no alternative."

I scanned the area, deciding where I'd run when he finally made his move, which I was positive was imminent. He was much larger than me. If he got his hands on me, I'd lose.

I took another step back and he mirrored me with a step forward. I needed to expand the distance. I needed a better lead.

Then I spotted a couple walking down the

sidewalk.

He dropped his hands and shook his head. "They won't hear you. You're just making this more difficult."

"Yes, they will. Charlie did."

"Charlie saw you. He didn't hear you. And the only reason that happened was you were getting a little help from us. You haven't transitioned completely yet. You won't be fully here until you do."

"You people are crazy. That's the most insane thing I've ever heard."

"Then go ahead and scream."

I didn't need a second invitation. I let out a holler that should have been heard all the way to Florida but, even though there were people walking down the sidewalk across the street and cars passing continuously, it was as if I hadn't opened my mouth.

I gripped my head frantically, wishing I could force the situation into something comprehensible.

I turned my attention back to him to find he'd gotten closer. Harold was still in the car, observing everything from the rear window.

"Don't come near me."

He still approached.

"I don't know who you people are, or what, but you need to leave me alone."

"I can't leave you here."

His words had the opposite effect on me

than he intended.

"I told you, don't come near me!"

He sighed and shook his head. "Not the answer I wanted to hear. Always the hard way, no matter what we do, it always goes down like this with transfers. Look at your hands. It's getting worse already."

I didn't need to look; I could feel the tremors running through my body. Nothing felt right anymore. They must have done something to me.

I eyed up the expanse. I knew this area like the back of my hand. I could lose him if I got a lead on him.

I took off in a sprint but only made it a few feet. An arm around my stomach hauled me off the ground and swung me back around toward the car and the open door. I knew it!

I kicked and clawed at his arm but nothing budged him. I screamed out of principle, even though I feared it was futile.

I jerked my head back to head butt him and heard a grunt.

"Don't do that again. The only thing it's going to do is piss me off."

Now that I knew I'd found something effective, I tilted my head forward to try it again. He saw it coming though and I was on the ground and being pushed toward the car before I could take my shot.

"Get. In."

I'm not a quitter. Never have been, never will be. If he wanted me in that car, he was going to pay dearly for it. I clung to the frame of the door as he physically pushed me through. I felt stronger than I'd ever been but I was still no match for the man trying to force me inside and I was losing ground at a rapid rate. I flipped and kicked out with my legs, I came within an inch of my target.

He followed me inside the car and I immediately tried to make it to the other door but he caught me by my legs and yanked me back in.

"Don't break her," Harold said as I lay on my stomach on the one seat with a knee in my back.

I'd forgotten he was even there until he'd spoken.

"Don't bother getting up, Harold."

At least he was winded.

"Seriously, Fate. If you injure her, it's going to be a lot of paperwork for me." My cheek pressed against the seat cushion, I had a clear view of Harold as he waved the papers.

"Unless you want to dodge a kick to the groin, shut up. She's my problem now, remember? I'm trying to help her and she almost took me out," Fate said from above me, mostly out of sight but uncomfortably present in the pressure on my back.

Harold merely "huffed" in response but said

nothing while the bully on top of me continued.

"You knew this was going to happen. This is why we shouldn't have transfers. If I let her up, she'll jump out the door. Is that better?"

"I didn't get any other candidates. She wasn't my choice."

I was being pinned down by a psychopath. I felt like I couldn't get enough air in my lungs and I renewed my struggle in earnest.

"Stop." His knee pressed further into my back.

"Look at her," he said from above me. "She's a mess. You should just pass and send her on her way."

"It's too late now, anyway. She signed."

"You know as well as I do they never think logically right after they die. Just rip the contract up and send her back."

"I can't rip up the contract. She'll just have to adjust and deal until the trial period is over." Harold was getting more and more flushed as the argument over me continued.

"Give it to me and I'll do it." Fate's hand reached out toward Harold, palm up and waiting.

"I can't."

"Why?"

"Because it's gone already."

"You're lying. It's not possible." His weight lifted off me as he reached further toward Harold. It was just enough freedom to push the car door open and try and launch myself out of the moving car.

I saw the road speeding by inches from my nose before a hand on my shirt yanked me back in before I face planted it on the asphalt.

"Are you insane?" he said as he pushed me back onto the seat.

I opened my mouth to scream again but shut it. I'd almost tossed myself face first out of a car going fifty miles per hour. I would've broken my neck.

Maybe he was right, because that was a bit insane.

"And it had to be her?" Fate said.

"I showed you the memo. It had to be her and it had to be you."

"Why? She's just a girl. Murphy or Crow could've handled this."

"I don't know. She's a transfer. I'm not sure they could."

"Get off of me," I said.

He leaned over, his face close to mine.

"Are you going to be stupid? If you try and leap out of the car again, you are going to kill this body and effectively die twice today."

I didn't respond and he didn't let up.

"I can't breathe."

"Are. You. Going. To. Be. Stupid? Answer me."

"No."

"I don't know if I believe you."

"I'm not going to jump out of the car. Now get off!"

"And no more kicking."

I felt the pressure on my back retreat and I pushed up quickly. He was still sitting next to me, his side against mine, a looming threat. Or begrudging savior, considering I almost broke my neck, but I'd be quite happy to lose him and quick.

The adrenaline of the fight leaving me, I started to shake even more violently. Tears were flowing down my face and I didn't care. I was starting to believe I had died. I was pretty sure I was also having a mental break of some sort. Well whoop de do for me, checks all around.

I looked at Harold, trying to pretend Fate wasn't in the car.

"What was that back there? That feeling of impending doom when I saw Charlie?" Even with my sanity teetering on the edge, I knew it wasn't just in my head. It had been palpable.

"That was the universe at work. There are certain things that it will not allow. Know this, and know it well...it will never let you disclose any of its true secrets."

"What would have happened?"

"Exactly what you thought. That's why you stepped away, isn't it?" Fate spoke this time.

"Why did you just drop me off if you knew this was going to happen?" Even in my altered state, and I was positive I wasn't thinking right anymore, I could see it as the set up it was. They'd dropped me off knowing exactly what I'd go do.

"Transfers are predictable." I could almost feel the baritone of Fate's voice. "They all do the exact same thing. Sooner or later it happens so we try and get it out of the way early. It's normally messy but not usually this bad."

I sat back against the tan leather, tears still streaming down my face and I realized I'd made the largest mistake of my life. Or death.

I was loosing my mind and Harold was still sitting there, his lap full of papers, just another day at the office.

Fate didn't budge from my side. I could feel the tension in his body where it pressed against my side. He was waiting for me to *do something stupid*.

"I don't want to do this." I kept shaking my head from side to side. "I wasn't ready. I don't want to die. I'm too young."

Harold shook his head. "Few do."

Fate shifted next to me. "Death isn't reserved for the old. It doesn't sit idly by and wait for you to do everything you wanted. It comes on its own timetable, whether you're ready or not."

"Then put me back or send me wherever? Send me where I was supposed to go."

Harold barely glanced my way before he responded. "I can't. Not now anyway. Even if I use the trial clause to terminate you, there is a mandatory thirty day period before you are eligible."

He shuffled through the papers until he found the one he was looking for.

A sheet of paper was slipped in front of my face, his pen pointing to the spot that was in boldface that I knew stated a time period.

I pushed his hand and paper away and looked to the side.

"Thirty days. I'm stuck here, on Earth – alive but dead to everyone who matters to me."

"Yes."

A month wasn't that long. I could kill a month. I dragged a hand across my cheek. "If you could just drop me off at that condo and pick me up in a month when it's time—"

"No, that won't work. Non-involvement voids the termination clause."

I turned to Harold, ready to beg, flat out grovel if need be. "I made a mistake. I thought I was going to be able to talk to them. I can't watch them grieve for me. I just can't. I can do anything but that."

"I knew Texas would've been a better fit."

"The location doesn't matter. I know they're there." I was having a hard time speaking. My teeth were rattling in my head like I was stuck in a snowstorm.

"Look at her," Fate said. "She might not make it anyway. Not all of them do."

There was an edge to his voice that made me want to back further into the corner of the car.

"You should've passed when you saw it was a transfer." He leaned forward, toward Harold, and I got the impression he wanted to throttle him. The way Harold leaned back, he seemed afraid of that exact thing.

"How many times do I have to tell you I couldn't? I had to fill the spot."

"And I have to deal with this."

"This will run its course in a matter of days."

And then I stopped caring what they were saying. Something very bad was happening to me. I couldn't stop shaking or catch my breath enough to get a word out. I pulled my legs up and tried to shrink into myself. I closed my eyes and pretended I was alone. I needed to get a grip.

"Camilla, this will pass," I heard Harold say.

"And if it doesn't?" Fate asked. "She's a wreck and it hasn't even been an hour. Can't imagine what she'll be like tonight. And if she doesn't make it, it's doing irreparable damage. She'll be a nut case in her next life."

"We needed a Karma. She's it, for better or worse. At least for the next thirty days."

I wanted to know what he was talking about but I didn't trust myself to speak. And this was all *before* the real pain started.

Chapter Three

"You've got to eat."

It was him. Fate. He was holding a sandwich next to my mouth and I tried to shove his hand away. Everything hurt. It felt like every nerve I possessed was on fire at the same time. My skin hurt where it touched the bed. I'd turn but that just made something else hurt.

"You're adjusting to not having your human covering anymore."

Even the sound of his voice seemed to be louder.

"All of your senses are overly heightened right now, but this will only last another day or so."

I moaned at the thought. Another day? I couldn't take another minute.

"I feel like I'm dying again."

"But you're not. I won't let you." He pushed the sandwich to my lips. "Eat."

I tried to shove the food away but he grabbed my wrist. The firm contact on my skin made me gasp but no matter how I pulled back, he wouldn't let go.

"Eat." I took a bite of the sandwich just to get him to let me go.

"Please, just leave me alone," I said after I swallowed.

"I wish I could."

He wouldn't leave until I ate and drank some water. Then I passed out again.

***

I awoke in a strange bedroom that I guessed was in the condo I'd initially been given the keys to.

Sitting up, I felt surprisingly good, considering what I'd felt like a day ago.

I clearly remembered Harold driving us back to the condo. Beyond that point, all my memories were filtered through the lens of agony. I'm not sure how I made it to the bed I was now lying upon. I was in the same clothes I'd worn when this all began, however long ago that was.

I pushed greasy locks of hair from my face as I looked to the bedside table. A sandwich, sitting barely eaten by my bedside, jogged a memory. I'd begrudgingly taken a few bites and only because of the threat of Fate, the animal that had stayed here with me.

Nursemaid he was not. All I remembered was while I'd writhed in pain, he'd screamed for me to toughen up. That I was being weak. When I wouldn't eat, he forced it on me.

I felt his presence in the room and I pushed myself up into a sitting position.

"So you're up?" he said, looking at my disheveled state. His features were hard and angular, nothing you would describe as pretty, but still if he wasn't such a scary bastard I would have described him as handsome.

"Get out."

"You're welcome."

"You think I'm going to thank you?"

"Somebody will come by tomorrow to bring you into the office." He strolled out of the room and I heard the condo door shut.

So this was to be home for the next month. I looked around the bedroom. Everything was new, from the comforter to the dresser with the large mirror above it. There was an ocean painting hanging on the white walls, as if to clue you in that you were at a beach, just in case you somehow forgot. The place looked like a summer rental before it acquired that well-worn look after a few seasons of use and profit.

The ceramic tiles were cold under my feet as I crossed to the door, avoiding looking in the mirror, afraid to see the foreign reflection.

The rest of the place was quaint, with a small galley type kitchen and a breakfast bar that opened to the main living area. All low-end beach motif decor that screamed don't forget where you are. Definitely a summer rental. It made sense. There would be fewer long-term residents asking nosy neighbor questions.

Glass sliders overlooked a view of the ocean and the people tanning on the sand. They were as blissfully unaware of what might await them; as I had been, not long ago. I was jealous of them, lying there in the sun, just another day of living. I'd kill for one more day. A chance to say goodbye.

People often say a quick death is better. I guess in some ways it is, but it sure didn't feel like it right now. Long deaths have one big benefit. You get to say goodbye. Nobody understands how important that is until there's no time for words.

But after everything, life still went on, even if mine technically didn't.

I walked back inside, turning away from the sunny beach, full of people. I felt too bitter to bear exposure to their happiness.

I looked down at the table, the phone Harold gave me lying there, dead. How ironic? When I was alive, I couldn't stand to be without my charged cell phone.

I walked past without touching it. I couldn't find a reason to plug it in. It would only serve as a reminder of who I couldn't call and what those people might be doing right now, like burying their child. They might be staring at the ground and grieving for a fiancée who was still here, but might as well be just as dead as the body in the casket for all it meant to their lives.

I pulled out a chair and sat at the white-washed wood dinette by myself, wondering what in the hell I had agreed to.

My new body didn't let me stay in my

catatonic state very long. A hungry growl erupted from my midsection that made me realize, I might not be exactly human, but I seemed to have a lot of mortal needs. And I had to pee. That shouldn't be a big deal, but it was. I didn't know if I could go into the bathroom and *not* look at myself, but this body wasn't giving me any other option.

The need overcame my hesitancy and made it easy to make it into the bathroom without looking. Making it out was the problem. Who knew good hygiene would prove to be my downfall? If I could've just not looked up when I was washing my hands.

I let out a small sound when I saw the image. It was me. I knew this face, this body, that there would be a mole on my left knee if I looked, but this wasn't the body that I'd just left dead and mangled. It wasn't the face of my parents' daughter or the image of Charlie's fiancée.

Staring with gray eyes that were eerily similar to the ones I'd had before my death, I raised a hand to my almost black hair, so different than the blond I'd been. I touched my cheek, watching my actions mirrored. I was prettier than I had been in life. My eyes were a little bigger. I ran a finger across a fuller lower lip.

A knock on the door jolted me from my intense fascination with my new image.

Harold walked in before I could get there.

"I thought you weren't coming until tomorrow?"

"I wouldn't have, if you'd answered your phone."

We both stared at the dead phone sitting on the table.

"It's...dead. I know." Dead, dead, dead, just like me. I couldn't seem to get past that word.

"Please keep it charged from now on."

If it were only so easy to fix my own dead state.

"Why do I recognize myself when I don't look like I used to?"

He was already looking down at papers he was holding in his hand.

"Harold?"

He looked up, as if not understanding the question and then the details seemed to click into place for him.

"Oh, that. I always forget transfers don't remember." He scribbled on his paper a moment before he finally continued. He swirled a finger, encompassing me. "This is how you really look and will look in your true form for all of eternity. If you go to heaven, hell, purgatory or whatever is beyond, this is your form. That body in the ravine was just a shell, a loosely formed portrait. When your essence is squeezed into a mortal mold, it never matches up the same."

I toyed with a lock of my hair, still adjusting to the different texture. "So I've always looked like this on some level? I guess I figured you would give me a new body or something."

"Well, that's silly. You think we have stray bodies just lying around?"

"Uh, I guess..."

He actually rolled his eyes at me before he tucked his papers into the case he was holding.

"Do you have everything you need?"

I shrugged, having no idea exactly what I should need. "Not sure."

"There's food in the fridge and my number is on the phone if you ever get around to charging it. I'll be back tomorrow morning for you."

Chapter Four

It took me about two hours to convince myself that going out wouldn't be a bad decision.

I'd showered and changed into some clothes I found in the closet. They were all my size and, considering I was the only dead chick living here, I assumed they were for my use. I'd briefly wondered if this apartment had been used by another female employee, but they all still had tags. I was still the same size as I used to be, if a bit more endowed.

There wasn't a computer in the condo and Harold had given me a dumb phone, perhaps the last in existence. The thing looked like it should be dropped off at the Museum of History with its flip screen.

I didn't have money to buy a newspaper but I could still walk to the library.

But what was out there? The beach looked normal but what about other places? Would I see ghosts now? I wasn't a chicken, but I'd always been freaked out by that sort of thing.

Oh no. I *was* that sort of thing. Ugh!

Taking a deep breath, I opened the door, afraid of the monstrosities like myself I might find as I left the condo.

I stepped out and the sun was shining and the birds were chirping. It was the nicest day we'd had in ages. A couple of bunnies scampering about and it could have been the start to a Disney flick. I'd officially crossed the threshold into "out there" and it didn't look spooky.

I pocketed the keys to the only home I had. Normally, I would've hopped on my bike for a trip like this but, if not for that small reminder, walking along like this, I could pretend everything was fine. I could almost lull myself into believing I was simply taking a walk, like any other day in my life, not death.

The library was pretty empty but the kids were still in school, and if you were off, you were reading on the beach right now, not cooped up in a building.

I went over to where the newspapers were and flipped to the section I needed. There I was. There was nothing that could replace the feeling you got from seeing your name in the obituary section.

Camilla Fontaine, 27, of Surfside Beach, died in a fatal train crash. Camilla, a highly esteemed public defender, had dedicated her life to the defense of the under privileged. She is survived by parents, Lawrence and Debra Fontaine, and her fiancé, Dr. Charles Knight.

They'd buried me this morning. It was for the best it was already done. I wouldn't have been able to stay away from my own funeral. Some deep masochistic need would want to see the casket lowered and covered in dirt just to confirm it had happened.

I put the paper back and drifted out of the library, half incoherent and half devastated.

I wondered what my casket had looked like and how many people had shown up? What was written on my tombstone?

I saw a car I recognized pass and started to lift a hand to wave at Jimmy, the guy who delivered for the local pizza shop, but dropped it quickly. He didn't know me anymore.

I should just turn around and go back to the condo but I couldn't. I didn't want to sit there, thinking. I needed to see my grave. This wasn't going to be real until I saw my grave.

***

I didn't need to read where I'd been buried. There was only one cemetery our family had been using for all the long generations we'd lived in South Carolina.

I walked through the gates and toward the section where my grandparents had been buried a few years back. They'd passed within a month of each other. I'd always imagined Charlie and I would be the same. We'd have kids, grow old and wrinkly, with faces that showed a life well lived, and then move on together. If I controlled the world, no one would die before their laugh lines had time to set in.

I was almost on top of her before I saw her. It felt like someone shoved a hand into my chest and twisted with all their strength. My mother was kneeling in front of a tombstone that I knew would have my name carved upon its shiny new surface. I'd never thought about how such a simple act of carving a name can impart such finality.

I took a couple of steps and felt the grip of death settle upon my shoulders. I halted instantly and then backed away. The weight lifted with my retreat.

"I get it," I said to no one or possibly everyone. Who knew what exactly constituted the universe, "I won't go any further."

I found a spot to settle in underneath the shade of an old oak, leaning against the rough bark and grateful for the support. I watched my father approach her, his normally perfect Marine posture now slightly hunched, a physical ramification of the emotional weight he carried.

He stopped by her side and, with a hand on her arm, he used his own waning strength to help support her. I saw the expression of grief on their faces. She turned into him, and although I couldn't hear her, I saw the sobs wrack her body. His arms circled her as they shared their emotional grief with the only other person who could understand.

I slid down the tree, not caring how the bark scratched my skin, and sat at the base of the trunk as I watched them leave the cemetery. At that moment, I didn't feel rage or a burning desire for revenge, only defeat and a hollow sadness I couldn't imagine living with, but couldn't fathom how to fill.

Chapter Five

After a night of wallowing in a depression that threatened to destroy me, I'd awoken with a determination to not think at all. I wouldn't think of my parents, the career I'd lost, the friends I had, nothing. As stupid as it might seem, it was the only way I was going to hold it together and get through this next month. Too painful? Don't think about it.

I only had to get through a month. I'd spent at least part of my teens not thinking. I had the skill set; it was just a bit rusty.

I shuffled through the clothes hanging in the closet for something to wear as I determinedly didn't think about the bad stuff. Problem was, I had no idea what type of attire a job like this called for. I wasn't even sure yet what that job *was*, exactly.

I ruled out formal business attire, mostly because I couldn't find anything appropriate. So, will it be corporate casual as I mete out the universe's justice or jeans and boots so that I'm comfortable as I even the score?

It was ten A.M. when I heard the knock at the door and I still hadn't figured out what to wear. Even in death, I still struggled with wardrobe decisions. Some problems just never go away.

I didn't budge from the closet, knowing

Harold would let himself in and no one else would be here. It wasn't as if I were getting calls from friends. I was dead. The dead didn't get visitors. Even if I mailed an invite, no one would show up. They'd think it was a sick prank.

Harold's footsteps echoed through the condo.

"Harold, what should I wear?" I yelled out the open bedroom door.

His bushy red head popped into the room, then looked me up and down.

"What's wrong with that?"

"Jeans, flip flops and a t-shirt?" I looked at his white button down and bow tie.

"Yes, let's go."

Ah, he didn't like it; he just didn't want to wait. I'd file that information away for when I might need it. Harold's weak spot was patience.

"I'm not making my first impression in this." I shooed him out of the room and threw on a little black dress that would be appropriate for many different occasions.

"Ready," I said as I left my room. I went to grab my purse out of reflex, before I remembered I didn't have one. I settled for grabbing the cell phone and headed out to...who the hell knows?

I saw Hank waiting out front, with the stretch Mercedes, as I shut and locked the condo.

"So, boss, where we heading?" I asked once I'd gotten in the car.

"Work." Harold settled into the other seat and was nose deep in papers before I could get my next question out. Harold wasn't much of a talker.

I took the opportunity to get my own head together. Today was the first day I actually felt like myself and if I wanted to get through the rest of this month, there were certain things I couldn't do. Seeing my parents was one of them. That had been a huge mistake. I was stuck for now and I had to remain calm about the situation, and work within its confines, until I got out of here. I'm a logical, sane woman. I could handle this.

One internal pep talk and fifteen minutes later, the Mercedes pulled into the lot of an unassuming three-story office building. I got out of the car and took in the average structure on Highway Seventeen. I'd driven past this exact location hundreds, maybe thousands, of times in my life and never given it a second glance.

"This is work?" I slapped my hand against the brick. "This is where the powers of the almighty universe reside?"

"Yes."

When we approached the door, it had one of those black boards that listed all the residents hanging on the wall next to it. I read through the list quickly. It included everything from an accountant's office, counselor, and a dentist on the third, exactly what I'd expect from a structure like this.

"Here?" I turned from the board to Harold, who was already waiting for me just inside the door. "This is where *work* is? The universe and all that? Just sitting in an innocuous office building, on regular road, in the middle of South Carolina?"

"Yes, our offices reside within this building."

"Then how was I going to live in Texas?"

"Commute."

"From Texas?"

"Yes."

He pointed to the lettering on the large glass windows framing the door above him. "This building is owned by UFU, LLC. If you looked that name up on Google, UFU stands for Units for Use, LLC, but the real name is Unknown Forces of the Universe."

He stopped talking abruptly and moved inside. Harold wasn't much of a teacher. If he were human, I'd think he might be diagnosed as having some sort of social disability.

I circled through the doors after him into the average looking, if slightly dingy, lobby. The dark brown tile gave me the impression it hadn't been decorated since the seventies, and not well even then.

We made a left when we hit the carpeted hallway. We passed an ancient looking elevator that made me glad it looked like we were on the first floor and proceeded past several doors.

"You might be tempted to visit other offices, but I would discourage that."

"Why?" I had no intention of visiting, but you couldn't have a statement like that thrown out there and not ask why. Well, some people could, but my life was about knowing every detail of a situation. Being dead hadn't changed me much.

"Until you know what you're dealing with, it's inadvisable."

He stopped at the final door at the end of the corridor. The plaque by the entrance read "Life Management Associates."

We walked into a typical looking waiting room. It had chairs that looked like they'd actually been used and tables littered with fliers that read "Be the best you, you can be!" and "Find your passion, unlock your future!"

"This is Trudy." Harold pointed to the young redheaded female sitting behind the Formica desk—another fabulous piece leftover from the rocking 70s décor—in the front room who looked to be barely eighteen.

We smiled at each other in greeting as I followed him to an interior door across the room. He held it open and I walked into a space that could've belonged to any small company. If

I had to make a movie set for an office scene, this was exactly what I'd make it look like. There were desks scattered throughout and people milled about here and there, until they noticed our presence. Then one by one, all heads turned toward us. And stayed there.

Luckily, I was used to a courtroom full of people staring me down. These people didn't have a thing on Judge Arnold when he was missing a golf tournament because I had requested an emergency hearing.

"Don't mind their curiosity. We haven't had a new recruit for quite some time."

I nodded, wondering what some time meant to these people, with a frightening suspicion it was a lot longer than my personal frame of reference.

I followed him as he walked to the back of the long open office to a smaller managerial six-by-six and the only separated area.

"Please," he said and waved a hand toward the chair, as he sat behind the only desk in the room.

As far as offices went, it wasn't exactly ostentatious with its gray metal desk, filing cabinets, and brown commercial rug. The plain white walls didn't do much to help add any character to the setting.

The room itself held almost no interest for me, except for the door behind his desk. It was plain, like everything else in the office, but there was a one-inch crack between the bottom of it and the floor, and the most brilliant light I'd ever seen was shooting rays out of the gap.

"What's behind that door?"

"Retirement. When you finish your trial period, that is where you will reenter," he said, not bothering to look up from where he'd seated himself behind the desk. "I'd like to talk to you about your position."

I forced my attention to Harold. He was as odd as my hazy memory had hinted at. He looked like he should be strolling around an economics convention, not dealing in death and retribution. And I couldn't help but feel like there had to be more than what met the eye. If *this* was the guy calling the shots, there just had to be.

"Which is what, exactly?"

"Karma."

"Could you elaborate on that?" I repeated, squinting my eyes and staring at him in confusion. He still wasn't explaining exactly what I was supposed to do.

"Yes. Karma."

"I don't understand. I thought Karma was when you did something good, it would come back to you and the same thing if you did something bad."

"Yes, exactly."

"But you said it was my job? I don't understand what I'm supposed to do." How many other ways could I ask him? This guy was really in charge?

He leaned his head in his hand for a minute and I had the distinct impression that this was out of character for him. He mumbled something I couldn't hear except for the mumbled word "transfer." Then he shook his head, as if pulling himself back together.

"The universe has a certain balance it maintains, but it will occasionally fall out of balance. This is usually caused by people slipping through the cracks, who have a sort of natural immunity to the universal forces and need an associate to go in and manually adjust them. If they go too long, they can sometimes throw the system and balance off violently."

I nodded and smiled, still unsure of exactly how I was going to come into play. How would I fix anyone?

"Let me give you a very simple example. You are familiar with WWII?"

"Of course I am. I'm dead, not stupid."

"Everyone in this office tries to make sure that everything runs pretty much the way it should and nobody cheats the system. When we don't do a good job, you end up with people like Hitler. That's what happens when no one is paying attention. The better we do our job, the calmer the world."

"So everyone here is in charge of karma?"

"No. Just you. Everyone has their own

department. *You* are Karma." He pointed toward me dramatically, the way someone would try and accent a meaning to a person who didn't know the language.

"I'm not sure I'm adequately suited for this position. Even for a month. I'm more of a "bygones be bygones" kind of person. Don't you need someone a bit more vengeful?"

He looked down at the file spread on his desk. "I would disagree. Your file said you would be an excellent candidate."

"May I see that?" I asked, eying up said file on his desk. How much did Harold know about me? Everything? That was an uneasy feeling. Even the best of us had our secrets and even though I considered myself a decent human being, I didn't think I fell into the saintly category.

The file didn't look big enough for my entire life to be in it. It didn't even look thick enough for a short story. Maybe just a highly edited Wiki version?

"No, absolutely not." He shut the Manila folder quickly, as if I were going to jump up and try to peek. The guy took neurotic to a whole other level.

Okay, the file wasn't that important. I needed to keep the peace and simply explain in better detail how I'd made an error in judgment. Be nice. My southern mother had always said you caught more bees with honey than vinegar.

She had tried to drill it into my head since I was a small child. It wasn't something I'd come naturally to, that was for sure, but it was a valid tactic, even if that wasn't the lesson my mother had meant to instill.

"Harold, when I agreed to work for you, I was under the duress of seeing my dead body. You can understand how jarring that can be, right? I wasn't thinking clearly at all." It sounded logical enough to me, but I wasn't sure if he'd ever had the pleasure of dying and his manner didn't scream naturally empathetic.

He cleared his throat and I could tell by the set of his mouth that I wouldn't like the next words. "I'm sorry, but that's not how things work here. Like I told you, there's a mandatory one-month trial period. An active one-month."

He leaned back in his chair and pushed his glasses up closer to his face. His almost black eyes, artificially enlarged from the lens, stared at me in a bit of an awkward way. I wasn't sure if there was a bite to follow up his bark but his magnified beady gaze sure made the situation less than desirable.

Still, beady gaze and all, I had to try one last time. Perhaps a different angle. Regardless of my record, he clearly thought I was an idiot; maybe that was the way to go. I had no problem playing a stooge if it got me out of here quickly.

"As you stated, I'm a transfer. You really don't want me. I'm a horribly slow learner. The mistakes I've made in my life, geesh, you'd squirm if you knew." I twirled a finger in my hair for effect and wished I had some chewing gum to smack.

"Yes, I'm well aware."

He was? Hey, wait a minute; I didn't think I'd done too badly for myself. What were these jerks writing about me in that file?

"Fate will help you with that."

And just like that, I had bigger problems. I wasn't just stuck here; I was stuck with him. "The guy who *helped* me so far?"

"Yes."

"No."

"It has to be him." Harold threw his hands in the air, as if why am I bothering him? Not his orders.

"Then I'll work alone."

I'd be clueless but peaceful. There was something wrong about that guy. There was something too bossy or too intense. I couldn't even describe exactly what it was about him that was too much, but it was.

Even the brief moment I'd actually been in my right mind around him, it was as if his presence exerted some sort of gravitational pull, stronger than a normal person's. As if his intensity could throw me out of orbit. And I didn't want to go out of orbit. I had enough things to handle besides ping ponging around.

"Non-negotiable. I've got orders." Harold

folded his hands and rested them atop his desk, littered with paper.

"From who exactly?"

"The universe." His chin notched up a hair.

"Would it be possible to speak to this universe person? I'm sure they'll understand that there is a personality conflict." It was time to bump my complaint to upper management.

"No one speaks to the universe."

"Then how do you know what to do?" I leaned in a little.

"Simple. Through my orders." His eyes started to twitch.

"Which you get how?"

"My memos."

"Then you can send a memo to the universe. I won't work with him."

"I'll file your complaint but it won't matter. And don't forget, as I've already explained, it has to be an active month."

Twenty-five days. I've dealt with worse for longer. One case in particular came to mind. The guy actually tried to bite me when we lost. Harold didn't seem inclined to bite and he didn't get into my personal space. I could deal with him.

On the other hand, Fate looked like he might be the biting sort.

"Do the last five days count toward the thirty? Time served and all?"

"Yes."

"These first days were highly unpleasant. Do you think I could get extra credit for those? Maybe, I don't know, you could knock off a day or two? Like they do in jail for good behavior?"

He squinted his eyes and tilted his head. I was going to take that for a no.

"Follow me." He stood and headed out of his office and back into the main room.

We'd barely taken a step out the door when I saw him; Fate, supervisor from hell. His eyes met mine and it was as if all the cells in my body had decided to wake up. Which was quite ironic, considering I was technically dead.

The room could have been packed wall to wall with people and it wouldn't have mattered. It couldn't be attraction, because I hated him. In my human life, if someone had treated me the way he had, I would have set them straight and then never spoken to them again. But I couldn't seem to stop the awareness I had for him and it made me dislike him even more.

I broke eye contact first as he walked over toward Harold and me.

Fate stared straight at me but didn't actually acknowledge me, not even the slightest tilt of the head. But he dismissed me pretty clearly when he turned and spoke only to Harold.

"Anything with her?"

"Doesn't appear to be, but it's early."

"Any what? You can direct your questions

about me directly to me."

He shifted his attention fully back to me and I wished I'd kept my temper in check. His presence was more intense up close. I should've just shut up and let him go along his not-so-merry way.

The first time I'd interacted with him, I hadn't been in my right mind. Like so many things in retrospect, it was crystal clear just how out of whack I'd been. I never would've agreed to this if I had been thinking clearly.

Then, when I'd been writhing in pain, I couldn't see past the intensity of what I was feeling.

This was technically my second coherent contact with Fate and the full impact of his presence seemed to get worse with subsequent exposures. Twenty-five days was suddenly a lifetime.

"Have you noticed anything different, yet?"

"What?"

"You said to address you, so I am. Have you noticed anything different?"

He *knew* he was making me uncomfortable. The corner of his mouth quirked up. Worse than him doing it on purpose was that little twitch of the lips meant he didn't care if I knew he was doing it on purpose. Maybe he even wanted me to know? What was this guy's problem? Decent folk didn't openly mock you and admit to it. They would feign ignorance. Rude man!

"Nope, nothing out of the ordinary here." And there was no way I was going to let him know how much he was indeed getting under my skin. I raise your smirk with a full on, double row of pearly whites smile. Take that, you ogre in man's clothing!

He didn't respond, just turned back to Harold. "Your office," he said and then strode off in that direction, making me wonder who was really in charge here.

Harold claimed to be calling the shots, but it certainly didn't look like that right now. And if Fate was the secret power holder, man, things just weren't looking good. He seemed to dislike me even more than Harold

"Luck?" Harold said and waved over a raven-haired beauty with the reddest lips I'd ever seen outside a Vogue Magazine, and not an interior spread but a glossy bright cover.

She walked over toward us, hips sashaying in a way that would captivate any human male alive. I say alive since she didn't seem to have any affect on Harold. Every time I thought I peeled another layer of the onion back on this guy, he revealed another skin of strange.

"Would you show Karma around?"

Karma, the truth of the name settled into my skin like a lotion I was allergic to.

"I've got a few matters that need my immediate attention." He nodded to us and made to leave.

"Wait, what about my killer? When are we going to go get him?"

"Your killer?"

"Yes. You said I could get my killer."

"Sure. Try and get him."

"How?"

"I don't know." He shrugged and threw his hands up, in a "why are you asking me" kind of way.

"But you said—"

"That you could right the wrongs, not me. I don't do that sort of thing."

"But I don't know *how* to do anything."

He looked toward his office, where Fate waited. "That certainly isn't my shortcoming."

I watched Harold walk away from me and directly toward the office where Fate had basically ordered his presence. Dead or not, shouldn't there be some sort of professional standards?

And another weird thing was Fate and Harold's relationship. I couldn't quite put my finger on what was wrong but there was tension there and I couldn't tell if they liked each other or not. Normally, when I look at two people, and see them interact, it's obvious. Not with those two.

Luck drew my attention back as she clucked her tongue. I found her looking me up and down in an appraising way, which I ignored, trying to make the best of the next month. After all, it would be nice if I didn't have to hate everyone I worked with. Even a dead girl needs a friend.

I plastered on another fake smile. "I'm Camilla. It's very nice to meet you."

Her lips formed a moue as she didn't reply but kept appraising me. "Yes, you are definitely a transfer, all right."

I wasn't sure what she was seeing that I didn't. What was I doing that screamed different? Broadcasted me as the transfer they kept labeling me?

"I just don't know why he did it, not that he listens to anyone," she continued.

"What exactly is a transfer and what's so bad about it?"

"Murphy!" she called out to a man wearing a long tan coat and a hat that would have looked normal on Humphrey Bogart.

We both took each other in as he walked over. He looked like he was in his early forties, with patches of gray that were winning the war for real estate at his temples. Did that mean these bodies aged? No, I didn't think so. Harold said this is what I'd look like throughout time. Murphy just got a bum deal I guess.

"Karma?" he asked as if he already knew the answer.

"Actually, it's Camilla."

"We all go by our call signs, here," he explained.

Luck hopped up on the desk, crossing her legs and showing off a really nice set of five inch red heels.

She punched Murphy in the arm to get his attention. "Tell Karma what a transfer is. She's got questions."

"A transfer is someone that was mortal first. After they were created into existence, they took a human shape for a while before signing on here."

"Neither of you were?"

"Nobody in this office was. We haven't had a transfer in a while. Doesn't tend to work out."

"Why?" This didn't bode well.

"When your being is first created, you understand the universe and the surroundings. When you're placed into a mortal body, the human shell insulates you a bit and your connection is dulled. It's like listening to someone talk under water. Even when you are broken from the shell, you're still at a disadvantage." He sat down on the desk next to Luck. I could tell they were tight knit, in a buddy kind of way.

"What happened to the other transfers?" I asked, watching the two of them for reactions.

"Almost all of them quit at the end of the trial period."

"You said almost all. What about the ones that didn't? Why aren't they here?"

Murphy started fiddling with a pencil he'd

picked up off the desk and Luck nudged him. "You tell her."

"Why do I always get stuck doing this?" Murphy asked in an annoyed voice.

"You talk to the new people and I help you supplement your income. That's the way it works. Are you trying to break our deal? It's only been seventy-five years. I should've known you'd renege."

"I'm not breaking anything."

"Then keep talking!"

Murphy turned his attention back to me now that their squabble seemed to be resolved.

"Sometimes the things we do can be dangerous when you aren't as in tune. Accidents have happened." He was back to fiddling with his pencil and the two of them were looking everywhere but at me.

"So we can die again?"

"There's death and then there's nothing. No retirement to a cushy mortal life, maybe a famous actor or just incredibly rich. Your energy is reabsorbed but you aren't actually anything, anymore."

Wow, this really sucked. I was recruited to do a job I didn't know how to do and when I failed at it, which had a high probability, I ended up even worse off than dead?

"By the way, I never introduced myself. I'm Murphy. Of Murphy's Law?"

"And I'm Lady Luck. Luck for short."

"So, how does this..." I waved a hand to encompass the office, them, everything. The entire situation was beyond surreal and made me doubt the reality I was in. But if I was going to be doing things that were dangerous, I needed to start gathering information yesterday. Twenty-five days now seemed like an eternity.

"Well, in my case, I help spread the luck around. Murphy is sort of my counterpart, spreading the opposite." She patted him on the shoulder. "You're just all sunshine and happiness, aren't you, Murphy?"

"And what exactly is Harold?"

"He's middle management." Murphy picked up another pencil and started to play mock drums as he spoke.

"Then who exactly do we work for?"

"The universe." He hit an invisible cymbal.

"That's what Harold said, but is it a person? Have either of you seen this universe person or entity?"

"Nope. Everything is through Harold. It's a lot to take in, especially as a transfer. Why don't we get you settled in. Just try and lay low until your month is up," Luck said. She motioned to the group of four desks clustered together that they were sitting on. "This one is mine." She patted next to where she sat. "That's Murphy's, next to me and that's the one the Jinxes share. They don't use it, though."

"Jinxes?"

She nodded and rolled her eyes. "They're out in the field right, but it's not an introduction you want to rush."

She got up and walked to the last remaining desk and pulled the chair out. "And you can have this one."

"So, we work here, in this office?" I sat down in the offered chair in front of my desk and opened a couple of the empty drawers. The place didn't seem like somewhere I'd be in danger, but no one had told me exactly what it was I would be doing yet.

"No, we just like having desks," Murphy explained, completely straight-faced.

I looked around at all the others in the office, no one hiding their curiosity at my presence and I was quite sure I'd fallen down the rabbit hole. This is why you always read contracts before you sign them. First contract I didn't read thoroughly and this is what I got.

"That's the Cat Lady, over there," Luck pointed in the direction of a woman reading a gossip magazine in the corner, a black cat weaving itself through her legs. "We call her Kitty for short."

"Why is a cat lady here?"

"Not *a* cat lady, *the* cat lady. Black cats? She sends them out right before someone is about to get really screwed." She pointed to short little stubby guy walking across the room. "That's our leprechaun, Bert. He used to be in a different office, but got pulled over here for clover detail. I'd introduce you, but he's in a real bad mood."

"What's clover detail?" I looked about for some paper feeling like I should be taking notes.

"Too many people were finding four leaf clovers. Some leprechaun jerk thought it would be funny to get a little free and loose with the clovers. Now Bert is in charge of monitoring the numbers. The leprechaun responsible got early retirement." Luck's eyes widened at the end of that statement.

Murphy held up a hand next to his mouth and whispered, "Poor as dirt and stuck in a boarding house, now." Murphy pointed to a Goth looking guy by the water cooler. "He's Crow. He sends out a crow before death."

"What about the guy in the jockey outfit?" I watched as he crossed the room and exited.

Luck perched next to me, a hip on my desk. "He's actually in one of the offices down the hall. He's in charge of the Night Mares." She looked at the door to Harold's office and tilted her head in that direction. "And you already met Fate. The hand of Fate, to be exact."

"Fate, as in destiny?"

Murphy nodded from where he sat across from me. "When a person is fated for a certain destiny, but things aren't lining up the way they should, he steps in." Murphy put on a pair of reading glasses and pulled out a newspaper.

"I'm surprised he's talking to you or helping out." Luck handed Murphy a pencil, which he eschewed for a pen.

"Why?"

"Hates transfers."

"If being a transfer is such a problem, why did I get recruited?"

This interested Murphy enough to look up from his paper. "Now, that is the million dollar question."

I took a seat at my new desk, not sure what else to do. I opened up the rest of the drawers to see if there were any office supplies. When I looked back up, Luck and Murphy were already walking away from me. I guess that was the end of my introduction.

So I sat there, alone. Eventually, I stole an extra newspaper from the corner and did the crossword. When noon rolled around, a strange woman showed up and laid out a buffet along the wall. She stopped at my desk and said "Eat," which ended up being the last word said to me for the entire day, until five.

I picked through the food and selected a small turkey sandwich, which I nibbled at but had a hard time finishing. Nerves had always dampened my appetite and this situation was bringing them out.

Throughout the day, people came and went, doing who knew what. I'd read the entire newspaper and five different gossip mags I'd snagged from the front waiting room.

Occasionally, someone would come near me, but no one actually spoke. I pretended to ignore them. They could stare all they wanted. I'd be out of here, soon enough. I liked crosswords and gossip mags. I could do this for a month standing on my head, no problem.

At five o'clock, the driver, Hank, strode through the door and headed toward my desk. "I drive you home," he said and turned on his heel, expecting me to follow. Hank was a man of very few words.

I went to grab my stuff before I remembered I had none. I was going to have to buy a purse, just to get rid of the feeling I was leaving something behind.

"Do you know when we get paid?" It felt like an awkward question, since I wasn't doing anything, but some cash would be good if I wanted to eat something I actually liked.

"Harold."

I took that to mean *ask Harold, I have no clue*, and I let it drop. At least there*was* food in the condo. It had cable T.V. and it was beachfront. As long as I didn't think of Charlie, my parents, my friends...basically, as long as I didn't think at all, I could get through this.

I'd decided this was a very short-term purgatory for making a bad knee jerk reaction when I'd known better. I could handle

beachfront purgatory that came with gossip
mags and cable.

Chapter Six

How wrong I was. Day eleven of beach front purgatory and I was ready to kill my already dead body just to escape the boredom. I leaned my head on my palms as I watched the people in the office walk around. I knew I must have looked frazzled but I was past putting up a good appearance.

Other than a few nods of acknowledgment that another body was a few feet away from them when I walked in the door, that was the extent of communication.

Hank picked me up every day and dropped me off at five. I hadn't seen Harold for days. He'd said I had to be here for an active month, but if this was what he considered active, I might as well be laid out in a coffin. There was nothing to do. People just strolled in to the office and strolled back out. I wasn't even sure what the purpose of this place was, exactly. No one seemed to do much of anything.

It wasn't even a good office. My newspaper was already second hand by time I got to it. I knew this for sure because Murphy's sweaty hands left smudges all over the words.

The catered lunch was stale and I caught Kitty, the cat lady, double dipping her celery in the ranch dressing. Not to mention when she brought her cats in they tried to use my leg as a scratching post.

I guess I couldn't blame them, I felt like a piece of furniture myself. I must have been putting out that vibe.

Luck was there the least, if you didn't count Fate. Most of the time, it looked like she'd been the one getting lucky, unless she meant for her hair to look like that and put on her shirts backwards as some sort of fashion statement.

As for me, it's amazing the damage boredom can do to a personality. There wasn't a person in the office I hadn't nit picked to death in my head. Even Bert, the leprechaun, who I'd never shared two words with; I'd daydream of calling in false four leaf clover reports just to see his green loving butt run out of the office in a tither.

No wonder this place was full of jerks. It should be a secret training ground for those inclined to go postal.

So, when I saw Harold step into the office that day, I was ready to tackle him to the ground harder than the biggest NFL linebacker just to get some answers. I chased him down as he walked into his office, giving him barely a foot of distance as we crossed the threshold. There was no way he was shutting his door and kicking me out.

"Harold, I'm cracking up over here. What exactly am I supposed to be doing? All this sitting around stuff better be counting towards the thirty days since I'm here every day, willing."

"You're waiting." He dropped his armful of papers onto his desk.

"For what?" I stood with my hands on my hips, blocking the door.

"You'll know when it's time."

"What am I waiting for?"

"You'll see."

"Can you tell me when this thing I'm waiting for might be coming?"

"I can't say. It's always different."

No wonder the world was a mess. These people needed a course in being proactive.

Be nice, I kept telling myself. Catch more bees with honey, not vinegar. Honey, honey, honey. I just didn't know how much longer I could be full honey when I was choking on acid. I wasn't naturally a sugary sweet person to begin with.

"I've acquired an automobile for you and the necessary documents to drive it." Harold reached into a drawer and handed me a Manila envelope. "The keys belong to the white Honda Civic sitting at the curb outside."

I peaked out the long rectangular office window.

"That?" The thing had to have been fifteen years old. One of the doors was primer gray, in comparison to the scratched white exterior of the rest of it.

Someone had just handed me a car. I should've been happy. No one had ever given me a car, before. Even though I came from an upper middle class family, my parents always believed a car was something I should earn. I should be grateful. But gosh darn it, I did die to get this job. Wasn't that worth at least a used Cadillac, or at the very least something that looked like it was going to start on a regular basis?

I swallowed back the complaint and opened the envelope that contained the keys and documents. I had no idea where he'd gotten a photo of me for my fake license, but it didn't matter enough to bother asking.

The license read Carma Walters. It sounded like a fortuneteller at a carnival, but it was better than nothing. I took my envelope and headed out. At least I'd procured wheels. It meant another level of freedom as the next twenty days slugged by.

"Call me when it happens," he said as I left.

"You got it. Whenever this mysterious thing that no one can explain to me happens, you'll be the first person I notify."

The clock ticked five just as I made it back to my desk. I nodded politely at the people who didn't speak to me as I passed them on my way to the door.

***

I fell asleep around nine after a busy night of watching Battlestar Gallactica by myself and a pizza and cookie dough ice cream binge. I was already onto the third season. It's amazing how much TV you can watch when there is absolutely nothing else to do. I was tired of spending my nights alone waiting for *something,* that no one could explain, to come.

That *something* finally came at six in the morning. I woke up in a sweat, not knowing why, and then bam, a vision of a man making alterations to financial retirement accounts. Draining them completely. It didn't stop there, either. I saw him arguing with an older woman before killing her.

The same man entering a coffee bar. The clock struck twelve as he was ordering a drink. I knew that coffee bar.

And then it was gone. It had been like having a dream while I was wide awake. Was that what I'd been waiting for? A weird daydream certainly wasn't the earth-shattering event I'd expected it to be. And seriously, were the people in the office that communication impaired that they couldn't say, *hey, you're going to get a weird daydream*?

I got up, made some coffee and called Harold, filling him on the latest development.

"Now you go there," he said.

"And do what?"

"How should I know? You'll find out when it's time."

Honey, honey, honey. I only had nineteen days left. Deep breaths and big beehives full of honey.

"Are you sure I'm going to find out?"

"I'll meet you at eleven. You did know the place, correct?"

"Yes."

And then he hung up.

I drank another four cups of coffee while I waited to leave, just to make sure I didn't lack for energy.

I pulled up in front of the office at ten fifty-nine A.M., and Harold was already waiting, staring down at his watch.

"You're almost late."

"Technically, Harold, I'm a minute early."

"Which is almost late."

The car door made a horrible sound as he got in. One might describe it as the automobile equivalent of a death rattle. I hoped the old Honda had a life expectancy of another eighteen days.

"What exactly was that I saw?" I asked as I pulled out of the lot with Harold in tow and horrible exploding sounds coming from the vicinity of the Honda's rear.

"We need to make a stop first and then you have to go the coffee bar you saw."

I turned out onto the highway and just when

I thought I'd have to pry the rest of the details from his bony pale hands, he started to talk.

"You are now essentially syncing into the universe. The person you saw is someone that has been escaping balance, probably for generations."

"How can he have escaped for generations?"

"He was doing it in a past life."

"These people get away with it for that long?"

"Yes. For whatever reasons, the universe hasn't settled his score and now you need to."

"But how?"

He tapped the clock on the radio. "In about forty minutes and I don't know how. Only you and the universe know."

"But that's a problem because I don't know. The *universe* hasn't bothered to tell me that."

"You'll find out when you get there."

After almost two weeks of no answers, watching TV in solitude while I knew my parents and Charlie mourned me, having to deal with bad attitudes, and that was only if I wasn't being completely ignored, my honey well had officially run dry. All I had to offer now was vinaigrette. Bon appetite.

"Harold, we're treading in dangerous waters. I've got no honey left." I gripped the steering wheel, trying to hang on to the temper set off from too few explanations and far too many expectations.

"I don't have honey. If it's such a problem, go to the supermarket."

I turned and glared at him. "I'm not surprised you have no honey."

His face made it clear he thought I was crazy. I didn't care. If I was starting to lose my mind, they were to blame.

I pulled up to the address of a sprawling beach mansion. Before I could ask what we were there for, I knew.

Fate was heading toward the car. Two things came to mind. That better not be where he lives and he better not be coming with me.

"Did you need to talk to him for a minute?" I asked Harold, clinging to hope.

"No. He's going with you."

Harold ignored my scream of "Absolutely not!" and got out of the car anyway.

Then he was there.

I saw Hank pull up in the Mercedes behind me as Fate took Harold's spot and sat in my front seat. I didn't want him in my Honda.

Neither Fate nor I said a word to each other in greeting.

He finally spoke first. "Do you plan on driving? I've got things to do besides babysit you."

"I was hoping if I ignored you, you'd get out."

"Wish I could. But the bottom line is you

need to learn the ropes and I'm the best equipped to teach you."

No wonder I had no honey left.

I put the car in gear and my Honda's engine whined slightly, as if she resented his presence as much as I did.

"This is my job, so don't think you're going to get all bossy on me either."

"Whatever, transfer. We both know you have no clue what's going on." He hand cranked up his window and turned on the air conditioning full blast, which made my old Honda wheeze like it had a pack a day habit.

I white knuckled the steering wheel and headed out. Eighteen days left, that was it.

I pulled into a spot near the coffee bar, after stewing over his last comment the whole ride over. If Harold didn't know, I bet he didn't either.

"Fine. You're right. I have no idea what we're here to do. Why don't you tell me?"

"It's your job. I won't know until you do."

"If you, the so called experienced one in charge, are clueless," yes, I'm petty and that dig was extremely necessary to my emotional well being, "how am I supposed to know?"

"Because, this is how it works."

"Well, thanks for the big heads up." I shouted at his back, since he was already getting out of the car and heading toward the coffee shop alone.

It didn't look like he was planning to wait for me but I knew I had to do this, active participation and all. I got out and took my time making it inside.

Even if I wasn't particularly fond of him, I wasn't sure I was ready to go it alone, not after I found out I could literally vaporize myself. Even if Fate was a bit of an ass, I didn't doubt his competence.

I found a free table toward the front windows when I entered, while he was in line. I heard the girl at the cashier giggling flirtatiously and caught Fate smiling back, equally friendly. So, it was just me he instantly disliked.

When he returned with two cups I was actually surprised. Did he buy me a coffee?

He sat across the table, and I forced the words "Thank you," out, even if it felt like chewing on sand to do it.

"And now?" Between my dislike of him for how he treated me and the unsettling feelings I had being near him, I was watching the second hand on the clock tick away all too slowly.

"Now we wait."

Ten to twelve, six more revolutions it had to swing around. Neither of us bothered to make small talk. Of all the things I wanted to know, I didn't bother asking him or we wouldn't even make it ten minutes. Silence was the best option when it came to him.

The second hand did its final turn and I

looked out the window, not expecting to really see him, the man from my visions. My breath caught as I saw the guy approach the building.

"Stay calm."

I didn't reply. "Go to hell, you arrogant jerk," didn't seem like the correct response and I knew, for some reason, I overreacted to Fate. But I couldn't think about that right now, I had a job to do.

As the man from my visions got closer, more flashes popped into my head; horrible images that made my stomach turn. A picture of a hive appeared in my mind and then a tree. Now, this might sound odd to some people, but I've always loved trees and when I notice a particularly nice specimen, I always take note, so I knew this was the old oak in front of the building we were sitting in now.

And just like that, I realized what I was supposed to do. But was that really it?

The man entered the shop and I watched as he got into line to order a drink. I looked at Fate, having no one else to turn to, and then a strange thing happened. Fate and I had an honest moment.

He touched my hand and looked at me with what seemed sincerity, the rancor that had existed between us since almost the very first meeting disappeared. "Go with your gut feeling. Whatever you are seeing is the right way."

"I'm afraid."

"If you do what it showed, you'll be okay. Just follow the visions."

He broke contact then and our small moment of truce seemed to fade the minute he pulled back.

My mark, as I decided to call him, took a coffee and sat down a few tables away.

I got up and went outside. His convertible was parked under the old oak, directly under the beehive.

Good thing I had jeans on. I walked to the base of the huge ancient tree. It had a lower branch that made it perfect for climbing and, having scaled many in my youth, I was a bit of a pro. I looked around, making sure no one would see me climb into the tree, when I realized Fate had followed me.

He stood directly under the hive, arms folded and waiting. "No one will see."

"How do you know?"

"They just won't."

"How is that possible?"

"Does it matter? Just do what you have to do."

Would it kill him to be pleasant for more than one minute? I kicked off my shoes then gripped the branch in my hands and hoisted myself up, all while muttering curses at him under my breath.

The branch wasn't as strong as I hoped and it swayed with my weight. My fingers dug into the bark until my nails hurt. My memories of climbing were a lot more fun than the current reality.

I crept close to the hive, waiting for either the bees to start going crazy or the branch to break with me landing on my ass at Fate's feet. What a wonderful time that would be. Well, there was always the bright side; maybe if I fell while the bees were chasing me, he'd get stung in the process.

I paused two feet from the hive. My fear taking over, I couldn't seem to force another step forward but I had enough control to halt a movement backward.

"They're going to attack me," I mumbled to myself.

"What?"

I looked down at where he stood safely on the ground, safe and useless. I wanted to drop the hive on his head.

"Nothing," I shouted down at him.

"Just do it."

"You just do it." Good thing he wasn't human. He'd have no friends at all if it weren't for the freaks at the office. If they were his friends. Maybe they didn't like him either? I was technically a freak now too, and I certainly wasn't looking to spend time with him.

"I *can't*. You got the order. I wish I could."

Order? That's what we were calling a few flashes? This business, for lack of a better name, had some serious gaps. Lots could be left to interpretation with this but I went with the hunch.

The fact that I'd be stuck with him until I got this done urged me forward.

"Okay, bees, just you and me, boys." I edged out further on the limb. Probably about twenty or so bees were buzzing in and out of the hive as I closed the final distance and, at some point soon, they were going to be mightily pissed off.

"I just want you to know, I didn't want to do this to you. Personally, I think it's very wrong to involve you in all this ugliness."

"Why are you talking to them?" Fate's hands had shifted to the equally unhelpful position of resting on his hips.

"I'm making friends. You wouldn't know anything about that."

I crawled closer and closer, waiting for them to decide to attack me. They buzzed by my head, a few landed briefly on my hands and arms, but no one stung...yet.

I made my way to the hive and perched next to it. This was it, I knew what I thought I should do, but this could go bad quickly. So far, the bees had left me alone but once I yanked the hive loose, I imagined I'd get their wings in a bunch.

I looked around, knowing I'd taken a while. No one was in the parking lot or seemed to notice me at all from the huge windows that had clear sight.

"We don't have all day."

Wow, I really didn't like him, but he did have a point. Both shaking hands out, I grabbed the hive, turned my head away, with eyes squinted shut, and yanked it loose.

Hmmm, no stinging? I opened an eye the tiniest slit. It was idiotic really. Seeing the bees or not wouldn't change their mind about attacking me. And yet, I couldn't bring myself to fully look at the mad swarm that was surely about to vent their anger.

When I did look, I saw the bees were still calm. Huh?

"Come on!" Fate screamed from underneath.

I looked at his handsome face and I swung a leg, eying the distance between my foot and his head. Nope, not close enough. I guess he gets to keep his straight nose today.

I tucked the hive under one arm, expecting a full on attack at any moment and shimmied down awkwardly with only one free arm.

"Can you take it?" I asked, trying to hand him the hive so I could make the final jump down.

He stood back arms crossed. "Can't touch it."

"Not even for a minute?"

"Not my choice. Right now, even if

someone were to walk out here, right by this spot, they might notice me, but they wouldn't see you. If I touch that, which is part of your job, all bets are off. You stay to assignment and you're shielded. It's when you step out of the boundaries that it can go badly."

I huffed a bit and then looked at the hive. "I apologize for the jolt ahead of time."

I jumped the five feet or so down and managed to hang onto it. I froze there in a squat as I waited for the mad swarm that would finally decide it was time to let me know they weren't happy about their relocation.

"You getting up?"

I looked under my arm where I had tucked it. The bees that were flying around followed me but none of them seemed overly upset, even after that jump. I stood slowly, not wanting to rock the hive.

The mark's convertible was sitting right under where the bees' previous home had been. I could see an image, as clear as a photograph in my mind, of the hive sitting in his back seat.

My hands froze as I lifted the hive to put it exactly how I envisioned it and I froze. What exactly would this lead to? Not many people actually died from bee stings. It just sucked.

"Do. It."

"Shut. Up." I didn't bother looking at Fate. I just stood there. Could I really do this? It was rare, but there was still the chance I could be murdering this man.

And then, like a jolt to the system, more images of the people he'd abused flashed through my head. An older couple with bare cabinets.

I looked upward. "I don't know who's running this show, but you made your point. He's got it coming."

I placed the hive onto the floor of the back seat of the open convertible and stepped back.

I looked over to Fate. "Now what?"

"We take a seat and watch the show. Make sure it goes smoothly." He walked over and looked at the hive, still calm.

"I don't know if I want to see it."

"You do the deed, you see it out."

I blew out a long breath. I'd never intentionally hurt someone and, no matter who this person was and what he'd done, I'd still prefer not to see it happen.

"No one likes this part."

And just like that, a little glimmer of the person he could be showed through a bit. Was it just me? I knew he made me more agitated. Maybe something about me triggered him as well.

He walked away without another word.

I headed over to a bench in front of the strip mall about fifty feet away. Fate found a spot about thirty feet down from me. I was glad for the distance.

A minute later, when the sound of thunder rumbled, I was glad I was under the overhang. My mark dashed out of the coffee shop just as the rain started. First thing he did was put the roof back up on his car.

I looked upward. "Nice touch."

And then the mark got in the car. It didn't take long for the screams to start. Even from where I sat, I could see the cloud of bees swarm up in the car. That's when I really started wondering what I'd done.

I had a gut reaction to the pain I knew I'd inflicted. I leapt to my feet to go and help him, but Fate got to me first and wrapped a hand around my forearm.

"You can't."

"What I can't do is this. Let go of me." I tried to pull free but instead of making headway toward the car, I was being towed further away by Fate.

All I could do was watch. There was a big difference between wishing bad on someone who's done harm and inflicting it yourself. The magnitude of the difference was hitting me hard, right now. In theory, I could've hurt someone evil like this all day, everyday. The reality was a lot harder.

People heard the screams he was making even through the closed car and ran to help, but couldn't get the doors open.

They banged on the windows and screamed

for him to unlock the doors. Someone screamed for a knife to cut the canvas top but by time one arrived, who knew how many times he'd been stung.

I couldn't break free of Fate but he'd stopped tugging me further away, so we stood there, arms outstretched in between us, as we both watched the horror of what unfolded.

"Will he die?" I asked.

"It takes ten bee stings per pound to kill a human. I'd guess he was about a hundred and eighty pounds. That hive probably had about 45,000 bees. Yeah, I'd say he's dead."

"I just killed a man."

"It'll get easier."

"I hope not."

He dropped his grip but it didn't matter now. I could hear the sirens of the ambulance as we walked toward my Honda. The good Samaritans had helped the man out of the car and laid him on the cement. His body didn't move. The stingers were so dense, patches of his arms appeared gray from a distance.

I could hear the people talking as we passed.

"What a fluke!"

"The hive must have dropped from that branch with the wind."

"Can you believe what just happened?"

I imagined the coverage on the news later today, talking about the crazy coincidence of a hive dropping and lying dormant in the back of a man's car until he got in it. A freak accident, they'd call it.

It's what I would've thought, a week ago.

Now, I knew better.

Chapter Seven

Everyone scattered out of my way as I stormed into the office and headed directly for Harold's door. It was shut but I didn't bother to knock.

He looked up as I walked in, the door slamming into the wall in my wake. He pushed a hand through his hair, which just made it stick out more.

"This is the job?" I asked as I stopped on the other side of his desk. "I'm an assassin?" There was a chair but I ignored it, opting to pace instead. "You said right the wrongs of the universe! Not kill people!"

Harold held his hands up in front of him. "It won't always be killing."

"How often? Every other time?"

"I don't know."

Harold got up from his seat and went to shut the door. I guessed he didn't want everyone to hear me, but I personally didn't care. They could all hear as far as I was concerned.

"Oh good. You're here," I heard Harold say and looked to see Fate walking into the room. Harold closed the door behind him.

I looked at the both of them now. "I'm not doing this job."

"Can we discuss this calmly?"

I sat in the chair in front of his desk and

took a deep breath, forcing myself to relax. "You want calm? This is me calmly telling you, I'm not doing that again."

I sat with a disgruntled Harold at his desk in front of me and Fate leaning against the wall behind me.

I turned around in my chair. "Is there something wrong with one of your legs?" Everywhere he went he was leaning on things. Like the vertical space he occupied wasn't enough. He had to hog up as much horizontal area as he could possibly get, too. It wasn't like you could miss him when you entered a room, but that just wasn't enough for Fate.

"Does my leaning bother you?" he asked.

I turned my back on him again. There was something very unsettling about being around him. I always wanted to kill him and the fact that I found him attractive on top of that made me want to torture him first.

"Do you know how your human form was killed?"

Of course I knew. I was there. It was a stupid question intended to throw me off balance and it did.

I'd been avoiding thinking of that day. If I did, I'd remember my parents were just miles away and yet I couldn't speak to them. I'd miss Charlie and all the friends I'd lost. The only way I was mentally surviving this situation was to push what had happened from my mind. I was living day by day until I left.

"Do you?" Harold pressed.

"Harold, you know I do. Make your point." It was one of the reasons I'd agreed to this in the first place and I resented the reminder. How could I not?

"All of those people robbed of the chance to even say goodbye. Have a few last words with their loved ones," Harold continued.

"If you don't get to your point soon, I'm leaving. And not in a calm fashion, either."

The last thing I wanted was to hear him talk about something I'd experienced first hand. Even when I did let myself think about it, I didn't know what to do. I knew I had a limited amount of time and yet I'd kept forcing it from my mind, not wanting to deal with what happened.

"You know you have to actively participate for thirty days."

"Calling it active participation doesn't change that fact that you want me to be an assassin for hire for thirty days." I stood, unable to stay calmly in my seat and slammed my fist against his desk.

"It's either active for thirty days or a thousand years. Don't be stupid about this," Fate said from behind me. "Even if Harold wanted to, you've got to be active for him to have the ability."

I slumped back into my chair and just shook

my head. They had me. They knew it and so did I.

"To help the situation become more palatable to you, we might be able to help you get the person who orchestrated your train crash."

"Now you're going to help? Didn't you tell me it was *my* problem?"

"We've reconsidered."

I stared at Harold and then looked back at Fate. There was something more going on but I certainly had no clue what.

"Do you agree?"

"I'm thinking." What were they getting out of this? And I didn't believe for a second that they weren't getting something. But did it matter? I didn't know how to find him. At least I could walk away from this situation with a certain amount of peace this way. As long as I was still walking away that was.

"And this doesn't extend my current contract?"

"No."

"Fine."

Fate pushed off his favorite place on the wall and walked out the door saying he'd be waiting out there.

"Why's he waiting?"

"He's going home with you."

"What?"

***

"Don't get too comfortable." I threw my keys on the counter, and if he thought he was getting a key to this place, he was highly delusional.

Neither of us had spoken since we left the office.

"Don't worry, I've already got a key," he said as he walked into my kitchen and opened my fridge.

Thanks a whole bunch, Harold.

"Why are you doing this? And don't give me some bull about having to listen to Harold." He was hogging up all the space in my tiny kitchen. What if I wanted to get in there? I'd have to squeeze in past him? If they hadn't dangled such a tempting carrot, this would be intolerable.

"I have my reasons." He took a glass from my cabinet and poured the last bit of my iced tea into it.

"Which are?"

"Which are none of your business."

"I still don't understand why you have to sleep here."

I saw him roll his eyes and I gripped the counter to keep myself from trying to physically drag him out. He finished my iced tea. You don't take the last of someone's iced tea!

"Because, I need to try and sync into your

past fate. We're more in tune to pick up things when we're sleeping. The closer proximity to you when I'm asleep, the more I'll hopefully pick up."

"Shouldn't you just be able to do that?"

"No, it doesn't work that way." He looked at me and paused. "And to complicate matters, it's your past, so it's even harder."

"So now what? We're stuck together until you start picking up on the murderer's trail?"

"Pretty much. If it's going to work, I'll get something in the next few days."

He took a couple of sips, made a face and tossed the remaining contents of tea in the sink. "What brand was that?"

That was it, I was on Fate overload.

I walked in my room, grabbed a pillow and a blanket and threw them on the couch before I shut my bedroom door a little more firmly than necessary.

Chapter Eight

It took a while to sleep after the beehive experience, but when I did, it was surprisingly deep. No more flashes of any type. When I woke up, I was still in shock. I was officially a murderer.

Fate was gone in the morning, so at least we didn't have to car pool. I drove to the office in my little Honda with the images of the bee stung body lying there and his screams fresh in my mind.

I parked my car outside work and went in, trying to pretend it was just another day. The usual crew were all there; Luck and Murphy looked to be gossiping off in the corner, Kitty was sharing her coffee over at her desk and I still hadn't met or seen any of the Jinxes.

I walked over and grabbed a discarded newspaper and settled at the table near the windows. It was partially obscured by the alcove it sat in. I liked it better over here. I was still technically at work but now it was a mutual choice to be separated. They didn't want to socialize with me and I decided to return the favor.

Just as I sat down, three boys on skateboards shot through the office. They looked to be around ten or eleven. What were kids doing here?

They zoomed in between the desks, knocking over files as they went and I heard someone scream "Jinxes!" and it all made sense.

All three sets of eyes scanned the room and froze on me. They kicked their skateboards into full gear in my direction. I was just about to jump out of my chair, when they skidded to a stop, inches from knocking me over.

All three were blond with blue eyes. They looked like angelic brothers but it was clear they were anything but.

"Hi," the kid closest to me said. "I'm Bobby, that's Billy and Buddy." He hooked his thumb in the direction of the two standing slightly behind him.

"Nice to meet you." I hoped.

"So, you're the new Karma?" Either Billy or Buddy said, I wasn't sure which. The three of them were forming a half circle around me, their eyes roving up and down me in the most uncomfortable manner.

"Yes. My names Camilla."

"So, Karma, you're single, right?" Billy/Buddy said.

"Having died recently, I haven't had a chance to date, as of yet."

"Move out of the way, Bobby. She's not interested in you, are you, darling?" The one on the left said, shouldering his way to the front.

The other one stepped forward now as well.

"Don't let the bod throw you baby cakes. I'm an old soul and I'm all man in the sack." His eyebrows rose while he smiled.

I was trying so hard to keep a neutral face it was impossible to speak without giving up the ruse.

"Hey, don't laugh at us," Bobby said when I couldn't control myself anymore. "We might look young but we've got some mad skills."

"I'm sure you do."

The three of them were foul, crude and all-round distasteful. I kind of liked them. They reminded me of most of my clients. It felt a bit like home.

In unison, all three heads perked up as if they were listening to something I couldn't hear.

"Billy?"

"Got it, Bobby." Billy was now staring down at his watch.

"What's going on?" I asked and got a finger signaling to give them a minute.

And then suddenly, Bobby dropped his arm and Billy and Buddy cursed.

"What happened?" I asked again.

"Some chick was just talking about how her trip couldn't be postponed again. She knocked on wood before the minute was up," Billy explained.

"That knock on wood thing really works?"

"Yeah. You get a minute to use it. Cuts off the signal to us," Bobby said.

"People use it less and less, lately." Buddy's eyes had an evil glint as he smiled mischievously.

Across the room, Murphy went on an epic sneezing rant, which I wouldn't have thought twice about except for the Jinxes' reaction.

"Cover your mouth, you degenerate!" Buddy screamed.

"What do you think tissues are for, old man!" Billy chimed in.

Bobby looked at his two cohorts and me, and then uttered, "Who *does*something like that? What an animal."

The other two grunted and huffed, agreeing with him, then turned their attention back to me again.

"You know, no one talks to you 'cause you're a transfer. Fate keeps telling everyone you'll either leave soon or die, so it's not worth getting chummy, but we don't care what the rest of these dweebs do. We're trendsetters, not followers."

I heard the office door shut and turned to see Fate walking in behind the caterer.

"Yeah, gotta go." And just like that, the Jinxes took off to the other side of the office.

After laying out the food, the caterer made one last trip in, carrying a cake in the shape of a cat paw, which she put off to the side.

I got up and grabbed a tuna sub and a can of Diet Coke. I made a quick glance at the cake that read "Happy 1,000 Anniversary Kitty" before returning to my seat.

A thousand years? Hell no! Literally, I'd tell them to send me to hell before I sat here for a thousand years.

I looked around the place, pretending to read the newspaper, as I sat and ate alone. The air conditioning kicked on, sending a draft my way, letting me know Crow must have taken off his shoes again. He liked to go barefoot about the office and the odor from his shoes alone could bring a grown man to his knees.

I couldn't eat for the smell. I put my tuna sandwich down, scraping my arm on the edge of the broken table in the process.

One of Kitty's black cats jumped up on the table, looked at me, then the tuna.

"Knock yourself out." I pushed the sub toward the cat, which meowed in reply and then dug in.

I sat back and thought about how I would not be able to exist like this for the next 1,000 years. I missed my life, my friends, having family. If I'd had a bad day at work before, I could call someone and talk it out afterward, instead of having to drown myself in Battlestar Gallactica reruns alone.

I worked in a dump full of weirdoes with no social graces, who treated me like *I* was the outcast. Thirty days of this was my max.

I tucked myself a little further back as I

heard them laughing at some joke. Even Fate was laughing. I think it might have been him who made the joke. It was probably a hateful joke too, most likely at my expense.

I cringed. This place was turning me into one of those bitter people. The "secret haters" I used to call them. Didn't matter what happened in their lives, they were miserable. Now I felt like one of them.

Crow was lighting some candles on the cake as Kitty went over. The worst was I didn't know what to do as they gathered around the cake waiting for her to blow out the candles. I felt rude sitting here but they weren't looking to socialize.

The mutilated Happy Anniversary song over and the candles out, Murphy took a knife and started to cut the cake and dole it out to the group. I was looking down at my paper when I saw Murphy heading over with a piece of cake for me. It was such a simple gesture and yet it felt like the world to me.

I looked up and smiled at him as he covered the distance. And then there was Fate, stopping him with a hand on his arm.

"What are you doing?" he asked.

Murphy looked at me, and then Fate, before he spoke in a hushed tone. "I feel bad."

Fate's head was shaking and I couldn't understand what he said next but it didn't matter. They could keep their cake.

Fate's back still toward me, I got up and walked over to them.

"It's for her own good," Fate said.

I should've kept walking but I didn't.

"What's for my own good?"

"That you realize you don't belong." He didn't flinch as he spoke but stared at me and I matched it with my own venomous gaze.

"Whatever. Keep your cake."

Murphy opened his mouth but shut it quickly when Fate gave him a small shove.

It was noon, five hours before quitting time, but I didn't care. I grabbed the keys to my Honda off the empty desk and headed out.

I tried to keep my gaze averted as I made my way to the door but it didn't help.

"Fate, I think you made her cry," I heard Murphy say.

"Let her go," he replied.

Chapter Nine

I'd stopped on my way out of the lobby and searched the board. There had to be another option for getting out of this mess besides Harold. That's how I ended up here. The plaque on the door read "Grief Counseling." Who *else* could it be?

I grabbed the doorknob and then paused. If this was the reaper – the real deal as in death in a dingy robe with a sickle – did I really want to meet him...or her...it?

Why not? He couldn't look too much worse than Crow did. I had nothing but time on my hands and all I did was sit around that office all day. I'd just say hello and introduce myself as someone new in the building. When you thought about it, I was really just being neighborly.

And while we were getting acquainted, if by some chance the subject came up about me looking for an early exit from this particular situation, what harm was done? If he could hurry me along out of my contract a little quicker, I certainly wouldn't snub my nose at the offer.

I turned the doorknob and pushed in to the reception area. No one was there, but at least it didn't look dark and scary the way I'd feared. I guess I was being judgmental, assuming it would be all spiders and cobwebs. It looked similar to our own waiting area. Just like our place, there was a door on the far wall that led to the back.

"Hello?"

I was just about to knock on the interior door when it opened.

The room was black, without a glimmer of light escaping.

"Come in," a deep male voice said from somewhere within all that darkness.

Sometimes judgment calls are more accurate than you hoped.

I came here uninvited. I couldn't go running now. I wanted out, after all. What if this was my way back into the system? I refused to be a sissy.

I took a step in and the lights shot on all of a sudden. A slender man who appeared to be in his sixties with thinning white hair sat behind an antique wood desk. The walls were lined on either side with leather bound books.

Yep, I'm judgmental.

"Sorry about that. I had a headache and the lights were bothering my eyes." The deep voice that had bid me entry now sounded quite high and nasally.

"Did you take anything?" Did ibuprofen work on the reaper? This man couldn't possibly be death, sitting here all calm and nonthreatening in his three piece suit.

"Yes, but over the counters never work well for me."

Did Death just tell me Advil didn't help his head? This had to be an assistant.

"Have a seat. I'd heard we had someone new in the building."

Death seemed so friendly. Weird that he'd have the best manners of any of them so far.

"It's nice to meet you. I'm Cam...Karma."

He held out his hand, and right before I grasped it, he introduced himself, "I'm Death. So nice to meet you."

I paused my hand in mid reach but then I faltered. I wanted to go back into the system and he could probably help me do that. But not before I handled matters here. If there was a chance at getting my murderer, I couldn't walk away.

"It's okay." He smiled and looked down at my hand.

"I'm sorry." I grasped his and shook. Treating Death like he had the cooties didn't seem to be a smart idea.

My hand clasped his and a frigid cold shot up to my elbow, and might have spread further if he hadn't let go.

He looked down at my hand and his. "Wow. Sorry about that! You've still got some human on you. Wasn't expecting it."

"So, you could have, you know, killed me?"

"No. I only deal in live humans. I just

meant touching me might feel uncomfortable. It's a little like chewing on tin foil. Feels unpleasant but isn't really a problem." He sat back down and motioned for me to make myself comfortable.

I sank into the seat, trying to hide the disappointment. It was nice thinking I had a back up plan just in case the thirty-day trial period turned into thirty years.

"I take it that's not what you were hoping for?"

"To be honest, no. I was hoping that you might be the escape clause I was looking for."

"I'm sorry. I wish I could help. You do seem to have a brilliant soul. It would've been a pleasure to help you along. I do so like the bright ones."

"Thanks."

"So, how do you feel about being here for a little while longer?"

I relaxed back and sighed. There was something strangely comforting about the Reaper. I guess that was the dichotomy of death. Sometimes it was frightening but every now and then in the right moment in life, it was warm and welcoming.

"I made a bad choice and now I'll have to live with it." How many times had I told my clients that same thing? More than half of them would then reply that they hadn't been thinking clearly. Drugs, emotional duress, the list went on and on. I'd righteously told them that they'd better start making the right choice or they'd end up in jail.

Now look at me. I was using the same tired excuse about not thinking clearly. I was as full of bullshit as they had been. I'd thought I could cheat death. There are a lot of things in life you might be able to cheat and get away with. Death isn't on the list.

"But how do you feel? It's a huge change for you."

"I don't know. A bit frustrated I guess..."

He leaned forward, resting his elbows on his desk and nodded. Why am I telling the Reaper about my emotional state?

"Do you actually do counseling?" It was a crazy thought but he did sound like one.

"Yes. I just got my online degree."

"You got an online degree in counseling?"

He smiled widely and nodded. "Of course, I had to use my alias. It's not like I could matriculate as Death but I did all the work myself. Wow, some of that reading was quite lengthy too."

"In addition to..." what would be a politically correct way for describing sucking the life out of someone? "Reaper *activities*?"

He nodded. "Ever since Fred moved in, he's been referring them to me."

"Fred?"

"The human accountant downstairs. We

golf together on Wednesdays." He pointed to the corner near the door where a new club leaned against the wall. "Just bought it off EBay last week. Can't wait to try it out."

"There's a human here? Does he know about all of this?"

"No. He doesn't. He didn't know what the building was and we had an open office. It was something of a paperwork slip up that no one's been able to figure out. He was such a nice guy that we all lobbied to let him stay."

"And Fred gets you clients?"

"Well, he got me my first couple but I've taken to it like a fish to water so now those clients have been getting me referrals. Fred has been a wonderful human to have around." He stood and took a framed photo off his bookshelf of three guys on the golf course. "That's Fred, Dennis and me. Dennis is the tooth fairy. He's even dabbling in dentistry now, because of Fred. Have you met him yet?"

"The tooth fairy?"

"Yes. He golfs with us a couple of times a month."

There was a rap at the door, then a young man poked his head in. "Hey, Doc. Your two o'clock is here."

"Thanks, Tim!"

I stood up and couldn't stop shaking my head. Where did the craziness of this place end?

"Thanks for talking to me."

"Any time! Door's always open!"

***

After the party gone wrong and the idea that *he* might be waiting at my condo, I needed a drink badly. I pulled up to a bar I'd known my whole life but had never frequented. It was one of those local joints that didn't get much of the tourism crowd. Being a public defender, I was always worried about running into one of my clients here. It was the perfect place for how I was feeling.

I walked into the mostly empty dim room. The Joker by Steve Miller played on a jukebox in the corner. A couple of guys shot pool, the balls clanking and cigarettes burning in the ashtray.

I grabbed a stool as far away as I could get from the few other patrons. A middle-aged bartender who would have looked at home in an old western approached me.

"What'll you have?" he asked, slapping down a peeling cardboard coaster.

"Something strong."

He nodded and returned with a bottle that appeared to have red wax dripping down its side. The label read Maker's Mark. He poured a shot and then placed a coke beside it.

"You might need a chaser."

The smell of it alone made my eyes burn

and my stomach do a flip-flop, but I threw it back in one gulp anyway. Trying to keep it down, I'd never been so happy to chug a coke in my life.

I pushed the shot glass forward and nodded toward the bottle.

"Another coke, too?"

"Definitely." I slid the empty coke glass forward.

"Want to talk about it?" he asked as he refilled both.

"Nope." *Not unless you want to die today.*

"That bad, huh?"

"Yep."

I was still none the better after three shots, a sugar high and a fuzzy feeling later.

"What's got such a pretty girl looking down in the dumps?"

I hadn't noticed him sit beside me until he spoke, probably due to the aforementioned fuzziness. I knew he was older by his voice but, when I turned toward him, I hadn't expected someone looking down a decade.

"I'd love to share but I'm not at liberty." If he only knew how honest I was being.

"Then just listen."

"Thank you for the offer, but trust me, you really can't help me with this."

"You need to listen," he chastised and even threw in a finger pointing for good measure.

I was wondering if I had a choice. He

seemed intent on having discourse and I was pretty sure I couldn't drive. A taxi would take at least ten minutes to get here so I guess I was hearing him out whether I wanted to or not.

"I've witnessed war, death, disease and every other type of atrocity you can imagine, let alone the ones beyond your fathom."

I'd been staring forward but now I looked back at him. He was old enough to have gotten around the block a few times and seen a few wars. But there was something about the way he said it that made me start to wonder who, exactly, this man really was.

"I knew you had good instincts." He smiled as if he knew what I was thinking.

"Who are you?"

"I work for the company. You could call me a recruiter." He took a sip of a draft beer he had in front of him.

"Do you work in the building?"

"We don't all work out of the building." He leaned a little closer as to not be overheard. "Now listen to me, I know you plan on quitting at the end of the trial period. That's not a good idea."

"Why not? I hate this job."

"Doesn't matter. This is where you're supposed to be."

"Fate doesn't think so and isn't that his department?"

He shrugged. "He doesn't understand, yet."

"But you, as a recruiter, do?"

"Yes."

"Do you want another refill?"

I turned to the bartender, and waved my hand over the glass shaking my head.

When I turned back, the old guy was gone.

Chapter Ten

When I woke up at one in the morning, my head was pounding, but that didn't seem to slow the visions. Image after image appeared, of a small woman being repeatedly struck in the face by this huge man. I watched him pushing her dead body off a cliff into the ravine below. I saw her falling, dark hair flying among flailing limbs.

They were in a dense forest with tall pines and maples all around. I'd never been there, but I somehow knew exactly where it was.

But how was I supposed to get to Pennsylvania by three A.M.?

I grabbed my phone and dialed Harold, who answered on the first ring. It made me wonder if he was a night owl or simply didn't sleep. I needed sleep; if he didn't, what *was* he? Hopefully I wouldn't be around long enough to figure it out. Put in my days, take out a killer or two in the process and get out before I was stuck.

I explained every detail to Harold and then repeated it all over again when he didn't respond.

"It hasn't happened yet and I have to get there. How?"

"Are you supposed to stop it?" he asked.

No. I wasn't. I'd seen the log he'd used for

the final strike to her head. I saw it placed in his trunk. The traces of her blood I'd add to his clothes. I was supposed to make sure he got caught.

It was time to see how many details Harold had about the assignments.

"Yes." There was no way in hell I'd sit there and watch him beat that woman to death without trying to stop him. If he didn't know exactly what the job was, I didn't feel it necessary to inform him.

There was a pause, a long one. Maybe he did know? Maybe he got a memo or something?

He finally spoke. "Tell Fate. He'll get you there."

"I don't want to ask Fate," I said but he'd already hung up. I knew he'd heard me but didn't want to answer. No, not Fate. Not again, especially not this time, when I was going to go off plan. If he knew this woman was meant to die, it could really mess me up.

So I did what any reasonable person would do. I called him again, and again. Then a few more times after that, for good measure. Fifteen minutes later, and after an unknown amount of ringing, I conceded defeat and accepted that he wasn't going to answer and awaited my dreaded Fate.

Ten minutes of aggravated pacing in the bedroom later, I forced myself to go and ask Fate. He'd been on my couch, feigning sleep, when I'd gotten home, so I knew right where to find him.

I walked out of my room and saw him lying there. He looked handsome, the perpetual scowl he always had for me smoothed away by sleep.

I sighed and meandered across the room, stopping to rinse a glass and put it in the sink.

"How long is it going to take for you to tell me?" I swung around, startled by his voice. He was still lying there with his eyes closed. Did he know I'd just been staring at him?

"Why are you pretending to sleep?"

"Having your eyes closed isn't a pretense, it's called resting."

"If you know, why do you need me to tell you?"

There was a quick upturn at the corner of his lip. A micro-expression, it's called. A small snippet of someone's true feelings that slip out sometimes, before the person realizes. I used to look for them all the time as a lawyer. He was amused, even if he didn't want to admit it.

I couldn't understand what he'd find amusing about this, but he was an odd bird.

"Your walls are paper thin. I heard you tossing around in bed, too. Not sleeping so hot, huh?"

Why would he even mention that? What was the point? He knew I was unhappy, why the reminder that it was affecting my sleep?

And I knew out of everyone I'd met, he was

the most likely to screw this up on me. But how was I going to get to Pennsylvania? Harold would just have to send someone else here to help me.

Fate sat up on the couch and then stood, stretching his arms out and hogging my living room. He walked over and leaned a hip against my table. He did that a lot. Leaned. As if he couldn't be bothered to exert the energy it would take to stand or something.

And he took up too much room; not physically, but he just seemed to eat up all the space around him. Why couldn't he be one of those people you forgot were there?

Then there was the other issue he had – he was too attractive and he knew it. Yes, he was good looking and well built, but so what? To put it nicely, he wasn't a nice person. He was the type of guy girls with issues would find attractive. I didn't have issues. I was a normal, healthy...

Shit. I kept forgetting I was dead. It didn't matter, I was still mentally healthy and that was all that mattered. No self-respecting girl would date him.

"I don't understand why it has to be you?"

I walked over and sat on my couch, trying to reclaim it. There was nothing left of my old life and I wasn't giving up anything else.

"Even if you weren't under my direction, most of the things you are going to deal with tie into a person's fate. If I go, I might not get the full details you do, but I'll be able to get a general sense of how things are supposed to play out. Murphy, Luck, even Crow, none of them overlap as much as we do."

"I did the last one basically on my own anyway. Why do I need you to come? All I need is for someone to get me there." *And I don't want you to know what I'm going to do.* If I'm going to be Karma, I'm making the most out the situation. If the universe thought it was fair she get beaten to death, it was obviously having slips in the system.

"Your last job was the equivalent of riding a bike with training wheels on it. It was almost full proof."

I didn't budge. I didn't want to work with him and I couldn't have him there. I'd take the risk of doing it by myself.

"I have to show you how to get there anyway."

"Harold can send someone else."

"But he won't. Don't forget, active participation. You start missing jobs and you aren't active."

He had a point. Thank goodness they didn't say anything about how I decided to participate.

I couldn't get there without someone's help and Harold wouldn't take my calls. I eyed up his "look at me lean on things, I'm so cool" face.

"Fine. But stop leaning on my stuff."

I stood and grabbed my purse. He pushed off from the table and followed me toward the door.

"I'm sorry you have such an aversion to people leaning on your furniture."

"Not people. Just you." If I annoyed him, he didn't let on.

"I'll drive."

"I want to."

"Sorry, but I have an aversion to your driving."

Yep, I annoyed him.

"You can't just dictate."

"Can't I? You can't get there without me so I think I can."

Just as I was trying to swallow the bitterness of that tasty bite, I noticed the car he was about to get into. Now, for the record, I'm actually becoming accustomed to my broken down Honda. She gets me where I have to go, even if a little slow.

But a Porsche 911? *Are you kidding me?* The jerk gets a Porsche? And I'm Karma. Shouldn't I be able to fix this, somehow? The fact that I didn't know*how* was making me feel very inadequate.

I stopped in the middle of the parking lot and looked up at the sky. "Seriously? I wasn't looking for you. You wanted me. Is this really fair treatment?"

Fate stopped and turned to watch me. "You

know, you're a little odd."

"Please, like you people have any room to talk." I walked over to the car and got in the passenger side, not surprised in the least that he didn't try and get the door for me. He sped out of the lot before I got my seatbelt on and the way he whipped down the road made it hard to breathe.

"Would you mind slowing down?"

"Yes."

"Why are you so horribly unpleasant?"

"You shouldn't be here."

"You are such a jerk."

"It's not just you, any transfer."

"I agree completely. You should do something about it. Maybe talk to the people in charge?"

"Harold agrees, but he was being honest when he said he couldn't get rid of you until the thirty days."

"What about the old man? Maybe he can do something?"

His gaze swung to me. "What old man?"

"The old guy that recruits?" The way he was staring at me didn't bode well.

"Harold recruits."

"Only him?"

"Yes. Who are you taking about? Are you talking to humans? Did you tell a human about us?"

There was absolutely no way I was going to

say anything else. He obviously didn't know the guy and the way he was looking at me, I didn't particularly feel like admitting to knowing about him, either. When in doubt, say nothing.

"I just figured there was someone above Harold." He was so arrogant that I couldn't help but get a little joy out of him not knowing something I did.

"No, that isn't what you meant at all."

"Don't tell me what I meant."

"Then why would you assume Harold's boss was an old man?"

"I was being sexist." The words tasted bad even as I said them. There wasn't a sexist bone in my body. My unlaughed giggles died a sad death in my chest, snuffed out by the false label of sexism. How short lived my glory had been.

"You are so full of shit."

"Please, Fate, let's not pretend you're insulted over unshared confidences."

He broke out into a deep laughter and something in my stomach fluttered. The scowl erased, a wide smile replacing it. How could such a jerk look so inviting just because he was smiling?

"Why are we at the office?" I asked looking to change the subject and get rid of the offending expression.

"It was closer than my place and I didn't want to leave my car in your lot." He got out and pulled his cell phone out of his pocket.

"Don't we need a plane or something?" I looked around searching for a hidden Cessna.

"I'm calling for a door." He held up a hand to me, gesturing for me to stop talking. "We're ready," he said into the phone.

A door?

I spun around looking at the dark lot.

"Shouldn't we get going?" I said to him. We did need to get states away and pronto.

"There."

Ten feet in front of us, a shimmering started until a set of doors appeared out of nowhere. They looked like they were made of platinum, but what was even crazier were the two guards in full armor that appeared next to them.

"I'm guessing that they would be the ones that stopped anyone trying to go through without permission?"

"Yes." We approached the doors and they glided open. On the other side of them, a forest appeared.

"And we can just call these guys up? How did they know where to lead us?"

"Yes. The number is programmed into your work phone."

"Why did I need you then?"

"They don't always like new people, even if they are supposed to be here. It's usually better if you travel with someone they know the first time."

Fate stepped aside to let me go first. I

hesitated right before I crossed the threshold and felt Fate's hand on the small of my back. If it was someone else, it might have been a reassuring presence. Him? It was probably to push me through if I tried to stop.

And then I took the plunge forward.

Chapter Eleven

I stood on the other side of the door as Fate came through after me and then it disappeared. Looking around, it wasn't so dissimilar to the forests of South Carolina, especially dark as it was. It was hard to believe we'd just crossed a distance that would have taken hours by plane in less than a minute.

"What time is it?" I asked as he looked down at his wrist.

"We've got about a half an hour to get to the locale."

It felt so odd that I knew instinctively where to go. If someone asked how I knew we had to walk north to find the couple, I'd ask them how they knew to drink water when they were thirsty. That's how natural and impulsive the urge was.

I took off in search of my job and Fate silently followed behind me. As we traveled in the dark in the middle of a forest, I wondered how I wasn't falling on my ass, tripped by a wayward branch or a boulder. Somehow, my feet always stepped somewhere sound.

I didn't falter until I heard the screaming coming from our destination. I only paused for a second before I took off at a dead run, knowing what was coming.

The hand on my arm jerked me backward.

"We aren't here for that."

"How do you know what I'm going to do?"

"Because I'm not a complete idiot and I know their fate. You don't need to run to plant the evidence. We'll get there in plenty of time for that."

"Get off me," I said. The lawyer in me wouldn't admit to anything. I attempted to yank my arm loose but to no avail.

"You can't save her. This is her fate."

Instead of pulling away, I stepped closer and got in his space. I'd handled my fair share of criminals, bullies and all around scary bad asses. Weakness didn't back them down. The only thing that happens if you run from a predator is a good chase.

"Get. Off. Me."

He didn't budge but held his ground. It was exactly what I'd expected of him but like I mentioned, I wasn't one to run.

Instead of letting go of my one arm, he grabbed the other and stared at me with an almost confused look. "How the hell did you think you were ever meant to marry that guy?"

"What?" The question was bizarre in its randomness but no less painful in the remembrance. "Don't talk to me about Charlie." The shock of the subject was quickly replaced by anger.

"You're right. It doesn't matter. The point is I'm trying to help you."

"And I'm telling you not to."

"I guess some people have to learn the hard way." He shrugged but dropped his grip on me. No sooner was I off and running again that I fell flat on the ground, face to the dirt and gasping to inflate my lungs. I turned to give him a dirty look, sure he was the cause of my fall but he was ten feet behind me.

I pushed myself up, ignoring the sting of nettle beneath my palms and took off running again. A low-lying branch that I knew hadn't been there a second ago knocked me hard in the head. The blow had been so bad that my head spun and my vision dulled.

I moaned, now flat on my back as opposed to on my stomach. I felt a hand run over my forehead and looked up to see Fate leaning over me. His eyes were trained on my forehead where I was sure a large egg was forming and, for just a second, he looked softer, then his eyes met mine and they hardened.

"Are you ready to give up yet? It will just get progressively worse." He stood up and crossed his arms. Standing in the same place from where he had just been squatting next to me

I stood up, a bit wobbly on my feet and without any offered aid from Fate.

"Are you done?" he asked after I wobbled slightly.

"I guess I don't have a choice." I brushed

off the twigs from my jeans and started walking again. How the universe knew I was willing to stay within my neatly penned box I didn't know, but nothing deterred my progress now. The desire still burned within me though.

I didn't consider myself bloodthirsty, but I wanted it today. I'd seen what that man was capable of. The snippets of what the woman's life had been like. She was probably better off dead than with him but why should she be the one whose life was stolen? If I was Karma, shouldn't I get some discretionary power?

"What if it's not enough? What if I don't agree?" I asked in a hushed voice as we approached their campsite. I could hear the screaming clearly now.

"We don't decide what the job is, we just do it."

"This doesn't make sense to me. If the universe can stop me from killing him, why can't it do this itself?"

"Some people are just born slightly out of reach."

"Of the universe?"

"Yes."

"But why not have me kill him like the last guy?"

"I don't know. Maybe rotting in a jail cell for fifty years is the way things need to play out."

"You're Fate. Is that what will happen?"

"If you do this, then yes."

Neither of us spoke as we walked the final distance. I knew exactly what was going to happen next. I'd seen it like a movie clip replaying in my head.

We stopped right outside their clearing and then Fate made a move to walk closer.

"What are you doing? Is that safe?"

"They won't see us because they aren't supposed to."

Fate walked into the area, not far from where they had their campfire. He was as clear as day, the fire illuminating him in an alarming way but neither of the occupants noticed him. But their chocolate lab was staring right at Fate.

The dog definitely knew he was there. I could hear a low growl but he didn't make a move toward Fate. The couple was too busy arguing to notice something amiss with their dog.

Feeling more confident, I stepped out beside him.

He leaned his head down slightly to the side. "You can talk."

"How do they not see us or hear us? Are we invisible?"

"We're just as tangible as we were a few hours ago, just shielded from view."

The man went back from arguing to screaming again. He was carrying on and on about her flirting with someone, all while she denied it.

The man was twice her size and loomed over the small brunette. Her hands were shaking as she cowered. He'd hit her before, even if I hadn't seen it, I'd know it. The evidence was there in her very stature, the pleading in her large eyes. She was scared.

I wanted to scream at her. *You knew what he was capable of. Why did you stay? Why didn't you leave before now?*

I cringed because I knew what was coming. His large fist connected with her stomach. I flinched with the pain she must have felt. And I also realized, whatever was going to happen, right now he didn't intend to kill her. He hit her somewhere that could be hidden and not on her face. So what was going to changed things? That part I hadn't seen.

I watched her bent over form, hoping the outcome I'd seen was wrong. Maybe it would be okay. She straightened and I saw a look in her eyes I recognized. Something had snapped. The fear was gone.

Oh no, lady, this was not the time to get some balls. This was a time for her to cling to fear because it might save her life. Fear isn't always bad. Sometimes it's the lighthouse on the shore telling you to steer out of the storm.

Don't do it. "Please." I looked upward.

Fate turned to me and I thought I saw regret in his face as well but he turned back to the scene quickly.

She straightened to her full height of a foot less than him. "You bastard! I'm leaving you and if you try to stop me I'll fucking kill you!"

His hands struck out and were on her throat. He actually lifted her from the ground just by her neck. She grasped at his arms and clawed at his face. Her feet kicked wildly but never hit their target. He was choking her to death.

I didn't think about what I should do or not do, I reacted. Fate lunged for me but missed. I caught myself before I fell over the log that appeared in front of me. I ducked a branch and then another one, somehow untouchable now that I was desperate. I leapt on his back before he even knew I was there, and with a knowledge I'd never had in my human life, sprang into action. I broke the man's neck with a hard yank to the side.

He fell to the ground almost instantly and I fell on top of him.

The wind kicked up and loud claps of thunder boomed in the near distance.

Fate was at my side almost instantly pulling me off the guy but it was too late. I'd heard his neck snap and he wasn't moving. Nothing to be done now.

He knelt down next to me until his face was an inch from mine. "What the hell did you do?"

I looked down at the guy and then back at

Fate. "I think I just gave him what was coming to him before he could screw that poor woman up any worse."

I motioned to the woman I'd saved. She was staring right at us, eyes huge. Uh oh, she was certainly seeing us now.

"How? You shouldn't have been able to." He was now looking right at the woman too, even though he was talking to me.

The woman was on her knees, still gasping air back into her lungs. Her eyes never left us.

"Who are you?" she managed to finally say with a raw voice, the marks on her neck already angry looking. "Are you angels?"

I wondered what type of religion this woman believed in that murder seemed like a saintly act. The guy had been such a bastard, I wasn't sure I should fault her logic.

Her eyes darted back to Fate. But if she thought he looked like an angel, she really had a screw loose.

"No, we aren't," I said.

"Watch what you say to her," he said quietly under his breath. "Unless you want her to end up dead after all your handy work."

"What's happening?" the woman said, looking from me to Fate.

I saw the minute he had determined the new way forward out of this. From his initial reaction, I knew I'd thrown a pretty big wrench into the plan so it wasn't a bad rebound time, all considering. It was better than mine anyway since I had no idea what to do now. My ideas had never gotten past taking out the big brute.

He turned to the woman. "Janet, you aren't going to tell anyone we were here. I know that's what you are planning to do right now. I also know the police will never find any evidence of us and you will land in jail."

Fate had a strong presence by nature, but concentrated and in control as he was right now, I couldn't take my eyes from him. He was potent. I didn't want to admit it, but he lived up to every ounce of what you would expect someone in charge of people's fate would be.

"Do you understand me?"

When I didn't hear a response, I forced myself to look at Janet who was nodding.

"You will tell them that he was strangling you when he accidentally tripped."

His presence was flawless but his logic was off. I cleared my throat to get his attention before I said, "That'll never fly in court."

"I'm cleaning up your mess. You did your part, let me handle it now." I held my hands up in surrender and let him continue.

He squatted down next to her. "Repeat that back to me."

She repeated it back to him verbatim. When she finished, he nodded.

"That is going to keep you out of jail. Do you understand?"

She nodded again and he seemed satisfied.

"One last thing. He's got money hidden. I don't know where, but it's there. You'll find it if you look. It's enough to keep you and the kids going."

Again, just a nod.

"You're going to be okay." He gently cupped her cheek, as he said it. Then he stood up and grabbed my arm like he was an uncouth animal, yanking me after him into the woods as rain started to pour down on us out of nowhere. The forest was lit with flashes of lightning.

What was that all about? Why could he be so sweet with her?

"I can't believe you did that." He wasn't screaming but he was beyond mad.

"I'm not sorry." And I wasn't, not even a little. Murdering the guy didn't even seem to bother me this time. Maybe it would later? Could I just be in shock? Nah, it didn't feel like that this time. Much less traumatic the second time around. I guess you really did get over it.

I'd had clients tell me that but I'd never believed them. I also never thought I'd have the opportunity to find out either. Life's full of those learning moments.

I think my words pissed off Fate even more because his grip tightened and no matter how quick I walked, he seemed to up his pace just enough to have to pull me along.

"You can act like a cave man all you want,

still not regretting it." It was the exact opposite. I was invigorated by what I'd just done. I'd saved a woman, who I didn't even know had kids. The life I'd saved her children from was enough to make me smile, in spite of the rain now pouring down on me, or the angry man dragging me through the woods.

He finally stopped but didn't let go of me as he dug into his pocket with the other.

"You can let go you know. I don't have anywhere else to be." I waved my free hand around toward the dark forest we were standing in.

He looked at me with such intensity I wasn't really sure if he wanted to kill me or fuck me. And not in an, *I want to have sex with you because you're so special and pretty.* It was more along the lines of *I have a penis and you aren't listening to me.*

Or maybe he did just want to kill me. I wasn't quite sure.

"Give it your best shot," I replied in response to the look. It might have been nice to know which way he was actually leaning. It wouldn't have changed the reply so I figured I had it covered either way.

"You think I couldn't?"

"No. What I'm saying is I know you couldn't." Geez, I really wished I knew if he meant murder or sex. I wonder if there was a way to slip that question in somehow?

He stepped so close I was afraid to breathe because I knew if I took a deep inhale, my breasts would graze his chest. He could be such a jerk but to my extreme annoyance, I was attracted to him.

"You overestimate yourself." His voice was deep and husky and wasn't helping out my attraction issue. Neither was the proximity.

I instinctively laid a hand on his chest—and a really nice chest at that—because I wanted to touch him and my body had gotten ahead of my brain.

I pushed him away to cover up my real motives for the contact and I was surprised when he acquiesced.

With a little space in between us, my brain started functioning again. Thank god he was never in the courtroom with me. It would've been ugly.

"I'm not overestimating myself at all. I know exactly who I am and I know what I'm capable of. If you think I'd be an easy mark, either as a human or as I am now, you need to brush up on your people skills. You don't know the kind of fight I have in me. I don't roll over for anybody, anytime. Ever."

"You think you could take me on?" His eyebrows raised, disbelief written in every ounce of his being from the spacing of his feet to the set of his shoulders. "You've tried before, just in case you don't remember. You couldn't even stop me from dragging you into the car and that was when I was trying to not hurt you."

"I was also out of my mind then." My stance spread a bit as I eyed him, both of us undeterred by the torrential downpour. "Go ahead, try it."

His hands went to his hips, and his deep-set eyes seemed to sink a little further, as he stared at me.

And then I started babbling like an idiot. "I have no desire to sleep with you. As you said yourself, I was going to marry Charlie. He was a good man and nothing like you. Just so we are on the same page, that will not be happening."

I saw his chest rise and fall as if my words infuriated him even further.

"I don't remember asking you to sleep with me." I thought he was done talking, but then he continued. "*Really*? You'd say no?"

"One hundred percent. No, one thousand percent." *And it would mostly be from the guilt I felt over wanting you so soon after losing Charlie.*

"First off, there is no such thing as a thousand percent and you'd melt like chocolate in my hands so you're full of it."

"You really think I'd stoop to sleeping with you after him?"

We stood there, sopping wet and staring at each other. Then in a flash of movement, he was up against me, one arm curved around my back, the other hand in my hair angling my face to his.

I opened my mouth to protest, but it was muffled by his own. The lines of our bodies fit together like they were meant to be one. I didn't want to fit so perfectly to him but it just happened. Just like I didn't mean to soften to him but I couldn't seem to not. I had just been about to get married, I shouldn't have gotten weak over a kiss, but that's exactly what I was doing. All my blustering about Charlie fell apart the second his body touched mine.

But in my defense, to call this just a kiss was an understatement. There was nothing normal about this. I hadn't known a kiss could even be this utterly consuming. I was a grown woman, not a teenage girl. How could I be so affected? He could've taken me there in the middle of the forest, right that second, and I wouldn't have given a peep of protest. Rational thought left the minute he was pressed up against me.

He pulled back suddenly and looked even more pissed off than before he'd kissed me.

His phone rang, breaking the tension between us and interrupting any chance I had of finding out what had made him so mad now. If anyone should've been mad, it was me. He kissed me and I acted like it was my first kiss, not to mention the guilt. How could I have just done that?

Fate answered it but said nothing until he replaced it back in his jeans.

"We have to go to the office."

He dialed another number and then spoke into the phone. "We're ready."

The spot in front of us glittered in the dark, signaling the doors imminent appearance just as golf ball sized hail started to shoot down.

I wrapped my arms over my head and left the forest not knowing if we would've ended up rolling around on the forest floor, beating each other or with limbs tangled in the heat of passion.

It was for the best.

Chapter Twelve

It had been raining and hailing just as bad when we'd gotten back to South Carolina. What were the odds of an unexpected storm hitting both places at the same time? It was the first real inkling the powers that be were pretty pissed. I felt like a school kid in the principal's office and I wasn't enjoying the experience. I was an adult. Being pulled out of my previous reality didn't change that.

I sat in front of Harold's desk, creating puddles with my drenched clothes and hair, as he flipped through his papers silently.

Fate stood holding up the wall off to the side, forming his own puddles. His shirt stuck to his skin, showing off the impressive physique I'd already felt first hand. The three of us were the only ones in the office – or the building, for that matter.

Fate hadn't spoken since we'd gotten back. The only contribution he was currently making to the situation was an occasional grunt of annoyance, as he'd shake his head, obviously replaying the situation over and over again in his mind. But which situation? Both had seemed to piss him off.

"Do you mind?" I asked after an especially loud grunt. "Your monosyllabic noises are very distracting." Getting literally weak in the knees during our kiss hadn't improved my mood either. If he thought I was going to be an easy mark and that he'd walk all over me now, he was very mistaken. The sooner he knew that, the better.

He looked like he wanted to lunge at me. I smiled brightly back at him, my hands folded on my lap as if I weren't the least bit concerned.

Harold's fingers finally came to rest on a sheet that he pulled to the top of the pile in front of him.

"I've been informed you went off plan. What happened tonight can not happen again."

"Sure," I said and waited to see if either of them realized that wasn't technically an agreement. It was more along the lines of *sure, I understand how you would feel like that*. If needed, I'd do it again the moment I left this office and I wouldn't hesitate for even a second.

What else was there to do in that situation? That brute would've killed that poor woman and left her children in foster care. If I was Karma, even if it was only for a short time, I was going to do what I felt I should.

Unfortunately, such thoughts didn't help my current quandary. Time to unload some of the responsibility, if possible.

"I was surprised I even could do that. Maybe you should have informed me of how surprisingly strong I am? This might have been averted if I'd had more knowledge."

"You leapt on the guy's back." Harold made a noise that was a watered down version of the ones Fate was making, and then continued. "The point is, it can't happen again. That man was not slated to move on for another fifty years." He waved the paper at me but not close enough to read. Harold really loved his papers. "Your actions have ramifications."

"I can see the problems that would create." *But I won't agree to not do it again.* Dodged another. His patience will wear out soon enough if I kept this up. As far as Fate, I wasn't even going to think about *him,* right now.

I watched Harold flip through some more piles before he finally looked up again. His lips were pursed and it looked like a couple of blood vessels were in danger of bursting.

"You wanted her," Fate said from where he was leaning, noticing how Harold was about to lose it.

I crossed my legs, making a squishing sound with the action. "I'm so glad you finally regained your ability to form words. The grunting was *very* unbecoming."

Harold cleared his throat, purposefully bringing the attention back to himself. "I'm telling you right now, that can not happen again. I'll have your word on it."

I was afraid it was going to come to this. They'd try and nail me down, maybe pull out another contract. I was a former lawyer, and not just a ho-hum one; I'd had a gift for it. They'd gotten the best of me once when I'd been weak and not in my right mind. That was galling enough. Let's see who got the best deal when I was in my right mind?

"I'd prefer not to commit," I said, like I was unsure if I'd be able to make it to a barbecue next week.

"You have to." Harold's face grew red as he stared at me. Fate was back to grunts and head shakes.

Then they said nothing. And the longer they went without words, the more suspicious I became. Time to start poking the bear and see what kind of teeth he really had.

"I told you, you made a mistake choosing me." I shrugged, silently inferring that this was their problem, not mine.

"You were the last name on the list of one," Harold said. "You think I would've chosen you?"

He thought insults were going to work? I'd dealt with and defended the dregs of society. I'd heard worse on a weekly basis. I decided to poke the stick in a little bit deeper. "That's not so good for you because I really don't like orders, and I'm trying to figure out why I'm supposed to be taking them from either of you."

Harold's breathing increased and his eyes flashed toward Fate for the briefest of seconds. He didn't know what to do with me and there was only one likely answer. He *couldn't* do anything.

I reclined into the chair and swung my arm off the back. Just to rub it in, because I didn't particularly like Harold or the way he treated people, I kicked my feet up on his desk and crossed my ankles before I spoke.

"You can't do anything to me, can you?" I posed it as a question even though I was certain of the answer. "Furthermore, I don't think this has ever happened, has it? I wasn't supposed to be able to do what I did and save that woman. And if the entire universe couldn't stop me, what can you do?" I saw Harold's eyes dart to Fate again, who looked like he wasn't listening anymore, even though I knew he was.

Harold rose and leaned forward. "I'll keep you here until you fall in line, contract or not. You want out? You better not pull one of those pranks again!"

I looked at him calmly, his head hovering above where my feet still perched.

"No, I don't think you will." I crossed my arms as I rocked my chair on the back two legs. "You don't like me. You'll get rid of me the first chance you can."

"How do you know I won't do it just to spite you?"

I laughed a little before I answered. "That's an easy one. You won't do it because that's what I'd do. When it comes down to it, I'll do anything to win. And you and me," I pointed back and forth between us, "couldn't be more different."

Harold was practically huffing now but didn't try and deny it. He stood over his desk while I continued to recline. Our silent standoff was finally broken by the sound of Fate's laugh.

"Why are you laughing?" Harold demanded.

"Cause she's right." He nodded in my direction but never actually looked at me.

"Now, gentleman, I'm exhausted and need to get some sleep, if you don't mind." I stood and walked out of the room, digging out my phone to call a taxi, since Fate had driven. I left the two of them to discuss me in private while I exited the building.

I was standing out front by the curb, the phone pressed to my ear, when Fate came out. He grabbed it from me, closed the lid and handed it back.

"I'll drive you," he said calmly.

He started walking to where his car was parked. Wait for a taxi for ten minutes or be home by then? I followed him to his car.

He didn't speak until we were on the road. "You came very close to crossing a line tonight." I'd thought he was calm. I might have been wrong. "Do not mistake me for Harold."

"Don't threaten me. It's not a tactic I respect or respond well to."

"Just like in a human life, there are lines you don't cross. If you put me in that spot again, I'll do more than threaten."

"And what would those lines be? I've got some lines as well and you seem to have no issue trampling over them," I said as he pulled into my parking lot.

"Don't press me."

"Why? And while we're at it, what exactly is going on between you and Harold? What do you have on him?"

"Absolutely nothing."

"But there's something there. I can practically taste the tension between the two of you."

"You've got two weeks left here." He pulled into my lot. "Is it worth it?" He nodded toward the door, silently telling me to get out, and I obliged him.

He peeled out of the lot. I guess he wasn't staying tonight.

***

Fate was still gone when I got up the next morning, or I thought he was. I heard him somewhere below when I went to have coffee on my deck

"She's sleeping."

Not anymore I wasn't. I didn't know who he was talking to and I didn't want to lean over the deck and alert them I was there. I slunk closer to the side, as far as I could get without hanging over the rail.

"Do you think she's going to lead us to him?" his unknown companion asked.

"I don't know, but she's the best tool in our box."

"And Harold?" The way he said his name indicated it was a question asked often.

"Useless, like usual," Fate replied.

"You going to tell her?"

"Definitely not. She's completely unpredictable. Head strong, stubborn—"

If Fate hadn't been cut off, who knew how long the list would've gone on, but it sounded like he was just getting going. I couldn't really fault any of his statements either. They sounded pretty true.

"And pretty hot. You working anything in that angle?"

"Not worth the cost," Fate said.

That stung a little. He didn't have a problem the other day.

"How's that?"

"She's too human."

"Which is exactly what you normally sleep with."

"You should leave before she gets up." Fate's voice. "I don't want to have to explain you. Don't come here again unless I give you the green light. Not while she's here."

"Sure."

I heard steps retreating and I ran back inside to see if I could catch a glimpse out the back kitchen window that faced the road. The back of a man with tattoos and long black hair walked away, with Fate by his side.

I didn't recognize him from the office but that didn't mean he wasn't from one of the other suites. If he wasn't, who was he? We weren't supposed to be able to even tell anyone else about us. I knew first hand how ominous that was.

So, the guy was either one of us and in the loop, or maybe the ominous feeling I had was just a loud bark with no real bite?

There was only one way to test it, and I wasn't ready to jeopardize someone's life to find out. I'd have to check out the suites. If he was in the building, I'd find him.

And if he wasn't?

And why did they care about my killer? What was the connection there because Harold didn't seem to care that much.

Chapter Thirteen

I was settled into my usual place near the window, newspaper spread out before me. The others in the office rarely approached so when someone said hi from right behind me, I nearly jumped out of my skin.

It was Murphy.

"Hi," I replied.

"Would you mind?" He pointed to the empty chair across from me.

"Not at all."

He fidgeted for a few minutes, shifting this way and that in his seat.

"Would you like a section?" I didn't particularly feel like sharing but I'd hand it over gladly if he'd stop staring at me the way he was. I was pretty sure he would decline, though. I'd already spotted his sweat marks on the business section.

"No, I'm fine," he said but didn't look it.

I picked up my pen to continue my crossword, for want of something else to do. I'd just pretend he wasn't looking at me funny, if that were possible. This office really was the land of misfits. Were they like this when they started, or was it something contagious in the bad food and dated decor that seeped into their systems after prolonged exposure?

"The thing is," Murphy started to say after a

few very long and awkward moments, "transfers tend not to stay long. We've been burned before, you know, getting attached and all. I think that's why we all listened to Fate."

I looked up again. Ever since Kitty's party, it had been pretty obvious Fate had discouraged the others from too much interaction with me.

I nodded, not sure what he was looking to get from me now. I was still a transfer, that hadn't changed and there was nothing I could do about it.

"He doesn't take to transfers well, but you especially. It's sort of odd how set he is on getting you out of here. In the past, he's just ignored them."

"Any idea why I'm so special? He hasn't talked to you about it?"

"No. But he never reacted this badly before. I know he seems horrible to you, but this is out of character. You know, he's been here longer than any of us. Maybe even longer than Harold."

"He was here before Harold?"

"I'm not certain, since they've both been here before me, but he's been around a long time." He looked around the room before he continued. "I probably shouldn't say anything but...I think Fate might've gotten worse after we lost the last Karma."

My pen point dug through the thin newspaper where I'd been writing a "T." I wasn't the first Karma? Why had that never occurred to me before, that there would've been someone before me?

"What happened? Where is she, or he?"

"I don't know. She was here one day and then gone the next. Harold said she retired."

"But you don't believe that?"

"Not sure."

"Was she a transfer too?"

"No. She'd been here since her creation. It was just strange how she never told anyone she was leaving." He was fiddling with his hat on the table in front of him and I could see how her disappearance still bothered him.

"Hey, Murphy, do you know all the people in this building?"

He seemed to perk back up a bit with the change in subject.

"Yep. Everyone. Too well, in fact. Same people year after year."

"Do you know a guy with long black hair and tattoos? Pretty tall, probably about Fate's build?"

His face scrunched up and he shook his head. "Nobody here fits that description. Why?"

"Nothing important. I got a weird vibe off someone on the street the other day and thought perhaps they worked here. My senses are far from fine-tuned. I'm sure it was a mistake." I started chewing at the tip of my pen, a bad habit that only reared its head when I was truly stumped.

"We haven't had anyone who fit that description in forever."

"But you used to?"

"Yes. Except for the tattoos. The old reaper. Him and Fate used to be real tight. He retired about twenty years back."

"Retired?"

"Yeah. Went back into the system, got reborn. He didn't say bye, either. Seems to be becoming a trend around here."

"You're sure he retired?"

The old reaper. It had to be him. It just fit too neatly. What was he doing at my condo complex, then? Did Harold know he was still around? Wasn't Harold in charge of people going back? He had to know.

"Harold said so."

So Fate wasn't the only one with secrets. I looked around the office. I hadn't seen him at all today, which wasn't that unusual, except I had a funny feeling in my gut. I never ignored those.

"Have you seen Fate today?"

"Only briefly on my way in, he was headed out. He looked a little rushed."

"Did he mention where he was going?"

"No."

That bastard better not have sucked up my energy, gotten a lead on my target and then dumped me. Anyone else I would've given the benefit of the doubt. Him? He got the benefit of the suspicion.

It just didn't make any sense. Why would he want my guy? There was a link here; I just had to figure it out.

I looked over at Harold's door, the light seeping underneath.

"Excuse me, Murphy. I've got to speak with Harold."

He smiled in my direction. "Just glad there are no hard feelings between us."

"Not at all." But there's going to be even more ill will with Fate if he's out there chasing down my murderer without me.

I rapped my knuckles on Harold's door and received a brusque response to enter.

"Where is he?"

Harold looked up from his papers then rolled his eyes when he saw who it was. Right back at you, buddy.

"Who?" he asked, like he didn't already know.

"Fate."

"I don't know." He didn't bother looking up from his papers this time.

"The agreement was for us to hunt down my killer together. I'm either in this or not. Don't think you people are going to use me and then give me the cut." I stepped closer to his desk. I'd riffle through the stacks of papers myself, if that's what I had to do.

"I don't particularly care about your

murderer. Is it really that important for you to be involved on every level of the situation if it's being resolved?"

"You might not care, but Fate seems to."

"No, he doesn't. It's probably just easier for him to handle it on his own."

Saying Fate didn't care was blatantly wrong. I didn't know why, but Fate wanted my guy. Was Harold covering up for him, or did he truly believe that Fate didn't care?

"Let me make myself clear now. The killer is mine. I'm either privy to every detail or Fate can figure out another way to get information."

"He doesn't care that much, Karma. I really don't think—"

Harold's words faltered as a yellow slip of paper materialized on his desk. Wow, they did just show up. I'd been somewhat skeptical of that.

Harold looked down and read it quickly. "Fine," he said through clenched teeth.

"What did that say?"

"It agreed you should know."

"Then where is he?"

"I still don't know—"

Another slip appeared on top of the last one. Harold looked down and then held it out to me. "This one appears to be for you."

58 Winding Road, Ogunquit

It was a small coastal town in Maine. I recognized the name. I should. I went there with Charlie last year. But I wasn't going to think about Charlie or what I did in my past life. That was still off limits.

"Do you need assistance getting there?" Harold asked.

I pocketed the slip.

"No. I can do speed dial as well as the next gal."

***

I parked in my development, not wanting to leave my Honda at the office when I didn't know when I'd get back. I wasn't sure what the space requirements were for the door guys, but I figured the beach was a safe bet.

It was a beautiful day with people soaking up the rays on the sand. I looked around and wondered if they would interfere with my gate. If it were an issue, they'd probably just not show.

I flipped open the ancient phone and scrolled down the huge contact list of three. Harold, Fate and Door Guys.

I pressed number three and waited. It rang once and then stopped.

"Hello?"

No answer.

"Uh, I need a door? I'm on the beach and

need to go to," I dug in my pocket real quick and read off the address.

Still nothing?

I held the phone out to make sure I had a signal. The screen showed a live call so I continued.

"Okay, I'll just hang up and wait here then."

When Fate had called, it had appeared pretty quickly. I pocketed the phone and looked around. It suddenly appeared in the middle of a gully, the armored guards standing next to the doors knee deep in water. The door guys probably didn't realize they were in the middle of water.

I looked around to see if anyone noticed the huge doors or the medieval-looking guards standing next to them. Nothing. Not even the girl who was lying in the door's shadow seemed to be aware of what was going on.

Okay then, looks like I was good, except for one tiny detail.

"Is there any way to shift this thing to the left? Just about ten feet or so?" I pointed to the spot I thought would work on a nice mound of dry sand.

Both of the guards shook their heads.

"Is it a technical problem or something?"

Another shake.

I got it. Apparently, some people were a little put out about getting hailed on last time.

"You have to know, the hail was an

accident. I didn't realize I'd cause a storm."

One armored hand raised and pointed to a dent in his helmet. They had been pretty big hailstones.

"I swear, it won't happen again." That might be a lie. It could possibly reoccur. "Intentionally, anyway."

His partner raised a gloved hand to point at a dent in his shoulder.

"Come on guys! They're barely more than dings."

Nothing. No response and it was tough to read an expression through a masked helmet.

I kicked off my sandals and rolled up my pants. Looked like I was going to be wading.

Chapter Fourteen

Fate was sitting in a corner booth at the luncheonette located at the address I was given.

He watched as I entered. If he was surprised, he didn't look it. He was relaxed back in his chair, a half eaten sandwich of some type in front of him.

"Why are you soaking wet?" He popped a fry in his mouth as he perused me.

Not, *why are you here?* or *how did you know?* Maybe even a, *sorry, I'm a complete ass on so many different levels.*

"The door guards are still a bit miffed over the hail. Why didn't you tell me?" I yanked back the chair and made a horrible little squishing noise as I sat across from him.

"He'll be here any minute." He pointed to his plate. "Want a fry?"

I leaned across the table, ignoring the fry he picked up and tried to hand me, trying to lull me into a side order distraction. "Don't try and disarm me with fries."

"It's just a potato." He dropped the offending fry onto his plate.

"What do you know and why didn't you tell me?" My stomach growled. They certainly smelled good, but I couldn't eat one now.

"I don't know anything, yet. I just got a glimpse." He shrugged and tapped a finger on the table. "I don't even know if it's your guy."

I nailed him with an accusing stare but said nothing.

"What do you want me to do? Drag you around on every vision I get *just in case* it ties in?" His eyes darted to the side as the waitress approached.

"Just coffee," I said as a she came to the table.

Fate watched her retreat before he spoke. "I don't even know what this is yet."

"Bullshit. You left me out on purpose. Me and you? We're partners. All or nothing. You want to suck my psyche dry, whatever exactly it is you do, for information and past life stuff, then you'd better be prepared to share." I might have ruined my hard ass approach when I took a fry off his plate after my speech. I should've grabbed lunch before I left.

"Fine."

"You go? I go. You know? I know." I just needed one more fry.

"I. Get. It. Jesus, you're like rain man. I'll tell you if you promise to shut the hell up with the *I go, you go* shit?"

Feeling smugly confident I'd gotten my point across, I gracefully ceded the floor so I could eat the rest of his fries.

"I got a lead on this guy and I thought he might be tied into this somehow."

"How so?" I had trouble getting those two

words out as one of the fries decided to put up a fight on the road to my stomach.

"I don't know yet or I would've said. *I know, you know*," he mocked in a false falsetto as he pushed his soda toward me.

The coke wrestled the rest of that stubborn fry down.

"Why do you think he's connected to me?" I asked, now that I could speak easier.

"Because you were there as well."

"What was I doing?"

"I don't know. Nothing really." He looked away, agitated at the question for some reason.

"I don't get it. Was it a vision? Where was I?"

"It was more...dreamlike." He cleared his throat looking everywhere but me.

"Was I talking to him or something?" Why was Fate acting so oddly about a vision, or dream he had?

"It wasn't that clear!"

"You don't need to get all testy. I just wanted some details." Sleeping on the couch was making his mood worse than ever.

"I don't have any. Just follow my lead. No crazy moves or breaking necks. Agreed?" Now that he was calling me a murdering freak, he had no problem making eye contact.

"No. Not agreed. This is a mass murderer we're talking about. Isn't my job evening the score? Why wouldn't I? If he's the guy, he deserves it."

He leaned forward, halfway across the table now. "No. Killing."

Something about this scene jarred my brain and I had one of those perfect moments of clarity. The kind where, just for a few crystal clear moments, your biases and delusions drop away and you see your reality for what it truly is.

And mine scared the hell out of me.

His eyes jerked quickly to the side and then back to me, a thankful distraction from the truths I'd almost been forced to contemplate.

"What?"

"He's coming. Don't look."

That was fairly easy, since my back was to the door. The waitress placed a coffee in front of me and I tried to busy myself, so I wouldn't stare or scream "bloody murderer" across the room.

Fate's hand gripped my arm briefly. "Look now," he said.

I glanced toward the man sitting a few tables away. Mid-fifties, balding and wearing a gray suit. If I were a normal human, I wouldn't have looked twice at him. But I wasn't anymore and there was something slightly off about this man. He was like that odd piece of broccoli that showed up in my pepper steak order every now and then.

I looked back at Fate and squinted my eyes

in silent acknowledgment. His face reflected my own expression.

"You ever seen him before?" he asked.

"No, never."

"You're sure?" There was a heaviness to his words.

"I'm positive. Why?"

He looked back at the guy and then me again. "When he walked in, it looked like he recognized you."

"Don't squint at me like I'm lying."

He leaned forward. "You'd better not be."

"Great, here we go again with the threats," I said mockingly, to hide the slight worry he'd instilled. I didn't know the guy, but what if he got it into his head I did? The clarity I'd felt moments before leaked over on to him a bit. I treated our situation like I knew Fate, as if there was a level of safety there, because we worked together. In truth, I knew very little and the more I found out, the less comfortable I felt.

We looked at each other, coming to some unspoken agreement. I didn't trust him and he certainly didn't trust me. Our cards were finally on the table. As weird as it was, it was the first solid foundation we'd had.

Our guy was sitting, minding his own business, at his table when Fate stood and pulled a couple of bills out. He laid them on the table and nodded toward the door.

I looked at the guy, then shook my head and

didn't get up.

His eyes widened, a silent *come on already, I have a plan.*

Fine. I got up and followed him out.

I stopped right outside the door. "Why are you trying to leave?"

He stopped as well. "Because I want to search his car."

"Ahhh, okay. That's a good idea."

"It's that dark gray Camry." He pointed toward the luncheonette. I followed him, eager for some clues who this guy was and maybe why he'd decided to kill hundreds of humans in one fell swoop.

"Watch for him." Fate opened the passenger door and then turned and looked back at me again. "You're supposed to be watching the guy, not me."

"Why? He can't see us and I want to look too." I tried to step around him to get to the glove box but he blocked me.

"Searching his car right now has nothing to do with a job. His fate isn't out of whack, or his karma. There is no camouflage."

His logic would make sense except for one problem. "No one saw the door guys and that had nothing to do with me fixing someone's karma. You just want to have all the fun."

"The door guys are the exclusion. They never get seen, ever. Will you watch the guy, now?"

I saw a woman carrying a child walking passed us, about twenty feet away. I smiled at the toddler in her arms. The child smiled back.

"You believe me now?" Fate said from behind me.

"Fine. Hurry up."

He turned back to the car as I stared through the windows. I could see the corner of the man's sleeve as he sat at the table.

"Got something," Fate said behind me. "Come on." He grabbed my arm and tugged me after him toward a Chevy Impala.

"Is there a particular reason you feel the need to pull me around after you?"

"I don't do that," he said and then looked down and realized that was exactly what he'd been doing. He dropped his hand. "You walk slow."

"No, you're just bossy."

"Get in."

"What? No Porsche?"

"Going for low key."

I slid into the front passenger seat. "What did you get?"

"He's at a hotel a few blocks from here," he said as he started the car. "We need to come to an agreement."

"What kind of agreement?"

"I don't want him killed. Not right away."

"Tell me why."

"I'm going to help you, but that's my

condition."

"What does any of this matter to you?"

"He's not a normal human. I want to know who he is."

"Okay." I didn't think that was the end of the story. I knew if I were planning to stay on, I'd want to know about people like him. As far as explanations went, I could live with it. "But he goes before my time is over."

We pulled into the hotel parking lot a few minutes later. Fate killed the engine.

"You stay here and call me when you see him," he said.

"Why don't you stay here and call me?" I suggested as I got out of the car. "Why do you get all the fun stuff while I'm supposed to be the watch?"

"Because I know what I'm doing."

"He's a curiosity case to you. He's my murderer. I want to know 100% you don't miss anything."

"I'm not staying down here."

"Neither am I."

We stood in the middle of the lot staring at each other.

"Fine," he finally said. "Take turns at the window?"

"Agreed."

We entered through a back door of the building as a guest was exiting.

"You know the room number?"

"Yes."

"Just checking."

I followed him up to the third floor.

"This is it," he said as he stopped in front of room three-fourteen.

"How do we get in?"

"If we were on a job, it would've just opened. But we aren't. Luckily, it's an old fashioned lock or this might've been a problem." He pulled out a small metal pick from his pocket and held it up to show me.

"Do you normally carry those types of things around?"

"Only when I think the occasion might arise." I watched as he inserted it into the handle. He made surprisingly quick work of the lock.

The room was classic moderate hotel, from the prints on the wall to the patterned coverlet. The guy was neat; not a thing was left out.

"I'll take the closet, you take the drawers." I didn't give him much of a choice as I was already standing in front of it. Gray, gray, gray – the guy sure liked his gray suits. Or perhaps he just liked to blend.

It was hard to tell exactly how long he was staying here, since there were four suits. With four, he could've brought a suit for every day or been having them laundered regularly, because he liked to pack light.

I felt in the pockets for any stray receipts

but came up with nothing. A small safe was tucked into the corner of the closet – shut. I turned to where Fate was searching through the drawers.

"Got any tricks for safes?"

He turned to answer me just as we both heard a sound in the hallway. His eyes stared at mine. As if of one mind, we were packed into the closet together less than a second later.

Now, if we had just played nice, and one of us had actually taken window duty, this all could have been avoided. But neither of us wanted the shit job, and as penance, were forced up against each other in a goddamn closet.

It was easier and worse for me. Being smaller and shorter, I could stand normally. It was worse because Fate was taller and larger, and in order to fit, he was wrapped around me.

The door closed and any squirming or shimmying either of us wanted to do was frozen. We'd left the closet slightly ajar, as it had been when we got there. It cut back on our room but also let us hear better.

Keys were tossed onto a hard surface, skidding slightly as they landed. A few steps further and a jacket was being shed. The springs of the bed compressed and shoes dropped, one after the other, to the floor. The T.V. was turned on. The only bright side was he must have had bad hearing, because the volume was turned way up.

This had the potential to take a while.

At first, he couldn't seem to settle on one channel. I tried to get as comfortable as I could, with my back to Fate's front. His left arm was around my waist, simply to avoid having it bang into the closet door. This would've been an awkward moment no matter what, but after the kiss in the forest, I was that much more aware of every point of contact we had. The way his forearm grazed the underside of my breast or when he shifted and I caught the graze of his stubbled jaw along my neck.

It still might not have been that bad if the moaning hadn't started. Porn, and from the sound of it, classic eighties stuff. Please tell me this guy was not really going to watch porn right now?

I shook my head and looked up. I only saw the closet shelf but it would have to do.

"This is payback for the forest, isn't it?" I mouthed the words, barely a whisper escaping.

I was pressed up against a guy I barely knew and didn't exactly like. Of course this didn't seem to deter my attraction to him, against my better judgment. At least it was dark, so he couldn't read the unease all over my face.

"Who are you talking to?" His lips were right near my ear as he whispered, causing a funny reaction through my body.

"No one. Shhhh."

I felt him try and shift his large frame away

from me but there was nowhere to go and he ended up closer, if that were possible. This set off my own tight space maneuvering.

"Stop squirming."

His arm tightened around my waist. Great. More contact. Just what I needed.

"I'm uncomfortable," I replied. The sound of the moans and accompanying music shielded our own noise.

"Stop." There was a husky edge to his voice that made me think he was becoming agitated. Like I wasn't?

"I'm claustrophobic. I'm doing the best I can." It felt like he was actually holding me closer, but it was probably just my heightened awareness of him, which I wouldn't have had if he'd kept his hands to himself the other night. Okay, that was a lie. I was always aware of him, it was just worse now that I had a feeling sex with him would be as good as I suspected.

Fate was like getting a big present with a bow and finding out the gift inside lived up to the packaging. I've received big presents before. They almost never measure up to the hype.

Fate was moving behind me, trying to rearrange again, but every shift seemed to bring him in further contact. His thighs were against mine and I felt his breath along my neck. If I hadn't heard him rejecting me with my own ears, I would've thought he was doing it on purpose.

My breath was getting ragged and the more I tried to calm down, the worse it seemed to get. What was wrong with me? Not dead even a month, with a fiancé and family left behind grieving, and I'm ready to play seven minutes in heaven with the first hot guy I'm near? Maybe this was why Luck always looked well tumbled. Was dying some sort of aphrodisiac or was I just turning into a bit of a harlot?

The T.V. was suddenly muted, alerting us to a change in circumstances in the room and saving me from rubbing myself up against Fate in the next few minutes.

With the new silence, I heard his phone ringing.

"Yeah." The man's voice was average and blasé, just like everything else about him. "No, I wasn't able to arrange it."

I could hear him moving around the room and my breath caught in my throat, my heart beat hard against my chest, waiting for him to open the closet door. I felt Fate's hand shift slightly, as if trying to gesture it was okay, which seemed so out of character for him.

"Because this isn't as easy as the other."

He stopped talking and I could hear the noise coming from his phone, even in the closet, but I couldn't make out the words.

"No. I wasn't saying anything of the sort. I'll get it done."

Another pause.

"You know the other one? She was at the cafe but I didn't approach her. There was a guy with her."

What?

Fate's hand shifted and his arm tensed around me, but it wasn't in reassurance this time.

I heard the phone hit a hard surface and then some grunting that made me think he was bending over to put his shoes on. Five minutes later the door slammed again.

I couldn't get out of the closet fast enough. I knew what that had sounded like and I knew exactly what Fate was thinking. He let go of me and I pushed out of the closet with him right behind me.

"You did know him." He was in my space with a very unsettling look upon his face. It was too close for comfort and, this time, I couldn't stop myself from backing up. Didn't matter, he followed me anyway.

"I have no clue who he is."

"Why does he know you?"

"I have no clue! Did you forget that I'm the one who wants to kill him? You're the one buying him time, not me. That isn't suspicious? There must have been five other couples there as well. It wasn't like the place was empty. Why do you assume he meant me?"

"If you're lying to me—"

"Yeah, I know. All sorts of scary things will

happen. If you think he's such a bad guy, why don't we at least try and catch him? Question him, something!"

There was a tense moment as he tried to stare the truth out of me but I didn't have anything to hide. It must have shown. He relaxed a bit and moved a few feet away, accepting me at my word.

But he still had to try and throw out another warning. "If you're—"

"You covered that already." That last comment could have gone either way. I knew we were fine when he smiled.

Fate moved to the window and stared down to the parking lot, looking for him.

"I'm still not exactly clear on why we aren't killing him."

"Because I think he's working for someone. I want to know who. He can't talk if he's dead."

"I don't have a lot of time left. He's the one who killed me. How long am I supposed to wait? Talk about shady circumstances, why do you keep trying to save him? I don't care who he talks to. If he's the one that did it, I want him dead."

"You seem to be taking to killing with surprising ease." He turned from the window just long enough to shoot me an accusing stare.

"My first assignment, you were there making sure I did a good job, which ended up with someone dead. Now I'm too eager? Make up your mind."

"You'll get your chance to kill him. Just not yet."

As long as I got him before I left...retired...whatever the hell they called getting out of this shit job, it didn't matter.

He moved away from the window. "He just walked out. Let's get out of here and see if we can tail him."

I noticed he was giving me a wider berth than he had as we exited the room, or maybe it was me. I'd had so much up close and personal time, I needed a larger buffer than normal as we made our way to the parking lot.

By time we got down to the car, it was too late. He was gone.

Fate scanned the parking lot. "We lost him."

"We'll just have to wait for him to come back. All his stuff is upstairs." I really should've eaten. I wondered what those snack machines had in them.

"He's not coming back."

Fate was standing by the car, looking a little too agitated for my tastes.

"How do you know?"

"Did you notice the bell boy we passed on our way out?"

I nodded. I remembered a guy his early twenties on our way out of the hotel.

"What's he got to do with this?"

"Because I saw an image of that kid emptying all the contents left behind in that room."

"Are you sure? Why would you know that?"

"I'm positive. He's going to get hurt in the process, break his leg because the elevators were packed and he took the stairs. While he's laid up for the couple of months, he's going to start playing online poker tournaments. In ten years, he's going to win the World Series of Poker in Vegas."

"I don't even have two weeks left and I just lost my chance of taking this guy out?" I stared at him over the roof of the car.

"You'll get another chance."

"Do you know that for sure?"

He paused long enough that by time he said "no," I'd already known the answer.

I got in the car and didn't speak again. I was so consumed with fury I couldn't verbalize it.

Chapter Fifteen

I hadn't spoken the entire way back to South Carolina. He probably thought I was doing it to be mean. It was a kindness. When we pulled into the drive of the beachfront mansion I'd picked him up from the other day, I was at least calm enough to talk. Maybe not pleasantly, but it was an improvement.

"And what if I wanted to stay at my place? What's so much better about yours?" Besides a few thousand square feet, probably a lot more bedrooms, what looked to be a wraparound deck and, well, whatever. It was still his so it wasn't that great.

"Besides the obvious reasons, I've got more bedrooms."

"So what?"

"So, I don't want to sleep on your couch like a homeless person."

We pulled into the garage. If I had plans to stay on, I might have a bone to pick with Harold over pay discrepancy. Fate was living like a CEO while I existed on a hot dog budget—and not even good hot dogs but the value packs.

I begrudgingly got out of the car and followed him. Inside, the place actually seemed warm and inviting. I could imagine resting on one of the brown leather sofas near the huge stone fireplace. Relaxing while I watched the waves break through one of the many sets of French doors that lined the eastern wall, facing the ocean. Even the high pile area rug on the knotty rustic wood floors appealed to me.

"Who was your decorator?"

"I was."

Sure you were.

"We need to lay down some ground rules."

"Tread softly. I don't even want to be here." I looked over at him and couldn't stop my eyes from rolling. Was he going to be one of *those* people? Don't do this, don't do that, don't touch this. He didn't seem the type, but you never knew.

"I think it's best if we share a bed."

My stomach did a flip-flop and my pulse instantly ratcheted up. "I'm not sleeping with you." There. I got it out. *Unless you kiss me into submission.* Oh no, where did that come from? I'm a harlot. I'd died and become a slut.

"I'm not asking you to have sex with me, just sleep next to me. I think it will help tap into what's left of your human psyche." He walked over to one of the couches that wasn't far from me, where he couldn't seem to stop himself from leaning his hip. He crossed his arms in front of him while he waited for me to respond.

"Oh." That was kind of disappointing. It was one thing for me to think it was a bad idea but I still wanted *him* to want *me*. Why didn't he want me? I was a cute dead chick.

"It's not that you aren't attractive, it's just not a good idea."

I wanted to crawl under a rock. He could tell I was disappointed? "When have I ever expressed any interest in sleeping with you? I really don't need a soft let down talk. *I* should be giving *you* the soft let down." I hooked a thumb toward myself.

"You're really going to try and deny this again?"

His eyebrows were raised and his facial expression screamed *you couldn't have forgotten this quickly how you reacted to me in the woods.*

I wrapped one arm around my waist, all of a sudden feeling self-conscious. I knew this shirt had made me look frumpy. I had the sudden urge to go change my outfit, but I wouldn't.

"Don't forget, you kissed me," I reminded him.

"Minor detail."

There was only one way to handle it now, own it and flip it. It was my only chance of hanging on to some pride. "Even if I did acknowledge that you might be attractive in a certain rough around the edges way, it doesn't mean I'd act on it. If you haven't noticed, I don't particularly like you and I'm not one of those girls."

"Those girls?" he asked.

"Yes, I'm sure you know the type. Girls

with issues."

"You think I can't get normal healthy woman?"

I scrunched up my face in a false apology. "I would be a bit surprised."

"If I wanted to sleep with you, it would be a done deal. But we work together so it's not a good idea. I don't do doe eyes." He pushed off the couch and actually used both legs for once.

"Doe eyes?"

"You know, the way human women get when they start liking a guy."

"You think I'd fall all over you because we had sex?"

"Pretty much."

"You're greatly overestimating yourself." Or at least I really hoped so.

"No. I'm not."

"Maybe I'm not the almighty Fate but I'm a grown woman. I think I could handle it."

"Yeah, I'm sure Charlie was a real powerhouse in bed."

The minute he mentioned Charlie, any teasing nature of the conversation died. I froze in my spot, my body growing unnaturally tense and the atmosphere changed drastically.

"Don't talk about Charlie." The tone of my voice made it clear he'd crossed the line. This was not somewhere he wanted to go.

He didn't respond right away. He watched me for a minute before he finally nodded, a silent acknowledgment, if not exactly an apology, that he had pushed too far.

I watched as he walked over to a drawer and wondered why the hell he'd even brought up my past with Charlie. The more time I spent with Fate, the worse I read him. It was the exact opposite of what normally happened. I should be able to read him like a book by now, but nothing ever felt normal around him.

He brought a handful of index cards back over and laid them on the wooden table between the couches and I walked over to see what he was up to.

"As of right now, this is what we've got," he said.

He used the word "we" and I knew it was an olive branch of sorts.

He scribbled "Karma", "Suit", "Big Bad" and "Target" on four index cards.

"Suit is the guy we saw today?"

"Yes."

"Big Bad?" I asked.

"Suit isn't calling the shots."

"You don't know that. There's no evidence."

"I know people. Suit's a lackey." He looked at me, eyebrow raised. "You're going to tell me you think he's in charge?"

My gut feeling was the same as his. "Keep going."

I watched as he arranged the cards in a

triangle with Big Bad at one peak, Suit underneath him, and then Karma and Target taking up the bottom two corners.

"You think Big Bad is really responsible for my death?" I tapped the name, a made up one for someone I wasn't sure even existed.

"Yes. Yours was a mass murder, but I think he had a specific target in mind." He stared at me, letting me know exactly what he was thinking. It better not have been me, that if it turned out I was hiding something...

"I told you, I've never seen that man before."

I rested my chin on my hand as I stared down at the cards, the one representing me next to target.

"What exactly do you think is going on?" I asked.

"We've had employees disappear without a word or a trace. I think it has something to do with your murderer. I don't think he's human."

"But what is he?"

"I think he's like us, and if he is, we should know about him. I've been doing this a long time and I've never seen him before." He leaned back on the couch.

"This is why you don't want to kill him. You think there's some other non-human group running around out there, messing with things? Killing people? I've never been big on conspiracy theories when there's nothing to back it up."

He leaned forward, resting his arms on his knees. "He was obviously talking to someone. Who? And there's been disturbances."

"What kind of disturbances?" I leaned back against the sofa while I waited for him to explain and realized this might have been the most civil conversation we'd ever had.

"Imagine that the universe, everything that is around us, every molecule of water flowing, the tiniest cell in the smallest insect is interacting with everything else. Then there's us, and we're wading around in this vast ocean of tides and swells. I've been feeling something bump against me. I can't see what it is but I know it's out of place. Like a leaf blowing against the wind."

"And you think that this guy is part of it?" The more I heard, the less I liked it. Even more so that my death might be wrapped up in this somehow.

"Yes. He feels out of place."

"I knew he felt odd but I couldn't tell he wasn't human."

"You're not connected enough, yet. You're only picking up on really obvious things. For a transfer, it takes a while."

Transfer. The word was starting to sound more and more like a slur. I wasn't going to argue with him. Less than two weeks left. He could call me a crazy bitch if he wanted. It didn't matter...or it shouldn't.

"So what now?"

"We wait and see if I get any more clues."

"And what if you don't get enough clues before I move on? Then what?"

"This new situation set up will help."

I stood, more tired than I should've been. I might as well get the inevitable over with.

"Bedroom's down the hall."

It was very irritating that although I was losing my ability to read him, his perception was still right on.

"I'm going in there." I pointed in the direction down the hall like I was preparing to enter a minefield. "You can't come in until after I fall asleep. I don't want to know you're there." Because even though I definitely won't be sleeping with you now, even if you begged, I didn't know if I'd be able to fall asleep with him next to me.

"Agreed."

"And I'd prefer if you were gone when I wake up as well."

"How am I supposed to do that?"

"You're the almighty Fate. I'm just a feeble brained transfer. You figure it out."

***

I woke up alone in his massive bed, confirming he'd found a way to manage. When I rolled over, I could still smell his clean masculine scent, proving he'd been next to me all night. The guy was a jerk but he did smell nice.

I forced myself to get up before I was tempted to take a suspiciously deep breath and I would do that under no circumstance. Wanting to sleep with an attractive man was natural. Trying to smell him took it to a new low—kindergarten crush kind of low. Even I had my limits when it came to acknowledging things. If I tried to breathe in his scent, I was crushing hard. Forcing myself out of bed lent me enough deniability that it couldn't be proved.

There was an adjoining bathroom but I avoided it and opted for the common one down the hall. It might have seemed ridiculous, but I drew the line at sharing a bed. I needed my own bathroom.

The house sounded empty and I hurried, wanting to get out of there before he showed up again. Nights and work time was enough. I wasn't going to hang out at his house all day, too.

There was a luncheonette not far from here. Since I didn't have my Honda, I'd walk there and get a taxi home after I got some breakfast and much needed coffee. This body might not have been physically addicted, but I was certainly still in need.

Stepping outside, it was a beautiful sunny

day. I loved this time of year. It was why I'd chosen to get married this month. And then I couldn't seem to stop the thoughts from rolling in. I wondered if my wedding dress was still hanging in the closet in the home I'd shared with Charlie.

"Camilla, I don't understand why you're so crazy, lately." He paused outside the cafe we were about to lunch in and squeezed my hands. "We're going to be married next week. Where are all these fears coming from?"

I looked into his almond eyes but the calm I usually felt when I was near him didn't come.

I reached a hand up and ran my fingers along his cheek. My calm Charlie. Everything was going according to plan, right now. I was marrying a kind man, who was my best friend. I had a supportive family, great friends, and a job I loved.

And yet, for days now, I'd been plagued by a foreboding so powerful I woke in fear every night. Knowing it was irrational had done nothing to quell it. Standing here, on a beautiful spring day, I couldn't shake the feeling that a dark shadow chased me.

"Honey, please don't worry, everything is going to be fine."

When he used to smile at me like that, it would make me feel like everything was right in the world. But not today, or for the last week. If

I could just understand why I felt like this, maybe I could get myself out of this funk.

"I don't know what's wrong. It's just this feeling I can't get rid of."

"Everything will be fine."

His hands brushed my hair back from my face as he looked at me with concern. "Fine." I hated that word. I didn't want fine. I wanted great and fantastic. But Charlie was a "fine" person. Never swung too much in either direction and that was what I loved about him. He grounded me, so I overlooked the choice of words, knowing it was petty.

"I'm sorry. I don't know why I'm acting like this." I smiled back at him but it was forced and he knew it. "Let's eat."

I tugged him along after me into the luncheonette.

Chapter Sixteen

"What are you doing here?"

I looked over to see Fate sitting next to me on the bench across from the luncheonette I used to go to with Charlie.

I didn't know myself how I'd ended up here. Once I'd started thinking about my life, I'd also started losing some of my control. I'd picked up my Honda this morning and the next thing I knew, I was driving to all my old haunts until I was sitting there, a stalking dead girl.

Charlie and I used to meet here at least once a week for a long lunch. Small tables lined the front sidewalk, where we'd sit when the weather was nice. If I squinted my eyes, I could see the menu board above the counter we used to order from.

"How did you find me?" I was resentful of the company. This was my place. And Charlie's. This was my life and nothing to do with Fate, or the office and the craziness surrounding it.

He leaned against the wrought iron back and rested an ankle upon the opposite knee. I'd never met someone who could make themselves so comfortable no matter where they were.

"Why are you doing this to yourself?"

"Doing what? Sitting on a bench?"

"Him." Fate was staring at Charlie, who was sitting by himself at our favorite table.

I looked at Fate's slightly squinted eyes, like he'd rather not see Charlie there.

"Why do you dislike him?"

His face relaxed instantly. "I don't like or dislike him. He's simply there."

I looked at him for another minute and then back to Charlie, eating by himself. I didn't want him to be alone.

"What are you accomplishing by doing this? No matter what happens, he's not slated to die for another sixty years."

"You know when he's going to die?" A week ago, I would've been surprised by that statement. Now I asked just for confirmation.

"Yes."

"Do you always know?"

"No, but he's got a strong destiny. He'll start up a chain of medical clinics for the under-privileged."

I smiled. He was really going to do it. Charlie had talked about plans for a clinic since the day I'd met him. "Do you know if he'll be alone?"

"He'll get married."

"I'm glad."

I broke my gaze from Charlie to look at Fate. His eyes, face, everything, was the polar opposite of Charlie's warmth.

"Let's go," he said.

I wasn't ready to leave. "Why do you care what I do? This has nothing to do with you or our arrangement."

"You're creating useless emotions. What logical purpose does it serve?"

"Of course you don't understand. You'd have to understand love, be able to feel it. Logic has nothing to do with this."

He stood up abruptly and I got the distinct impression I might have hit a nerve I didn't know existed. I was hoping he'd leave but he didn't. He stood in front of me as if resigned to some course of action I wasn't aware of yet.

"I got a flash. If you want to check it out, we have to go now." He looked down at his watch.

"Where?"

"Florida. We've got to leave now if we want to make it."

I stood and took one last look back at Charlie. His eyes caught mine and he gave me an awkward smile. It was the kind people give when they catch a stranger staring and they are trying to be polite. I smiled politely back and then went to follow Fate.

"I want to drop my car off first," he said.

"What about my car?"

He looked down the street where my Honda was parked and dismissed it quickly. "We'll tell someone at the office to come back for it."

I settled into the passenger seat and did a double check on my seatbelt. Fate drove like a demon.

"You were never meant to be with him."

I'd thought we had come to an unspoken agreement that we wouldn't talk about Charlie, but he seemed to want to change the rules again today.

"You have no idea what you're talking about. Please keep your opinions to yourself." I watched the road whiz by and wondered how many times I was going to have to tell him the Charlie subject wasn't open for discussion.

"Did you forget who you're talking to?"

"You don't know everything about him. You're just like the rest of us. You get flashes. The universe hasn't seen fit to make you all-knowing."

"Maybe not, but I know his fate."

"And that means you know every detail of his life? I don't think so."

"No. But I've seen souls who were fated to be together. Lifespan after lifespan, there is still a connection. I saw him look at you. Nothing. You're relationship with him was purely luck. I might not know love, but I know fate. You two were never supposed to end up together."

"Why are you doing this? Why can't you mind your own business?" I watched him across the small expanse of car and wondered why he couldn't just leave it be.

"I'm not saying this to be hurtful. I just want you to understand you didn't lose anything. You were never meant to be with him.

When you move on from this and get reborn, as he will, you still won't be together. You are clinging to a life that was never going to be."

I didn't scream but I came really close. "You don't get it because you have no feelings. You're a robot. Maybe I was human, which makes me a dirty transfer, but I like my humanity. I like having feelings. You have no idea what it's like to lose everything you are but still be there, so close that you could reach out and grab it—except that the second you did, it would fall like water through your fingers. So you might think you *know,* but in truth you have no clue. So please, shut the hell up."

I turned my head away from him, back to look out the window. He actually did shut up.

He didn't know if we were meant to be together or not. It was nothing but a guess.

The phone ringing through the speakers broke the silence a few minutes later.

"Fate?" the voice spoke through his car speaker system.

"Harold, you called my phone. Who else would it be?" Fate's voice had an edge to it that I hadn't heard before.

"I need you to come back to the building."
"Can't."
"This isn't optional."
"Neither is this."
"Mother's flipping out."
Fate groaned then hit the steering wheel.

"Be there in five."

He hung a hard left that sent me crashing into the car door and had horns blaring.

"What are you doing? We'll miss Bad Guy," I said.

"And if I don't get back there and handle this, it could be worse."

"I don't care who Mother is, or what's happening back there. I'll go on my own."

"Absolutely not."

"Who are you to tell me no?"

"I don't want you to go alone."

"Why?"

"I just don't and Florida is a big state, without having any idea what you're looking for."

"It's in our best interest for me to go. You can't withhold information from me."

"Hold me in contempt of court."

It riled me because there was absolutely nothing I could do. "If I don't get to kill this guy before I leave, I'll be killing you in his place."

"You're perfectly welcome to try." He smiled at me, practically daring me to do it.

I made a half groan, half scream of frustration as we pulled up to the front door and he got out. On the slim chance that perhaps whatever he needed to handle would be done quickly, I followed Fate to the second floor.

I barely got to read the door plaque— Mother's Landscaping—before we entered.

What could be happening at a landscaping business that would cause us to have to run over here and not continue to search out who the murderer was? But nothing was what it seemed here, which meant Mother wasn't really a landscaper.

The reception area was similar to our own office, but with images of beautifully manicured lawns scattered throughout. A young guy sat behind the desk, giving me a skeptical look.

"Tommy, let us in," Fate said when he stopped at the locked inner door

"Who's she?"

"Karma."

"Why's she seem different?" His head tilted to the side, as if a different perspective would help answer the question.

"Because I'm a transfer. Okay?" I blurted out before Fate could answer.

Tommy made an "oh" face, and nodded, as if it all made sense now.

"Tommy. The door?"

"Oh yeah, sorry, Fate."

I heard the wailing and screaming as soon as it swung open, so when I walked in behind Fate, I wasn't surprised at the chaos before me.

Clusters of people in jeans and t-shirts were everywhere, arguing loudly. If I had seen any of them working on a lawn, while driving down a residential street, I wouldn't have taken a second look.

They were all in heated groups, some screaming to let her do it, some screaming no. A little pixie of a woman was at the center of the chaos, being trailed by several brawny young men, as she paced around the room. Thick dark brown curls framed a peaches and cream complexion, which the blue of her suit complimented.

Her eyes lit as she saw us—or more precisely, Fate.

"Darling! You've come to visit me?" Her voice was so sweet it gave me a sugar high, but the kind that made you nauseous and turned you off chocolate bars for a year.

"I came as soon as I heard you were upset." He took her hands in his as he greeted her with a kiss on each cheek.

My head snapped back and forth between the two of them. Where had Fate gone? Who was this well-mannered guy? And why did it seem like he was nice to everyone but me?

The entire room seemed to cease all other activity as everyone watched their conversation, including me. Fate took one of her hands and laid it on the crook of his arm and strolled with her through the room.

"What has you so upset?"

"I want a blizzard and they all keep arguing with me! I don't care if it's spring. I'm in charge. Why do they all bother me with these ridiculous details?"

"Now, you know we've talked about this before," he said as he patted the hand resting on his arm.

My eyes went to Fate's hand as it then moved to rest on her lower back. He steered her toward what looked like an office and I watched the door close on the two of them.

As soon as the door shut, I was the point of focus.

"Who are you?" the group of fifteen or so landscaper-looking people asked, eying me up from the top of my pony tail, down along my sun dress to my sandals.

"Who are you?" I asked, throwing the question back at them. Most of them looked like normal men, but there were four who definitely weren't human. They looked like they could've been the original models for the garden gnomes.

"We're her Gardeners," one replied.

"We heard there was a transfer," the guy on his right said.

They were circling me in an uncomfortable fashion.

"Yes, well I'm it. If you don't mind, I'll just go have a seat over there and wait for Fate."

I moved away from the crowd. Only one followed me over. I sat down and eyed the office up, wondering what exactly Fate's relationship was with Mother.

"It's not like that," the guy who followed me said.

"Like what?" I replied, feigning disinterest.

He let out a chuckle. "You know what I'm talking about. What, you think you're the only one hot to trot with Fate? He doesn't dabble with coworkers."

"I'm not hot for anything." What was wrong with me? Was I broadcasting every thought in my head these days?

"I'm not blind. I saw how you watched him with Mother."

Him wiggling his eyebrows was my last straw. I got up and left the office, his chuckles taunting me as I closed the door. I wanted to go back to the cafe and watch Charlie, as sick and masochistic as that might have been. I wanted something I knew just for a while, a small taste of normal to keep me going. But the chance that Fate might finish sooner rather than later stayed me from walking out of the building. Instead, I went to go and sit at my table.

I was surprised at how many people were in the office when I got there. I grabbed a newspaper and went to the corner, as I normally did.

About fifteen minutes later, Kitty the cat herder walked over and stopped in front of me. It was the first time she'd ever approached me. As far as Kitty went, though, she didn't seem to talk to anyone too much, so it wasn't that insulting.

The black cat weaving in between her legs

nailed me with a stare, jerked its chin up slightly in what looked to be a greeting and then went back to rubbing its head along Kitty's leg.

I found Kitty to be slightly scary. It wasn't because she was large and intimidating; she was actually quite frail looking. It was the crazy that scared me. She looked like she'd just been let out of the mental ward for good behavior, but you weren't sure how long the sane spell would last.

I looked up, not exactly sure what to do with her. Didn't these people understand I'd already reached my crazy quota for the year?

"I sent you many cats."

Her flat, monotone voice didn't offer any hints to whether that was supposed to have been a good thing or a bad thing. Yep, this was definitely going to put me over the top.

"Uh, thank you? Are they at my apartment?" I wondered if I should go run over and see if this woman had shoved a herd of cats into my condo. How many were we talking about?

"No, before you died. I sent you cats. Many cats."

"That was you?" The hair on my arms stood up. I remembered them. I'd even mentioned to Charlie how I kept seeing black cats everywhere I went. I'd thought I was crazy.

She leaned in closer, her palms on the table. "You didn't have to die."

"What do you mean?"

"I only send cats when it's something that can be avoided. I knew what was coming, but it didn't have to be. You had a choice. You've had more choices than anyone."

"I don't understand."

She stood up straight and started walking away.

I grabbed her arm to stop her. "Please, I need to know what you mean."

"I don't know anything else." She pulled away, finishing a conversation that was sure to haunt me for the rest of my time here.

I could've avoided this?

Chapter Seventeen

When Fate didn't come back to the office by six, I gave up. Hank gave me a ride back to my Honda, which was still sitting on the street outside the luncheonette and miraculously didn't have a ticket.

We'd lost our chance at figuring out who the Bad Guy was for today, but Fate would get another lead. He'd better, after he blew this one on us. But who was Bad Guy after? And why?

I didn't know how long Fate would be helping Mother, so I decided to swing by the grocery store. I'd pick up a couple of things for my place and have a quiet night out on the balcony, overlooking the ocean. I didn't expect to see old guy perusing the produce when I got there, his Fedora sitting low on his brow.

I pushed my carriage over to where he was picking through some fruit mounds.

"Did you know I was going to be here?"

"What? I can't go shopping for some fruits and vegetables without looking suspect?" He smelled the tomatoes and then placed them in a bag. "Ripe tomatoes smell like the plant near their stem."

"Who exactly are you?"

"I'm Paddy, a recruiter. I thought we'd covered this." He moved over to the pineapples. "Now with these, you have to pull a leaf from their stem to check for ripeness."

I ignored his fruit ripeness course and got to the subject. "A recruiter no one knows?"

"I can't help it if all the young kids are too self obsessed to be bothered with an old man."

"Okay, well, it was nice to see you." I pushed my carriage over to the next aisle. I really didn't need apples that badly and I couldn't handle any more complications or lies at the moment. I didn't know who Paddy really was, and it was probably for the best he wasn't going to tell me.

Except it didn't look like he was done with me.

"So, what have you and Fate been up to?" he asked as he followed behind me. I turned around to go get apples. If I was going to be stuck with him, I might as well get what I intended.

"You mean the Fate that doesn't know who you are?" Granny Smith apples, bingo. I grabbed a few and turned to head toward the shampoos, hoping he would disappear like he had the first time I'd met him.

"If you want to find your man, perhaps it would be wise to target someone he wants on the grid."

"What do you know about it?" I asked, not surprised in the least that he did know. Recruiter my ass. "Just be straight with me, are you the guy in charge or something? If you are,

I've got a serious bone to pick with you."

I looked up from the Pantene and he was gone. If I wanted him to stay, he left. Wanted him gone? He stayed. This Paddy guy was pissing me off. I was tired of this existence of riddles and non-answers. People who treated me badly and then turned around and sweet-talked whack jobs who threatened blizzards in the middle of spring.

Losing the mood to shop, I grabbed a tube of toothpaste, a rotisserie chicken and checked out. I loaded up my Honda and headed back to the condo with his words "On the grid," repeating in my head.

I managed to get a few hours of peace before Fate barged in at eleven.

Without so much as a single rap on the door, he came in and planted himself right in front of the T.V., so all I could see was a sliver of poor Jimmy's suit.

"What are you doing?" He motioned to my reclined state on the couch.

"Watching Jimmy Kimmel?"

"You know what I'm talking about."

"I was going to come over after this was done." If I leaned my head against my palm, I could almost make out Jimmy's mouth.

"Bullshit."

"You're right. I was coming over after I watched Craig Ferguson. But, I would have left the minute it was done. Well, I mean, unless

something else good came on after that." I
looked up from the spots of TV to him and
shrugged. "You know how it is."

"Get up."

He stepped closer to the couch and loomed
over it. I, in turn, sank deeper into the cushions,
not wanting to relinquish my comfy spot.

"Can't we take a night off?" There was a
whiny quality to my voice that was cringe
worthy. I felt like a dog, begging for mercy as I
lay on my side and stared up at him.

"No."

"You don't want to be glued to me, either. I
think it's for the best. Maybe every other night
is a better idea?"

"You agreed. Get up or I stay here and
there's a lot less room here to pretend."

He decided to demonstrate this by
squeezing next to me on the couch, his hands
picking up my outstretched legs so he could
shimmy underneath.

I jumped up. I was not having any more
moments with Fate. It was much easier to forget
he was there in his larger home. Grabbing my
stuff I walked to the door and he followed me
out.

"Where's my car? Someone stole my car!"

Fate laughed where he stood next to me.
"No self respecting car thief would touch your
Honda. The Jinxes are driving it over to my
place."

"They're eleven. Why would you do that? Why not just let me follow you?"

"They aren't eleven. They just look it and I didn't expect you to come willingly."

"So you were going to kidnap me, if necessary?" I said as I followed him to his car.

"It's not kidnapping if you previously agreed," he said as he opened my car door. "Get in."

"It would still have been kidnapping. You'd never find a jury that would agree with you."

He shut my door and got in his side before he continued the conversation. "There's one huge problem with your logic—there is no jury system anymore. Not for us. If I say it's not kidnapping, who's to say differently?"

I hugged my purse to me. "What about Harold? What if I told on you?"

He looked my way, smiled and shook his head before he started driving.

A lifetime spent learning and working the legal system, all for nothing. There were no laws for me here. I was living in the Wild West.

I leaned my head back on the seat and sighed. "We need to talk."

"I thought that's what we were doing."

"I don't have a lot of time left. I don't like you, you don't like me, but it would be nice to get through this *experience* without being miserable every second of the day. Getting along with you, who I spend so much time with, would help."

I watched his face, expressionless as far as I could tell. "You're positive you aren't going to stay on?"

There was something odd about the way he asked, but the day had already been too long. I couldn't rouse my brain enough to try and figure out what Fate was thinking or why he wanted me gone so badly. I'd just accept it for what it was. "There is nothing about this existence that I find even the least bit desirable."

It was true. An eternity of doling out justice to the dregs of society was at the bottom of my list of must dos. There was only one murder left in me before I moved on and the target was most deserving.

In my human life, I'd wanted to become a judge. Maybe it was a good thing I'd never gotten to realize that dream. It probably wouldn't have been that much different.

"Okay. Truce."

Some of the tension of the day left me as he said that. I had too many other issues. I needed to save what fight I had left in me to take out the man that had killed me.

As we drove the rest of the way to his house, I kept thinking about what Paddy had said. "As far as figuring out who Bad Guy is, would it be easier to focus on one of his human targets? You know, someone on the grid, so to speak?"

He pulled into the garage and then paused. I went to open the door and he clicked it locked. "On the grid? Why'd you choose that term?"

"I don't know." I opened the lock but before I could open the door, he locked it again.

"That's an odd choice of words."

"And locking me in a car in the garage is an odd action. I don't know why I chose those words, now let me out of the car, psycho. We have a truce, remember? Bullying is not a healthy start."

"You, bullied? Sure, like that could ever happen."

He made a flourish of his hand toward the car door and I opened it and got out. I followed him out of the garage into his kitchen.

"A mortal would be a lot easier to track. Only problem with that plan is, we don't know who he wants."

He tossed his keys on the counter, poured himself a drink and headed to the deck without another glance at me. I grabbed my purse and then paused.

"Don't forget not to come in—"

"Got it," he yelled right before the door to the deck shut.

What a dick. I couldn't believe I found him attractive. I was an embarrassment to all self-respecting dead girls everywhere.

Chapter Eighteen

"Bob, it's great to see you!" I watched my father greet a friend who used to be in the service with him. The man entered our house, a gift bag in one hand and a bottle of wine in the other. "How long are you going to be in town?"

"Just a few days. I've got some appointments on the West Coast this Friday."

"You didn't have to bring anything," my father said as he patted him on the back.

"I wanted to." The man turned and looked straight at me, in a way that made me want to run to my room and hide. My father seemed oblivious to my reaction, and the slimy feeling this guy gave off, and was still smiling away.

The man handed me the gift bag. I didn't want to take it but I saw my father's face behind him giving me the look. The "Camilla, you're being rude again" stare. I reached out a hand and took the unwanted gift.

"I hope you like it." There was something in his eyes, the way he looked at me, that made me freeze up.

"Say 'thank you,' Camilla," my mother said as she walked in the room.

"Thank you."

"I bet you'll turn into quite a little lady when you grow up."

I nodded and then took off the first chance I got.

I shot up in bed, trying to catch my breath. I'd lied. I did know Bad Guy.

He had looked exactly the same twenty-five years ago and, even then, I'd known something was off with him.

I jumped out of bed and looked around the house quickly. After I was certain I was alone, I powered up the laptop Fate always left sitting on the side table.

My mother was big on ancestry so I knew every site to hit, complete with passwords. It took me about fifteen minutes to find Robert Reynolds. He'd supposedly died one year after that dinner. My guess was he'd been dead long before then.

No wife or children listed. His parents didn't exist. Robert Reynolds never actually existed.

I'd just cleared the history when Fate walked in. There was no way I was admitting I knew this guy now, not after his reaction to even a hint of recognition.

"Hope you don't mind, I borrowed your computer."

"That's fine," He said as he moved around the kitchen.

"What happened to the Karma before me?"

I saw his movements falter for a hair of a

second before he continued taking things out of the fridge.

"You want some French toast?"

"Sure," I stood up and walked over to the breakfast bar that faced the kitchen, waiting for him to talk on his own. I had a feeling this was a touchy subject and I didn't want to press. Fate wasn't the type you could push into a response, anyway. He was either going to tell me on his own terms or not at all.

"A month before she died, she came to me and told me about a man she'd seen. She said she thought he was like us. From that day on, she had become obsessed with him."

"What did she tell you?"

"Nothing but a description of what he looked like."

"Which was?"

"Exactly like Bad Guy." He placed a plate in front of me, but I noticed he didn't make himself one now. "The day she died, she called me and said she'd spotted him again. I asked her to wait for me to get there, but she said she had to follow him or she'd lose him again."

"And then what happened?"

"She disappeared. Harold said she retired, but it's a lie. She's dead."

"How can you be sure?" I forced down a bite but had lost my appetite as well.

"She wasn't due for retirement and Harold knew that as well as I. She wouldn't have left without saying goodbye."

"What about the rest of the office? No one else is suspicious?"

"I haven't spoken to them about it." He leaned on the opposite counter, his arms crossed in front of his chest.

"Why not?"

"I don't want them involved."

"I'm involved?"

"You have to be. You're also leaving. They aren't. It's better for them to stay out of it."

I pushed the plate away after I forced down enough to not be rude.

"So he must have known she was searching for him. Whoever he is, he knows about us." He certainly knows about me.

"Which means he's somehow like us," he said, finishing my thoughts. "But I'm fairly certain he wasn't ever with us."

"Why?"

"Because I've been around a long time." He walked out into the living area and I swiveled on my stool to follow him around the room.

"Is there anyway for this transition to happen accidentally?"

"It's never happened before, but I couldn't rule it out." He paused for a moment. "I've got a job," he said, and left.

With no other current leads, I decided to do a little office reconnaissance. I should probably be at work anyway, demonstrating my active participation.

An hour later, I was looking up at the black felt board that listed all the inhabitants and their office suites.

Then my eyes lit on "Custom Toys." He was real? I'm coming, Santa! I did a little hop in place before I caught myself.

It wasn't even a question of where I was going first, straight to the big guy himself. Santa. I wondered if he had a north pole. If he did, maybe I could visit it before I left?

I took the stairs two at a time to the third floor, Unit #307. I wondered if he had some reindeer hidden somewhere. Maybe the roof?

I swung the door open, expecting candy canes and big boxes with bows. Maybe some milk and cookies?

I was a little disappointed that it looked the same as our reception area. I was hoping it would appear a bit more...I don't know, magical toy land?

With no one behind the desk, I went over to the door that would lead to the back offices, and hopefully Candy Cane Lane, and rapped quickly. All the fun was probably back there.

"Coming!" said a high-pitched voice. The door opened a minute later to what could only be described as an elf. The inner child in me was screaming "YES! YES! This is what I was hoping for!"

"You're the transfer?" he asked, his voice

was high but with a strange raspy quality, like he alternated between sucking on helium and an unfiltered cigarette.

"Is your boss in?"

"No. He's on Spring Break. You know, it's our off-season? Even the big guy needs to get some rays in. He's down in Cancun, right now."

"Okay, well, I just wanted to drop by and say hello." I tried to look past him but all the lights were out and the blinds must have been down.

"Come back next month."

"But I won't be here."

He shut the door in my face.

I wasn't going to get to meet Santa? That just sucked.

I walked from the office, more disappointed than an adult woman might want to admit, and headed toward my next stop. Dr. Bright, the tooth fairy. It felt a little like the lame consolation prize.

I was trying to remember which suite he was in when it hit.

***

I leaned against the wall in the hallway, trying to catch my breath. It had come on so strong and suddenly, it had taken me aback. A vision of a woman lacing her elderly father's tea with cyanide hit me like a cinder block across the forehead.

They lived in a small house in a suburb right outside of Dallas, Texas. The clock on their kitchen wall struck twelve, as they were about to sit down to lunch. It would be the final lethal dose, but it wasn't his time to go.

The tooth fairy would have to wait. I ran down to the parking lot, the closest place that would be large enough. I reached into my pocket and dialed up a door. In spite of any animosity they might harbor for me, the guards appeared quickly right there in the middle of the pavement. The door showed too, what little of it there was. It only opened about ten inches wide.

"Oh, come on guys! I have to squeeze through that thing?"

The only response I received was the right guard raising a gloved hand. He pointed toward a different ding I hadn't seen on his armored chest plate.

"Okay, I get it. Still paying me back. I deserve it. I ruined your stuff."

I squeezed through the small spot, trying to mask my struggle. "I understand. I dinged your suits. We started off on the wrong foot but I'm really not a bad sort." Thirteen more days. "I just need to say, I'm a very nice person once you get to know me," I continued to speak as I pulled my leg through the last little bit.

Instead of any reply, they slammed the door. "If I were to hang around for a while, you would grow to love me!" I yelled at where the door had just been.

I'd been left in the middle of a playground, a few blocks away from where I knew my job would be. A dirt bike that had seen better days—hell, maybe even better decades—was lying in the dirt in front of me. I guess I was biking the rest of the way.

I yanked a handle free out of the sucking mud that didn't particularly want to let go. Wasn't there a drought, right now? Yet, here I was, smack in the only mud pile within sight.

I looked around and saw some kids playing baseball further away on the playground. They were completely unaware of me, even as I had to duck to avoid getting hit by their ball. I didn't think that had gone unnoticed by the guards either. They probably wanted me to get pegged in the head. I hopped on my so aptly named dirt bike and started pedaling away.

The house was right where I'd thought. It was a yellow ranch with dingy, white crooked shutters. It had an overgrown lawn, more weeds than grass.

I rode around to the side and leaned my bike up against the house. It was ten to twelve as I approached the side door. And older man sat at the table while a younger woman, who I knew was his daughter and soon to be murderer, moved about the kitchen.

I stood there for a moment, looking in the

screen door, making sure they wouldn't notice me. When she walked toward where I stood and looked outside, right past me, I knew I was in the clear. It was such an odd thing, being right there but invisible to her. She stepped away, her worn flip flops slapping her calloused heels as she walked back to where the man sat at the table.

I opened the door and walked in. My hand was shaking slightly as I shut the door. The woman was quite large and I wasn't sure how I'd fare in a fight. Track marks ran up and down her arms and I knew drug addicts could often be quite tough. I'd defended quite a few in court, but as their attorney, they'd had motivation to play nice.

"Now, Dad, I'm going to take this and cash so I can buy things for the house." She pushed a greasy strand of hair behind her ear and I wondered when she'd showered last. She looked at the check in her hand as she stood next to him by the table.

I walked over to where her purse sat on the counter and was about to riffle through it for the cyanide when he spoke.

"Hello."

I swung around to see the older man staring directly at me.

"You can see me?" I was ready to grab a knife to protect myself from the attack surely to come from the daughter, but she looked right past me when she glanced around the room.

"Who are you talking to?" she asked him.

"Her," he said and pointed to me.

"You've completely lost it. You're lucky I don't stick you in a home." The daughter went back to rifling through a pile of mail on the table.

I shook my head. "She can't put you in a home," I said to the man. "She wants your Social Security checks. How come you can see me?"

He shrugged.

The daughter stashed the check in her pocket as she opened another piece of mail that probably wasn't hers and walked in the other room.

"Are you here for me?" he asked.

I knew exactly what he meant.

"No."

"For her?"

"Not the way you think. I'm not killing anyone. I'm not Death." Not today, anyway.

I dug into her purse and found the cyanide.

"Goodbye," I said. I left the house, but I knew my job wasn't done.

I went to her car parked in the driveway. The doors were open and I lifted up the passenger seat mat. A small packet of off white powder was there. I took it and placed it on the back dashboard. I walked over to the back of her car and gave it a little tap before I hopped back on my bike and rode to the playground.

For reasons I'd never be able to explain to any sane human being, I knew after she left there, she would get pulled over a little less than a mile away for a bad brake light. Upon the officer approaching the vehicle, he would spot the bag of heroin through the back windshield.

Between her probation being violated and possession of an illegal substance, she would be incarcerated and spend the next three years in jail. The entire time she'd be wondering how the bag got there when she thought she'd stashed it under the rug.

I didn't know what would happen to the man but I hoped he'd find peace.

Chapter Nineteen

I hadn't seen Fate at all, that night. I knew he'd been there from the dent in his pillow. So when I got in the office the next morning, I went straight to Harold. I knocked on his open door to get his attention.

"Yes?" he said and waved me in, not bothering to look up, but he seldom did.

"Something odd happened." I slumped into one of his chairs.

He looked up briefly, shook his head and looked back down at his papers. "I'm not surprised."

"I went on a job yesterday—"

"Alone?" His head perked back up.

"Yes."

He looked me over, nodded and then looked down again.

"There was an older man there and even though his daughter didn't see me, he did."

"Close to death. When humans start straddling the line, they sometimes pick up on us."

"Ah." I leaned back in the chair.

"How are things going?"

I picked up a pen from his desk and started nibbling. My quasi partner was a bastard, I had an old guy who looked like he shouldn't even be breathing who stalked me, my murderer had been keeping tabs on me from childhood and the door guys hated my guts and made it their purpose in life to have me wade through dirty gully water and sink in mud piles.

"It could be worse." Technically, it could be. I still had pizza and coffee, after all.

Harold looked up at the exact minute a slip of paper appeared in my lap.

Maxwell Stein, Fort Myers Beach Pier

"What is that?"

I jammed the paper in my pocket. "Huh?"

"That paper! Give it to me." He stood, leaned over the desk and pointed to my pocket.

"Oh, that? It's just my notes." I stood and started edging toward the door.

"No, it isn't. I saw that show up. It should've come to me. That's my note. I get the notes."

"Harold, I don't know what you're talking about. I pulled that piece out of my pocket." I just kept shaking my head, as I got closer to exiting his office, hoping he wouldn't follow me.

"You're leaving at the end of your trial, right?"

"Yes. No worries there."

I could see him deciding whether it was worth pursuing the paper and then he finally slumped back into his seat with a scowling face.

I opened my phone and speed dialed Fate as soon as I got out of hearing distance. "Meet me in front of the office."

***

"What is that?"

I handed Fate the piece of paper. He looked down and then back to me.

"Harold give this to you?"

"No."

"Then where did you get it?"

"I just got it."

"How?"

"It just came to me."

"But why are you getting memos?" He was holding the paper in front of my face.

"Back off. I don't know why, but I did and I bet this is his target." I ripped the note from his fingers. "Are you in or should I find this guy alone?"

He pulled the slip from my fingers. "Come on," he yelled, walking briskly toward his car.

"Where we driving?"

"I want to drop my car off at my house."

"The Jinxes are upstairs. Why not have the kids drive it?" I already knew the answer. He probably didn't like them to drive *his* car, but it was fine for my Honda.

It didn't take long to drop it off and pull up a picture of the guy online so we could make sure we'd recognize him.

I let Fate make the call for the door guys,

hoping they wouldn't realize I was with him until after the door was open.

It didn't work. The door started opening oddly from the bottom up but stopped about a foot and a half off the ground.

"What the hell?" Fate asked, walking closer and bending down and trying to yank the door up. He turned to me. "What's the deal with this?"

"Ask them," I said pointing to the guards.

"They don't speak." He turned toward me, hands on hips.

"They point."

"No, they don't."

"I guess you don't know everything." I walked closer, but not too close, to the guard on the right. "Why is the door like this?"

A gloved hand raised and pointed to a ding on his shoulder.

I swung back to Fate. "See? They're still pissed off about the hail storm."

His face looked disbelieving. "You're mad?" he asked them.

They nodded and then pointed to me.

Fate motioned for me to follow him, as he walked about twenty feet away.

"Why is everything to do with you so strange?"

He looked at me as if I had some sort of explanation for him.

"What? That they're mad? I did dent their

suits. It's not that surprising that they're upset."
If someone stained the only dress I had, I'd be pretty pissed.

"That they're communicating."

"Have you ever tried talking to them before?"

He shook his head.

"Well, maybe it's not that odd. You can lack certain social graces, on occasion."

"No, you don't get it. Everything to do with you is odd."

"How so?"

"You want a list?"

"No. I don't need a list from you about how weird I am."

"You're a transfer. We haven't had a transfer in eons because they don't work out. You transferred over within a week of losing our other Karma. Spots usually stay open for a year or more. You're still so connected to your past life you never should have even been an option and yet—"

"And besides having no social graces, you stink at truces!" I walked away from him and back toward the doors, screaming over my shoulder as I did. "I'm doing what I'm supposed to do...most of the time."

He cut in front of me, dropped to the ground and rolled through the opening. "Come on," he called out from the other side.

I paused right before I dropped to the

ground myself. "I hope you both have a really nice day," I said to the guards.

They turned their heads away and stiffened. It didn't matter; I'd crack them.

I rolled right onto a sandy beach. Fate reached down and grabbed my hand, yanking me to my feet and letting go quickly.

"Hey, how'd I end up in this?" I realized I was in a gold bikini that I filled out quite nicely. A cute black wrap hugged my hips.

"Did you pick this out?"

"The guards did," he said but wasn't actually looking at me.

"Over here," he said, weaving his way through the people sunning themselves.

He was in bathing trunks but had a shirt on over it. Considering I was in a tiny bikini, the shirt struck me odd. He looked like he was in superb shape but maybe he had something under there he was uncomfortable with.

"I see him." He pointed to the distance. "There, the guy in the blue trunks and the surfboard."

"Are you going to try and get close?" Maxwell was floating around on his surfboard with a couple other guys.

"Not me, you."

"Me? Shouldn't the more experienced person do this one?" He was still staring out at the ocean. "Hello? Can you look at me for a second?"

He looked back at me and I immediately wished he hadn't. It was *that* look. I knew what could come from that look. Completely thrown off kilter, my tongue darted out to wet my lower lip while I crossed my arms over my chest. I couldn't decide if I should close the gap between us or run screaming down the beach in the opposite direction.

I realized I'd liked it better when he was telling me he wasn't interested. Disinterest was insulting but safe. That look scared me.

Sometimes I was lulled into thinking he was something he wasn't by his relaxed posture. Then he looked at me like this and my heart wanted to relocate out of my chest as I waited to see if he'd act on it.

He was the type of man that could consume me. After a man like him, I didn't know if there would be a *me* left. The scariest part of all was, when he looked at me like that, I wasn't sure if I cared.

"You know, it's probably better to keep track of where he is." I pointed toward Maxwell. "Keep looking at him."

There was a slight hesitation, a decision being made. I held my breath while I waited to see what he would do. He turned back toward Maxwell and the tension broke.

"What should I do?" I asked.

"Wade in and try and get a little closer." He laid out a couple of beach towels he had tucked under his arm, provided by the guards. He sat on one of the towels.

I kicked off my sandals and unknotted the cover. "Why am I the one going?"

"Because I can't pick up anything from him. It would be good if we could get a clue why Suit wants him."

"You can tell from over here?"

"Yes."

"Then shouldn't I?"

"No. You haven't been doing it long enough and you've got too much human left on you to be that sensitive."

I nodded. It made sense.

I watched Maxwell as I waded into the water, getting as close as I could but not close enough to arouse suspicion. I got about ten feet from him but I wasn't picking up anything. I lingered in my spot but it was futile. I waited until he started paddling out to catch a wave. Whatever Fate thought I was supposed to pick up on wasn't happening.

I waded back out toward the beach where Fate was reclined on the towel, shirt still on. It's not like he was pale and maybe had a fear of burning. What was with the shirt?

"Anything?" he asked, eyes still fixed on Maxwell.

"No."

He stood and grabbed the towels, not elaborating any further.

"Well?"

"Either his karma doesn't swing strong enough in either direction or it's you." He started walking back to where we had initially entered the beach and I followed.

"And?"

"I'm guessing it's you."

Fate stepped through the doors first.

"I'll be right there," I yelled when I lost my sandal in the sand. I grabbed my shoe and just as I was stepping through the door, I heard him.

"See you soon, Camilla," I spun around, just as the door was shutting, to see Suit standing there.

I turned to find Fate, but he was getting in his car. He paused half in, half out. "What?" he asked.

I looked over my shoulder, the doors gone. "Nothing."

Chapter Twenty

I pulled my legs up under me on the bench as I watched Charlie walk out of his office. He looked tired as he got into his car.

Did he look thinner, too? Yes. He did. He needed to eat. He was always working crazy hours. I used to bring him dinner, a lot of the time. Who'd make sure he ate now?

I wondered if he'd been sleeping. I knew it was hard for me. Between Fate and this job, now I had Suit tracking me and I was too afraid to even tell anyone. Like Fate had said, there was no jury here. Harold hated me and Fate didn't trust me. I'd just have to take my chances, keep my own counsel and hopefully get out of here before the situation escalated.

Charlie's car was pulling out of the driveway when I heard footsteps approaching.

"You've got to stop."

Fate was standing behind me but I didn't turn. I just wanted—no, needed— some time alone, away from them and everything to do with the office.

"I'm not looking for company, right now."

Instead of leaving, he sat down next to me.

"This is the problem. And your problem is becoming my problem."

"He doesn't even notice me."

"That's not what I'm talking about. This is

why you aren't picking up as much as you should. I bet this is why you couldn't pick up on Maxwell. If Suit wants him, there's something off and, for good or for bad, I bet it's strong enough to show up in his karma. You can't pick up on it because you can't let go."

"So what?"

"You said you were leaving at the end of the trial period, correct?"

"I told you I was."

"Then I only have a small window to figure out who this guy is. You're my best lead and you're screwing this up."

I edged over, further away from where he was sitting next to me. "How does coming here screw up anything?"

"The more you cling to your mortal life, the duller your senses and the less you pick up. Why do you think everyone knows something's off with you the second they see you? You practically reek of human."

I could hear the disgust in his voice and, if anything, it made me want to cling harder. I didn't want to be like them.

"I thought you wanted to get your killer?"

"Don't think you can throw those words out at me and I'm going to hop up and do whatever you want. What am I, an idiot? Just because we didn't get a read off of that Maxwell guy doesn't mean it has anything to do with this. I could never visit Charlie again and I might still stink of human. I don't know what your problem is with this, but it's your problem. I agreed to cooperate, and I am. Now back off."

I grabbed my purse and walked away from Fate.

"He wasn't even your soul mate," he said as he got up and followed me.

"You have no idea what we were to each other."

"Stop lying."

"I'm not lying to you."

"Lying to me isn't the problem. I know it's bullshit and I make my arrangements accordingly. You're lying to yourself and that is an issue." He stepped around and stopped right in front of me.

"Come on."

"What?"

"I want to show you something."

"What?"

"I didn't want to do this, but it's getting out of hand."

When I didn't move he grabbed my hand and yanked me after him.

"You're so bossy!" We walked to his car, where he opened the door for me and waited.

"Where are we going?"

"You'll see. Get in."

Charlie had left for the day so I didn't care enough to fight about staying. If I had to go see something with him to get him to back off, it was easier to just go.

I sighed extra loud, voicing my annoyance, but I got in the car.

We drove several blocks away and parked on the street. Walking between the houses to beach access, the sun was just starting to set. We stopped in front of a two-story beachfront house.

"Would you mind explaining what we're doing at the beach?"

"Now we wait."

"I'm not standing out here all night. Five minutes and I'm leaving."

He looked down at his watch. "Only need two." He tapped my shoulder and nodded to the house we were in front of, just as the sliders to the deck were opening.

When I saw the intense expression on Fate's partly shadowed face, the panic started. I felt lightheaded and my legs were weak, but I didn't tell him that.

"I want to leave. I'm not into peeping tom scenes."

He grabbed my wrist when I went to walk away. I tugged at my arm but he wasn't budging.

"You already know, don't you?" It sounded like an accusation.

I swallowed hard but didn't answer. He wasn't going to let it go so I was forced to let this play out. I looked at the house.

An elegant brunette walked out, followed by Charlie, both with a glass of wine in their hands. I knew all of Charlie's friends, and I didn't know her.

I stood transfixed, watching as the woman walked over to the railing and put her glass down on it. Charlie followed and placed his beside hers. Then, the woman's back to the railing, Charlie placed his hands on either side of her. I'd never taken a real beating in my life but I knew I would've preferred the physical pain compared to what it felt like now. I watched as he leaned in closer until there was no possible excuse left that could be made. His fingers threaded through her hair as hers found his shoulders.

They were oblivious to us watching. Why wouldn't they be? We were just two strangers, enjoying the beach on a nice evening.

"And he didn't just meet her. But you knew that, didn't you?" Fate was angry and I didn't understand why. I was the one watching my fiancé with another woman.

"Do you get some strange satisfaction out of this?" I looked at the ocean, the beach, the dunes that ran along it, and finally I looked at Fate. I looked anywhere but back at Charlie.

"I don't understand," he said, and I could tell he meant it.

"Why do you care? Yes, I knew. I didn't have any facts or details, but I knew the way women always know."

"Why did you stay?" His hands gripped my shoulders.

"I don't know." His hands tightened on me as he forced me to watch them on the deck together. They weren't kissing anymore, but he still had an arm around her as she nestled into his side.

"He met her two months ago. She's his soul mate. I can't speculate on what he would've done if you had lived. I don't know if he would've gone through with the marriage or not. I just know she is who he's supposed to be with and who he'll live out the rest of his life with. And now that they've found each other, even if they are reborn, they'll search for each other until the end of eternity."

"Thank you. I'm not sure I could've gone on another moment without being aware of that."

"You put Charlie on a pedestal and pretended your relationship was something that, deep down, you knew it wasn't. It was a lie."

Why was he doing this to me? I just wanted to get away, but I wasn't going to struggle with Fate and have him see how much it was bothering me. "Did you have to cultivate being this much of an ass?"

"I don't understand. With your work, you gave it every ounce of yourself, but your relationships are always disasters."

"I'm dead now, so I guess it doesn't matter."

"You still don't get it. I'm not just talking about this life, I'm talking about your last ten. You've done this over and over, and over again. It's exhausting to watch, even as a bystander. For fuck's sake, just once, don't settle for this crap!"

He finally let go of my shoulders and I moved quickly to leave. I didn't care how it looked anymore, or if I appeared weak. Right now, I was—and I needed to get away from here and Charlie and the harsh reality I'd avoided until now.

Then he was in my path. "You could have so much more and yet you accepted this? Why? Every other aspect of your life you live to the fullest, but then with him you take everything that you are and try and squeeze it into the little box so that you blend. Some people aren't meant to follow the crowd, they're born to lead it."

"That's all fine and dandy but, in case you forgot, I'm. Dead. So what crowd am I leading now?" I went to move around him, in the direction of the car, but he stepped in front of me. "You know what I want, right now? For you to get the fuck out of my way." I was on complete information overload as I watched him standing before me. There was a glimmer in his eye. I was about to lose it on a level I'd never done in my life and I got the distinct impression he was happy about it.

"You want to know why I stayed? Because I wanted it to work. Because it should've worked. Charlie was perfect for me in every way and yet, just like every other guy I ever dated, something didn't click and I was tired of it. I was too this or too that. So I tried to become what I thought he wanted. Is that what you want to know? I was tired. I. Gave. Up."

Somehow, whatever I said in my frustration finally calmed him down and he stepped aside.

"You're a real sicko," I said to him as I headed to the car. He stayed behind a few minutes before he followed, as if acknowledging that I might need some space.

I'd avoided the truth when I was alive and now that I was dead and it was too late, I couldn't escape it anymore. I felt myself wondering who she was, what was so special about her, what could she give him that I hadn't; but I stopped myself. It didn't matter. I wasn't even human anymore, what purpose did it serve?

The driver's side door shut and the engine revved to life. He wasn't saying anything at all now and I was grateful.

Neither of us spoke until we got back to the house and were walking through the kitchen.

"You look like you could use a drink."

I nodded. He was absolutely correct. I took the glass he handed me and threw it back in one gulp, which I had to struggle to keep down.

He refilled it for me. "If it helps, I do think he cared for you."

"To be honest, it doesn't." I held out my glass for him to top it off then I hopped onto the counter.

He leaned a hip against it a few feet away. "You need to understand something, people have different life forces. Sometimes a stronger life force overwhelms the weaker ones."

"What's your next line? I have no friends because they're all secretly jealous of me?"

He smiled and let out what sounded like a little laugh. "Actually, you have no friends because I can be a bit of an ass." He moved over and topped off my glass but didn't move back again.

"Yeah, forgot to thank you for that." I laughed at the absurdity of it all and then threw back the last of my glass.

I scooted off the counter and walked toward his room. "I'm going to bed now, in your room. Please wait until I fall asleep?"

"Just tell me one thing and I'll never bring Charlie up again."

The offer was too tempting to turn down.

"Why would you keep watching him when you knew what the situation really was?"

I took a shaky breath before I forced the words from my mouth. Hearing them acknowledged it in a way that was hard to run from. "Because I miss my life."

"But why not watch your old work or your parents?"

"He was the only part of it I could bear to see."

***

I fell asleep easily but woke an hour later. I wasn't alone anymore. He wasn't touching me, but I could feel his heat.

And, for some reason, it made me feel more alone than ever. I turned on my side, facing away from him.

"You okay?"

I hadn't realized he was awake. "I'm fine."

"You don't sound like it."

"Leave it alone."

I felt him turn in the bed and then his hand was resting on my shoulder.

"I told you, I'm fine. I'm trying to sleep."

His hand paused briefly before he withdrew it.

Chapter Twenty-One

I was sitting at my usual table when Luck sashayed over. She sat down next to me as if it were something she did every day. "How you doin' darlin'?"

I looked up from my Dean Koontz paperback. I could relate to his writing on a whole other level, now.

"Fine. You?"

"Nothing amiss?" she asked, disregarding my question completely.

"Nope." I forced a smile. What the hell did Fate tell her? I wanted to kill him. Wasn't his little set up enough? I get it. My love life had sucked. If he had told the whole office, it was going to be war.

She sat back, lips pursed in deep thought. "Well, this isn't making much sense at all."

"What would that be?"

"First he's all blustering about how we shouldn't be nice to you and now he's all over us *to* be nice to you. I don't know why I even listen to him. He never makes any sense." She tapped the longest red nails I'd ever seen on the table.

"Do you always listen to him?"

"Depends on my mood and how pushy he's being that day. He said it was better for you not to stay and he was being so…so Fate, if that makes sense."

"I think I know what you mean." I kept my face neutral.

"Him being Fate and all, most of us figured he knew what he was talking about. He always does. But then today he came in and told everyone to be nice. He's not much of a talker, so I figured I'd ask you. What changed his mind? You two getting it on or something?"

"No. Why would you even think that?"

"I guess the way you look at him. Then he told us to be nice. He's never wanted us to be nice to anyone, before."

This was nice? I looked around. She was the only one that had even approached me. My thoughts must have been obvious to her.

"Well, we aren't a really warm group to begin with."

"I thought Harold was in charge. Why do you listen to Fate?"

"I can understand the confusion. Harold is technically the boss." She did air quotes when she said "boss." "We listen to him as long as Fate doesn't tell us to do something different."

"Why would you do that?"

She leaned back in the chair. "I don't know, exactly. Just seems natural, I guess." I heard Elvis sing out from the cell phone she laid on the table next to her. She grinned when she looked at the number.

"I've got to take this. It was nice talking to you."

The entirety of my "be nice" squad now gone, I put the Dean Koontz novel in my empty desk drawer and decided to stretch my legs a bit.

I walked down the hallway, thinking about introducing myself to the tooth fairy, when I read the plaque to the office next to us. "Find Your Match." Who else would be better at telling me why my love life was a wreck, and according to Fate, for quite some time.

I should've asked him about that. How many lives of mine was he familiar with? And I hadn't had a decent relationship in any of them?

I tried the doorknob and found the office open. I walked up to the receptionist, who looked like a blond Greek god and was smiling quite warmly in my direction.

"Is your boss in today?"

"Oh yes, he's been waiting for you, girlie. He thought you'd have been by, already."

"Do you know who I am?"

"Of course! You're the transfer. He's been watching you for a while, now."

"Okay then."

Adonis held up a finger and lifted the phone. "She's here." He looked at me and smiled as he listened to the phone. He replaced the receiver and got up to open the inner door himself. "Go right in."

I felt like a teenager when I walked in because the only word I could summon up for the scene in front of me was *awesome*.

The place was swarming with cupids. What looked like young girls and boys in white with fluffy white feathers were literally flying around a pure pink and red room. Everywhere I looked, there were satin couches and velvet chaises. It was like Valentine's Day on steroids.

"Camilla?" a deep masculine voice called and drew my eye to a couch situated in the back of the room. A gentleman dressed in a black silk suit lounged on the sofa. He had this blond wavy hair that looked so thick you itched to run your fingers through it, just to test it out. And then he smiled. He wasn't what I imagined, even my imagination wasn't this good.

"Darling, I've been dying to meet you." He stood, waving me over. "So glad you stopped by!"

He kissed both cheeks and I couldn't believe his smell.

"You smell so good. What are you wearing?"

"Oh, that's just me."

He led me over to a seat on the couch he had been occupying. He held one of my hands as we sat, as if it were the most natural thing in the world. I wasn't normally a hand holder and yet I didn't mind.

"I figured I should say hello and introduce myself." *Maybe find out why my love life is a complete disaster?*

"I've been waiting for you." He turned his head in a way that had me re-situating myself in a more flattering position. "You're a very attractive soul."

"Why thank you! So are you!" My voice came out an octave higher and I felt like a teenager who'd just been complimented by the quarterback.

"I know why you're here. You've had a rough time of it."

"I have had some bumps."

He squeezed the hand he held. "Don't worry. I'm going to get you all straightened out."

"You mean when I get reborn?"

The door slamming drew our attention to Fate, who stood scanning the room, scowling until he locked eyes on us.

"Oh no," Cupid said. "Looks like the fun police arrived. We'll have to catch up later."

Fate was on us a minute later. "We've got to go."

"Why?"

His eyes shifted to the door and back.

Was that supposed to tell me something? I wasn't sure, but if I stayed with Cupid I was going to be giggling like a twelve year old soon.

Both Cupid and I stood. I wanted to know what Fate wasn't saying, and Cupid... I wasn't sure what he wanted. Cupid walked over to stand next to Fate and gave him a look like he was a ripe leg of lamb.

"She's *all* yours darling." Cupid grabbed Fate's ass before he walked away.

"It was nice to meet you," I called after him as he left.

"Don't worry, we'll be seeing each other again," he yelled back.

I walked to the door with a scowling Fate. A slight shake of his head indicated he didn't want to talk there and I held my peace until we got outside.

"Why are you scowling?"

"Did he touch you?"

"No."

"Didn't Harold warn you about visiting?"

"Everyone else seems to know each other."

"We also know what everyone's capabilities are. You aren't human anymore. This isn't like going to a block party and getting to know your neighbors."

"Why are you getting so crazy?"

"You're leaving soon. Just stay out of trouble."

I stopped walking and he followed suit a second later.

"Was there anything else?"

"I've been doing some background checks, and I want to take another stab at Maxwell, Suit's target."

I stood there for a minute. I wanted Suit, there was no doubt about that, but did I really have to do everything with Fate? Could I risk doing everything with him? What if he figured out there was a connection between us?

"We've got less than two weeks left before you leave. You plan on making a decision anytime soon?" He stared at me, clearly confused by my hesitancy.

"I'm thinking."

"About what? You either want this guy or you don't."

"Camilla!" I looked down the hall and saw Death with another middle-aged man beside him, standing where the lobby began.

I walked past Fate. "Hi, Doc," I greeted him, figuring it might not be appropriate to call him Death in current company.

"I'd like to introduce you to Fred. We were just heading out for some golf." Death patted Fred on his back as he said this. They were both dressed in golf shirts with little sun visors.

"It's nice to meet you."

"You too!" He turned to Fate, "I've got your return ready."

"Thanks, Fred," Fate said, smiling. "You guys have a good game."

"I'm sorry you couldn't make this round."

"I'll catch you guys next week."

I watched Death and the accountant head off to go play eighteen holes and then turned to Fate.

"Have you met everyone?" he asked.

"You golf with them?" I asked.

"What's wrong with golf?"

"You want me gone because I'm a transfer and you're golfing with a human?" I seriously didn't need to elaborate on this, did I?

"It's different." He shrugged a single shoulder, as if he couldn't even sell that bullshit to himself completely.

"Really? How's that?"

"We have to go if we're going to check out the lead. You coming or not?"

And the bottom line was I did want to check it out. I'd lost my first opening to take out Suit and I was running out of time. I'd have to take my chances. Worst case scenario: kill him quickly before he could talk.

"I'll be right out."

Chapter Twenty-Two

When I got back, the guards were already there with an opened and normal door.

"I figured I'd use the opportunity before they saw you," Fate said.

When he went to move through the door, I grabbed his arm.

"Give me a minute?"

He shrugged and watched as I walked over to the guards with my offering in hand.

"This is called compound. They use it on cars. It's not going to completely fix your dings but it will help."

I stood there, arms outstretched with a bag for each. Fate stood off to my side, watching intently. Just when I thought they wouldn't take my gifts, they reached a hand forward.

"I am truly sorry that my actions contributed to messing up your suits."

They both looked over their gifts, then they looked at each other and made sure the other guard didn't get something better. As if that wasn't adequate, they swapped, examined and swapped back. After a long few minutes, they both looked at me again. In unison, they did a single nod in acknowledgment.

"So, we're good?"

Again, another nod.

I wanted to smile and skip around but I held

it under control. Feeling content that I'd mended a bridge, I walked through the opening. It's not like I'd see them for that much longer but I didn't want to move on knowing I'd upset the guards.

"I don't get it," Fate said as the door closed behind us.

"What?" He was staring at me as if I were a puzzle he was missing a piece to.

"Why they communicate with you."

"What's so strange about it?"

"You're the only one. You don't think that's odd?"

"Considering the people I've met so far? No. I don't find it that strange. I'd find it more unusual if they did." I looked around the parking lot of an office park. "Where are we going?"

"There." He pointed to one of the larger buildings off to the side that anchored the development. "That's where Maxwell works."

"We're going to walk into his office? Won't that tip anyone off?" I looked down at the dark pants and blouse I had on. It fit perfectly. How did they do that?

"Not if we have an appointment. He's an accountant."

"We?" I looked at Fate in a black suit with a crisp white shirt he wore really well.

"Yes. Mr. and Mrs. Clark." He walked forward and yelled back, "Come on, honey, we don't want to be late."

I followed him into the elevator and pulled the collar of the blouse open a bit.

"It's warm in here. They need to turn the AC up a bit." I put a hand under my hair and lifted it off the back of my neck.

I looked over to Fate who seemed completely comfortable in his suit jacket. God, he looked really good in a suit—too good.

"Did you eat or drink anything at Cupid's?"

"No. Why do you ask? Would that have been bad?" I thought back and I definitely hadn't. I would have remembered.

He squinted his eyes, as he looked me over. "You sure? You're looking a little flushed."

"I'm not an idiot. I'd know if I ate something. Why? Would it have done something to me?"

"You didn't, so don't worry about it."

The elevator doors slid open and stopped the conversation. We stopped by the receptionist, who checked us in right away and then led us down a hall into a corner office. He was obviously a very good accountant. The office was plush, the chairs, the desk, even the lamp that sat on his desk all screamed that he was raking in the cash.

A minute later, Maxwell walked in and shook our hands.

"It's nice to meet you both." He moved around to the other side and sat behind the desk.

"Did you bring your paperwork?"

Fate handed him a pile of sheets he pulled out of a briefcase.

"So, Mr. and Mrs. Clark, how can I help you?"

"Please, call us Hank and Ruth. We've been thinking of doing some financial restructuring."

Ruth? Oh no, I so didn't look like a Ruth. Is he crazy? I was going to have to talk to him about choosing my own aliases if this was what he was going to come up with.

I watched Maxwell put on his glasses and start looking over the paperwork. I was leaning back in my chair, still dwelling on the poor choice of names, when a strange noxious odor wafted through the air, a strange blend of skunk and spoiled eggs. I turned my head in different directions trying to get a lead on where the odor was coming from when Fate reached out and squeezed my hand.

I looked to Maxwell and saw Fate do a single and ever so subtle nod of his head.

I looked closer at him. His head was bent and I saw what appeared to be cracks in his skin slowly appear, but he kept looking down at his papers like nothing was amiss while his skin was splitting open in front of my eyes.

Fate squeezed my hand harder and I forced my gaping jaw shut. It was just in time as Maxwell looked up briefly and smiled at us, before continuing to look our numbers over.

The cracks in his face didn't stop but continued to spread as I watched him. I was horrifically mesmerized as they grew larger, slowly spanning his entire face. Once they got to a certain size, yellow pus started oozing from them.

"Are you okay?" Maxwell asked. I hadn't even realized he was looking at me again.

I couldn't speak. I was having a hard enough time holding down the salad I'd eaten. Luckily, Fate stood up and covered for me.

"Darling, are you okay? You look a bit sick."

"Uh huh," was all I managed to utter and then Fate positioned himself in between me and oozing Maxwell.

Fate grabbed my hand and then circled an arm around my waist. "I'm sorry, she's with child and you never know when the morning sickness is going to hit. Can we just leave our documents with you?"

"Of course! And congratulations. I'll call as soon as I've taken a look," Maxwell said as he came into view again.

I tried to look past him as I forced a smile on my face. I think I mumbled out a "thank you," but I wasn't sure.

We walked out of the office and I could breathe again. The further we got from him the better I was feeling.

The fresh air hit me as we exited the

building. I moved out of the embrace of Fate's arm as the sun hit my skin and I felt normal again.

"Well?" Fate asked after we got a few parking rows away from the building.

"It was, well, I'm sure you know. I wish you had given me a little warning."

"I have no idea what you saw or felt in there. Every one of us experiences things differently. I got nothing from him again."

He stood there waiting for me to tell him what I thought.

"Well, if what I just saw was his karma..." I shuddered before I could continue. "He's certainly not on the good team."

"How bad?"

"With no point of reference, it's hard to say. But, I hope he's among the worst because I'd hate to see anything beyond that."

I breathed deep, enjoying the smell of the outdoors more than I had all week. "Why did it come on like that this time, when I got nothing from him at the beach?"

"You were closer to him for a longer time and perhaps…" his words died off.

I looked at him and I knew what he didn't want to say. I'd taken a step further away from my old life.

He dug his hands in his pockets and looked down for a bit before he met my gaze. "You know, I didn't do it to be—"

"I know." I broke the gaze. I did get it. This was his job. I wouldn't hold that against him. But I wasn't going to discuss it either, not anymore anyway because it was also my life— or had been.

Fate dug out his phone and called for the doors. They appeared before us and opened up to a lawn with the sprinkler system on full blast.

"Guys, I thought we were good?"

I received a single nod.

"Then what's with this?"

I didn't expect them to talk. Not with the way Fate had reacted to them even pointing. But then a single word came out.

"Funny," the guard on the right, the one I considered slightly more *outgoing* of the two, said. It sounded like a clap of thunder when he spoke. I felt the vibration of it go straight through me like I was upfront at a concert but I understood it perfectly.

"Funny?"

They nodded. I just shook my head. "I'm glad I can offer you cosmic entertainment."

"I told you, strange," Fate said from behind me.

I shrugged as I walked through the door and took off in a sprint through the sprinkler. It was the office building next to us and I could see my Honda from the lawn.

"Where you going?" Fate yelled from behind me as he crossed the lawn.

"My place to get a change of clothes," I said heading to my car.

"We need to talk. You've got stuff at my place."

"Can't it wait?" I said, pausing a few feet from my car.

"'Til when? We don't have that much time."

It was true. I'd be officially resigning in less than two weeks. I needed to make this experience count for something. If I left leaving a mass murderer behind, what was the point of it all? I needed something positive to come out of this. I *had* to have something positive. "Okay. I'll meet you there."

Chapter Twenty-Three

"Are you sure you didn't eat anything at Cupid's?" he asked as he watched me walk into his kitchen.

"I told you, no. Why do you keep asking?"

"Forget it," he said but continued to stare at me in a weird sort of appraising way.

I left him standing in the kitchen and sat on the couch, facing away from him to avoid his perusal.

"Did you pick up on anything else? Other than he was bad?" I heard him moving around the kitchen doing who knew what as he talked.

"No."

"Are you sure?"

I shook my head and sighed. "Yes. Are you sure your hearing is okay? Because I can't figure out why I have to answer every question twice." I grabbed a magazine lying on the table. I never would have pegged him for a Home and Garden reader in a million years. Maybe he did decorate the place himself.

"You know we're running out of time."

"Yes. You mentioned that. Unlike you, I hear things the first time they're said." Wow, what a pretty gazebo. I wonder if I could make a note of this and put in a request for my next life. I'd really like one of those. I'd heard you could do that.

He walked over and stood in front of me. "I want to bring in some outside help."

My head perked up. "I didn't know there was outside help?"

"Nothing company approved."

I threw the magazine back on the table. "Is this something that could get me in trouble?" He wasn't leaning on anything. For some reason, I found that alarming.

"Yes."

"Can you lean on something?" I asked.

"Why? I don't feel like leaning."

That did not bode well. What could be so important that it made him use both of his legs? This was some serious business.

"What is it?" I asked, hoping he'd lean soon.

"There is a certain person I want to call in, for our purposes, lets just say he's in the know but not with the organization."

Oh no, he just crossed his arms. "And what does he do?" I sat up a little straighter myself now.

"He might be able to open you up a bit more by shedding some of the humanness you still have clinging to you."

Now I was standing, too. "I don't want to shed anymore. I want a smooth reentry."

He followed me as I moved about the room. I didn't have a destination in mind but I no longer felt like sitting still.

"That has no effect on it. Where did you get that idea?"

"How do you know it doesn't? And I'm not sure I'm comfortable going outside the organization. That sounds like trouble to me." I crossed my arms now. I knew I should've gone home.

"It doesn't matter, since we aren't getting caught."

I laughed loudly at that one. "You know how many clients I've had who thought the same thing?"

"If you don't, you'll move on and we might never get the guy that killed you. You're okay with moving on and leaving this guy on the loose?" He crossed the room until he was only a foot away from me. "And I thought you actually had some balls."

"Really? You think you can goad me with that stupid ploy?"

He just stood there smiling at me.

"Fine. Do it. But, this isn't because of your stupid goad."

He didn't say anything, he just opened up the drawer on the side table and pulled out a cell phone.

He stared straight at me as he spoke into it. "Can you swing by?"

***

I sat on the couch with my snifter of Maker's Mark whiskey, which I was starting to develop a taste for. We were waiting for a guy named Lars. Technically, just I was, since Fate had disappeared into the garage, probably doing some other secret stuff.

Lars. Even the name sounded shady to me. I repeated it in my head and I couldn't help but scowl. That had to be a bad sign.

Lars showed up at the back entrance, which I guess was to be expected, considering how this was supposed to be secret. Yeah, secret in the shadiest kind of ways.

He had waist length black hair, black eyes and tattoos all up and down his arms that crept onto his shoulders. I could see this because he only wore a tank top. He wore black pants and one of those chain key holder type things.

He was the same man I'd seen with Fate in my parking lot. If the information I got from Murphy was correct, *Well hello, mister ex-reaper.*

Anyone who thought death warmed over didn't look good had never seen this guy. I nodded in acknowledgment as we both sized each other up. He liked what he saw and wasn't shy about it.

I was a little more reserved myself. He was attractive but the past occupation was a bit off putting. Orgasms are hard on the heart already. An orgasm delivered by death just didn't seem like a good combination.

"Fate," I yelled, "your company is here."

Lars placed his bag on the table in between us. He sat down on the couch across from me as we continued to size each other up.

He obviously already knew who I was. I knew who he was too, and yet we both sat there saying nothing.

"Lars." Fate came and sat next to me on the couch and I wasn't sure why I found that comforting. Maybe I figured Fate didn't want me dead. I didn't know what this other guy was about.

"You say anything?" It was the second time I'd heard Lars's voice and it fit his appearance perfectly.

"No. I figured I'd let you do the honors," Fate said as his arm went around the back of the couch where I sat.

"It's always such a pleasure." Lars's attention swung back to me. "What I have to do isn't agency approved. It's a two-step process. I need to tattoo you. The tattoo will block the universe from picking up on the next order of business."

I looked at his arms now, covered in tattoos. "Is that what yours are for?"

"Not these," he said indicating his arms. "And I wouldn't ask any other questions, if I were you. I'm taking a risk with this, and pretty girl or not, I don't like risks."

I was used to people with secrets but that didn't make me comfortable trusting them. The bigger and badder the secret, the less I trusted. I knew Fate had his share and I thought this guy might have even more.

"You can't tell anyone about this. You understand, right?" Fate asked.

"Not even Ha—"

"Don't say any names. Not yet."

I didn't exactly like Harold, or have any desire to confide in him, but being told I couldn't tell him didn't feel exactly right, either.

I looked at the two of them, Lars and Fate. I could see why they'd be friends. This is who I'd thrown my lot in with? What did I even truly know about Fate? He worked for the same company I did, and that didn't inspire any confidence either when I thought about it.

Really, what did I even know about the company or Harold? I'd been going on the assumption that we were the good guys, keeping everything in line, but what if that wasn't the case? Or not completely, anyway?

At least I knew I'd helped that man. I knew I'd helped the woman, too. Whatever the rest of them did wasn't my problem. People always talk about how you die alone. They don't talk about the one benefit to this. When you do die alone, you've only got your sins to contend with. I only had to live with myself and I didn't feel bad about any of those choices.

The two of them were sitting there, waiting for some acknowledgement or acceptance.

"After the tattoo, if I want to stop, can I?" I asked Lars since he had the supply bag and I assumed he be doing the tattooing.

"Yes."

"Nothing we do will carry over, will it? To my next life I mean."

"This magic is strong, so there will be a residual left. But the only reminder you might have in your new life is a birthmark where the tattoo once was. You won't remember anything about it, though, and it won't leave any other residual effects."

If I wanted out, this was probably the best time, before I even dipped my toes in the water. I looked at Fate. I couldn't read him anymore. I didn't know why or what, but something about him just kept screwing with my antenna.

I'd have to base my decision on Lars. He wasn't trying to sell me on this, but the best sales people don't do the hard sell. Yet, he truly didn't appear to care—maybe a little but he wouldn't be upset if I declined. Just in the time it was taking for me to decide, he'd already started to get distracted by the TV, and he wasn't faking it.

"What does the tattoo part do? Can you tell me that?" I turned to Fate, thinking he'd be more likely to tell me than Lars.

"It's a shield, of sorts. Right now,

everything you do as part of the agency is relayed back. Essentially, right now you can't have a secret."

"Certain people know everything?"

I didn't think I was a bad person but we all have secrets and I wasn't immune. I wondered what else was in the fine print that I wasn't aware of. I opened my mouth to say more but Fate's fingers brushed my lips.

"It doesn't matter what you think but watch what you say." He moved his fingers away. "They can't pick up on me or what I'm saying and Lars shielded the house before he came in, but that doesn't mean some of it can't leak out. Names are especially bad."

Seriously? They could track everything I did? Case closed. "Somewhere hidden."

"It's got to be, anyway," Fate said.

"Where do you think?" Lars asked, returning his attention back to me.

"What about here?"

Fate pointed to a spot slightly inside my hipbone that would fall right below my bikini line.

"You good with that?" Lars asked.

"It'll work. How big will it be?"

"About two inches in diameter."

I nodded and he started digging through his bag.

"I'll clear off the table. You might want to throw on a pair of sweat pants."

"I don't have any here."

"Take a pair of mine. Top right drawer."

I went in Fate's room and was thankful of the moment of privacy to think out my decision alone for a second. Was I doing the right thing? I didn't even really know what it was I was doing? But if I didn't, and the killer went free, what was this all for? Would they ever get him? I needed this all to be for something: the death, watching my parents grieve, seeing Charlie. It couldn't just be for dumb luck and then I moved on. I had to make this count for something.

I pulled his large sweat pants on and rolled the top down several times and the ankles up. Not exactly a fashion plate, as I walked back out, but at least I wouldn't get blood on my clothes.

"Hop up," Lars said from his seat at the table.

I lay down and tugged the sweatpants a few inches lower on my hips.

"What is it going to look like, anyway?"

He held up a tattoo stencil of a ying-yang sign.

"Karma?" It was fitting. When I first started this, I'd hated the name, and despised the job, but I found it was growing on me a little. Not enough to want to stay on, but I didn't hate it anymore.

"It's what you are, so the symbol will yield the most protection," Lars explained.

Fate turned a chair around and sat on it backwards, resting his forearms on the back. "And also a dead giveaway. Remember that. Harold can't see this."

"Well, I guess it's a good thing I don't find Harold attractive and therefore have no intention of dropping my pants for him. Huh?"

Lars pressed the stencil onto my skin.

"You want to see it?"

"Nope. It won't be there long anyway."

"Then I'll get started."

I heard the buzzing before I felt the sting. The tattoo gun felt a little like getting stung but nothing as painful as I'd imagined.

"So, what comes next?" I asked.

Lars stopped tattooing just long enough to hold a finger to his lips.

Fate edged his chair down closer to my head from where he'd been watching the tattoo.

"We can't tell you until he's done," Fate spoke quietly by my side. "Nothing about this is a normal tattoo. The ink, the way he is applying it, everything is steeped in heavy magic."

I leaned my head against the pillow Fate had laid on the table for me, as I listened to a baseball game being played on the TV. My thoughts wandered, occasionally broken by the cheering for a score or by the irritation of Lars moving the tattoo gun over the same area repeatedly.

I felt a cloth wipe over my skin again and

then Lars leaned back, taking in his work.

"Done?"

"With the tattoo, yes."

Fate stood up and leaned over me, peering at Lars's work. His fingers grazed over my stomach and sent tingles through me, making me feel flushed like I had in the elevator earlier today.

I looked down and Lars's handy work. I wasn't a tattoo expert but it looked pretty good to me.

"Nice work."

"I own the tattoo shop, Dead Ink, over in Myrtle Beach, so I've had some practice," Lars said as he eyed his latest accomplishment.

"Well isn't that convenient." Dead Ink? Talk about hiding in plain sight. I imagined all the people going in and getting reaper tattoos. Wow, if they had any idea how close to death they really were, I bet they'd rethink the subject matter.

"Do I need to cover it?" I asked as I hopped down off the table.

"No. This one needs to breathe."

"So what's the deal? How do you two know each other?" Sometimes the best time to ask a question is when you already know the answer. And how honest are you going to be with me? Instinct, of which mine was usually dead on the mark, told me probably not that much.

Fate stepped back from where he'd been

peering out the back doors. "Even though the agency will tell you differently, there are certain humans that are aware of us. Lars is one of them."

Liar. Why am I not surprised? "So what comes next?"

Fate took the lead, as Lars continued to pack up his supplies but was still listening to every word said.

"Now, we lift the veil."

"What else is there?"

He took my discarded snifter of whiskey, topped it off and handed it to me.

Chapter Twenty-Four

I stared at my reflection above the bathroom sink while Fate and Lars waited for me in the living room.

Did I really want to make this choice? My tour guides were proving to be less than honest.

What if I saw something I couldn't live with? But, knowing I'd only be here for a little longer, could I really not do it? Forget about the murderer. This was a chance to see and know the secrets of the universe. Who could walk away from knowledge like that?

I looked at my reflection in the mirror. Not me. I'd been born asking questions. And it was only for a little longer. It wasn't even that much of a risk. I'd be reborn clueless of any of this.

I turned the water on and splashed a little on my face and took a deep breath. I walked into the living room, picked up the snifter I'd left on the table downed the last of it.

"I'm ready."

Lars nodded and reached for his bag and headed out the door.

"Where's he going?" I asked turning to Fate.

"Prepping the grounds so that no one will interrupt." Fate edged in closer to me. It was clear he wanted to say something but it took him a minute to get to it. "You sure you want to do this?"

"You're having second thoughts? This was your idea." I waited for him to respond. If he kept looking at me like he was now I was going to need another minute in the bathroom.

"You're leaving after your trial period, right?"

"Yes, yes, yes. Stop asking me the same questions over and over again." I knew I was being testy, but couldn't he lay off how much he wanted me to leave just for a little while? I still had intact feelings, after all.

"Okay." He walked over and held the back door open. "After you."

We walked out into the starry night. No one was on the beach for miles except for Lars. A black blanket spread out on the sand was surrounded at foot intervals with burning black candles. Black? I would've felt a bit better if they had been white.

Worse than the color, why wasn't the breeze coming off the ocean causing so much as a flicker in the flames? It should have been impossible to keep them lit, but they blazed straight up as if the wind didn't stir at all.

"Lie on the blanket, in the center," Lars said.

I moved into place and lay down, feeling increasingly like I was about to be sacrificed.

I didn't become apprehensive again until I saw the knife Lars handed Fate. It looked like it could have taken down a buffalo.

"I'll start the chant. You know what to do," Lars said.

"Can we use mine?" Fate asked.

Lars looked surprised by the question but then shook his head. "No."

Fate nodded and took the knife.

"What's that for?"

"Everything has a cost. If you want to see the universe, you need to be connected to it."

He pointed to a spot near my wrist. "Right here."

"I won't bleed out?" The spot he pointed to looked pretty close the main vein.

"You might feel woozy but you'll be okay."

"Did you do this?" I might have felt better with a smaller knife. Did they have to use one that looked like it could amputate my whole arm?

He held up his wrist, Lars who was also listening held up his.

I had agreed to this. I held out my arm and looked away.

I heard Lars start to speak in a language I didn't understand. It didn't matter; I couldn't focus on anything other than waiting for the feel of the knife sliding along my skin, anyway.

A spicy smell hit my nose that I thought might have been from the candles, except then the air started to feel thicker too. It started to feel like breathing in a sauna.

I felt the burn of the knife where it slid across my skin. It was deep and my blood was warm where it flowed over my skin.

"You might want to see this," Fate said.

I hadn't planned on looking at my blood flowing out but his words made me curious.

Fate had my wrist slightly raised and I saw the blood flowing out but it wasn't dropping onto the ground, it was dissolving into the air leaving trails of pink mist. Whatever this process was, it looked like it was in full swing now.

Lars, who had been circling the ring of candles, stopped and made a hand gesture toward the sky.

I looked around and at first I saw nothing different.

"There," Fate said and pointed to a spot on the horizon. It was dark so I wasn't sure what it was I was seeing at first, when a dark shadow showed over the ocean and disappeared quickly. Then it happened again and I watched more intently. It was like a seam had opened up in the middle of nowhere and a dark shadow appeared. The ocean swelled unusually large in that area and it looked like a riptide had been left in its wake.

Then I saw more of them. Little shadows in all different sizes. I stood and walked closer to the ocean. Maybe I should have been afraid, but instead I was mesmerized.

"You good?" Lars asked Fate from somewhere behind me.

"Yeah," Fate responded.

I felt Fate lift my arm and wrap the cut as I stood there, looking out. The shadows were everywhere.

He squeezed my hand to get my attention and nodded toward a couple walking down the beach towards us.

"Is it going to be like Maxwell?"

"Remember, I don't see things the way you do. But there's more. You're going to see the universe at work."

It was almost completely dark now so I couldn't see it as clearly as I would've in daylight. The man had a subtle glow to him but the woman appeared dull. As they came closer, I could see the atmosphere around them the way you see heat waves on a hot summer day. As they moved, the clear waves around them shifted with them.

Then some of the woman's dullness seemed to spread toward the man's chest, diminishing the brightness over the area of his heart.

"He'll die next week from a heart attack." Fate said from next to me.

"You saw that shadow creep toward his heart?"

"No, I saw his fate spreading out in front of him and it didn't go far. Before this, if it wasn't a job, you could only see people that had strong karma, in one direction or another. In my case, it was if they had a strong fate."

"And this?"

"This..." he said as a single older man walked along by himself, with an aura so bright against the night sky it made me want to squint, "is behind the curtain."

"What exactly am I seeing?"

"The very balance of everything in the world. It doesn't touch us, though. And whatever you do, you can't let on that you see it."

"Why is it so bad?"

"This, all of this, Lars, seeing the true forces at work, all against the rules."

"What would happen if someone found out?"

"I don't know."

I sank down into the sand and watched as people came and went. Some of them appeared normal. Those were the ones that must have been in balance. Then some were so much duller it was hard to make them out in the night. The bright ones were the prettiest to watch. Sometimes they'd shine so bright they'd make the sand sparkle at their feet.

Swirls of dark would appear here and there, adjusting a wave or causing an especially strong gust of wind.

"This happens everywhere?"

"Yes."

"And you think this will help us with Suit?"

"It's not going to hurt. The more you're plugged in, the stronger our leads should be."

Lars called out from the deck for Fate and he went in without me.

I sat on the sand and watched for hours. Shadows would appear and kick up the surf this way and that. At one point, I watched a woman walk down the beach, and her flip flop got stuck in the sand. Just as she was about to fall, a shadow appeared underneath her and she managed to find her balance.

Everything was being controlled and micromanaged. And instead of having fewer questions, I had more. Who was pulling the strings? Who had this kind of power?

I'd think God, but Harold had made it seem like God wasn't doing the daily lifting down here. So who or what controlled all this?

I didn't go in until I couldn't keep my eyes open a second longer.

Lars's bag was sitting on the table but the house was quiet. When I got to the bedroom, Fate was sprawled out, asleep. I couldn't fault him for not holding to the bargain, as it was almost two in the morning.

I tried to keep my eyes averted as they adjusted to the dark. This was much easier to do until he turned in his sleep and the blanket moved down to his waist displaying a well-built and very *tattooed* chest. Now I understood why he wore a shirt to the beach.

I climbed into bed and kept my face toward the wall.

Chapter Twenty-Five

I woke in a sweat and waited for the flashes of a job. They didn't come. But something was wrong. Maybe something they did to me had a bad after effect.

"Fate?"

He mumbled something I couldn't make out at all. It might have been *I'm sleeping* but could've also been *Go screw*.

"Something's wrong with me." I could feel my heart pumping quicker than normal among other things.

He sat up in bed, with all sorts of naked torso action going on. Even sitting leaned over as he was, there was just ribbed abdomen and my pulse beat a little quicker.

"You're sweating."

"I know. That's because something's wrong with me. I thought I already established that."

He laid a hand on my forehead. "You're warm."

"Ergo, the sweat." I watched as he dropped his hand and moved his beautifully masculine arm away from me.

He had the nicest skin, all smooth and tan except where the tattoos ripped across his shoulders. I didn't even know I liked tattoos until this very minute. I felt like I could stare at his chest for the rest of my life.

"You're looking at me like I'm hamburger meat and you haven't had a meal in a while."

"No I'm not," I turned my gaze quickly. I hadn't even realized he'd been assessing me as I stared.

"I knew you didn't look right." He got out of bed, and I was grateful to see he had on a pair of nylon shorts. But still, way too much flesh available to stare at. "Goddamn fucking Cupid!"

"Seriously? Are you sure?"

He came and stopped by my side of the bed. "How are you feeling? Little excited perhaps?"

I couldn't even answer. It was too mortifying. I covered my face in my hands and groaned.

"I'd ask you some other questions to confirm but I don't think it's necessary. This is one of his favorite hobbies."

And then I remembered Mother's obvious infatuation. What if it was permanent? "Is this going to go away?"

"It'll wear off in a day or so, depending on your system. I've got some stuff in the kitchen that'll help you sleep some of it off."

I bit my lower lip as I eyed him. I didn't even like him. He was volatile and raw, the complete opposite of what I went for. He was everything I would have steered clear of in my human days. One look at his face, a second's glance at his eyes, would shred any pretense of humanity. Getting close to him would be akin to jumping into a volcano. And yet, in this exact moment of time, I couldn't stop my desire to feel the burn I knew he could deliver.

I couldn't stop staring at him.

"I won't sleep with you. I could be that man—actually, I normally am that man. But not with you."

I had to stop staring at him. "I'm not asking you to." I should've let the subject drop but I couldn't stop myself from asking. "But since we are on the topic, what's wrong with me?"

"You're the relationship type and, no matter how much of the human we pry from your clinging hands, it cloys to you, just like the girlishness of your perfume and ruffled skirts. I don't need you looking all doe eyed at me in the morning."

"You are such an ass." I got up and walked out of the room. My shoulder connected with his arm as I pushed past him but it wasn't very satisfactory since it didn't budge him at all and I ended up bouncing a couple of steps off my path.

I walked into the kitchen, swearing revenge on Cupid and determined to find some sleeping pills myself.

I looked upward and then spoke in a hushed tone so Fate couldn't hear me from the other room, "Look at what you've done to me! I will never speak to you again after this."

"Need help?" I turned to see Lars coming up behind me in the kitchen. What, did no one wear a shirt anymore?

I looked upward. *This doesn't change anything.*

"I didn't realize you were still here." I turned, the counter at my back, as he came forward and leaned against the opposite counter. Could I really sleep with Death?

"Long commute." He grinned as his eyes made their way up from my bare feet, to my thighs before the hem of the long t-shirt I wore to sleep covered them.

Maybe I could give this a try.

His hand came to rest on the side of the counter I leaned against. I knew the type of help he was looking to offer and my eyes drifted to his lips. I couldn't deny I was tempted, but for some reason it felt like eating low fat frozen yogurt when I was craving ice cream.

Still, I didn't turn away when he leaned in a little closer. Frozen yogurt tasted better than nothing.

I knew if it wasn't for whatever Cupid did to me, I wouldn't be doing this, but I couldn't figure out the harm in it. I'd be reborn in less than two weeks from now. I'd forget all of this. It was like a free pass. Why not?

"What are you doing?" Fate asked from the entrance of the kitchen. He was clearly speaking to Lars, not me. Now there was the ice cream man, but he was closed for business.

Lars's hand dropped from beside me and the gap between us widened a couple inches. "I was seeing if Karma needed a little help."

"I've got it covered."

I could almost smell the male testosterone party going on, but I couldn't figure out where Fate had gotten an invite. Hadn't he just turned me down? Was a girl supposed to starve?

It couldn't be jealousy, after he'd so graciously explained how he wasn't interested. What was his deal?

"I didn't realize you were up." Lars now moved to the opposite counter, a few feet between us now. "I was just looking for a bite to eat. You said you weren't hungry."

"Well, now I am." Fate stepped deeper into the kitchen.

Lars put his hands up. "My mistake." I watched as he started backing out of the kitchen.

Was this a joke?

"Oh no!" I yelled and grabbed his arm. "What are you doing? He doesn't make this decision." I pointed a finger at Fate.

He smiled and then pulled away. Lars nodded to Fate and then disappeared up the stairs.

Fate rounded on me as soon as Lars was gone. "What do you think you're doing?"

"Really? This is almost as bad as when you

ask twice. It wasn't obvious?" And still no shirt. Although if I was a guy with his chest, I guess I wouldn't have been anxious to wear one either.

"He wouldn't have fixed the issue."

"Why do you say that?"

"Because that's not how Cupid works. There's always a target."

I wasn't going to argue. I knew he was right. I felt it standing next to him. It was a fight to just keep my hands to myself.

"He might have taken the edge off, though." I dry swallowed as he got closer and closer to me.

"If you're going to do something about it, at least do it with the person it was meant for."

His arm wrapped around my waist and lifted me to the counter. He stepped in between my thighs and the long t-shirt I'd worn to bed hitched up in the process.

"When Cupid plays his games, there's always an intended target." His eyes were on my mouth as he spoke, and then his lips grazed mine as he said his last words. "You weren't intended for Lars."

He might have acted disinterested before, but with his hips pressed to mine, I knew this wasn't just for me. My legs wrapped around him, trying to bring him closer to me. His hands tangled in my hair as his lips covered mine. I felt like I couldn't' breathe and I didn't care.

There was something dangerous about

going down this road with Fate. There was no control here, only pure sensation, and intense, soul consuming feeling.

His arm wrapped around my hips and pulled me snug to him. He was carrying me somewhere, but I didn't care as long as he went with me.

And then I was falling backward and he was following me down. His hard body moved over mine, pressing me into the bed and all I could do was moan with the exquisite feeling. I couldn't get close enough to him. I wanted to crawl inside of him and the way he gripped me back I knew he was feeling it too.

Nothing registered except need.

What little clothes we had on weren't even removed but shoved out of the way and then he was pressing into me. It felt like nothing I'd ever experienced before. I didn't know if this was because of Cupid's interference, or it would've been like this with him anyway.

And then we were both coming and I didn't want it to stop.

We sagged in exhaustion. I was still in shock over the intensity of what had just happened.

He was still in me, resting his weight on his arms. His lips were tailing along my collarbone when he paused his actions and whispered against my skin.

"You're still going back, right?"

He didn't ask in a, *I'm hoping you might stay now*, he asked in a, *you know this changes nothing* kind of way.

I closed my eyes trying to keep control. I hadn't expected anything from him, hadn't been looking for it, so why did that hurt so badly?

"Of course I am."

I wanted to pretend he hadn't said anything, but I couldn't. Hyped up on Cupid's stuff or not, my pride was stronger than any love potion.

I stared straight into his eyes. "Get off."

"What's wrong?"

"Nothing. I need to use the bathroom." I wanted to scream for him to get off me but I wouldn't. That would let him know he'd gotten to me.

Did I see regret there? It didn't matter. I was too mad to try and find reasons for his actions.

He didn't initially move and I needed to get away from him.

"You're heavy. Get off me." I'd loved his weight a few minutes ago. Now I felt suffocated.

He finally gave and I slid out from beneath him in my urgency to get away from him as soon as I had room.

"Where you going?" he asked as I headed toward the door.

"I already told you."

I swung by the kitchen and found the sleeping pills and then found a spare room to go crash.

Chapter Twenty-Six

When I didn't wake until three in the afternoon I wondered if I'd perhaps taken too many of those pills. After my night, I'd wanted nothing more than to pass out into oblivion.

My muscles ached as I pushed myself up out of the bed. I cringed when I thought about what had happened last night. I'd felt like a cat in heat but it seemed to be gone, now. I'd be having a talk with Cupid just as soon as I ran into him—across a long hallway where I could keep a good twenty feet distance between us. But when I did, he'd be getting a mouthful as long as he didn't try and approach me or get too close. A nasty letter might be better.

I didn't want to think about last night and I knew instinctively there couldn't be a repeat. I didn't want one. I couldn't believe I'd been so consumed by him and then all he'd worried about was me hanging around. I dragged myself from the bed in one of his spare rooms when I would've rather hidden under the covers all day.

My hand on the doorknob, I hesitated and leaned an ear in. It sounded quiet and it was pretty late. He must have left, not that it mattered or anything. I opened the door and stepped out just like I would have if he'd been home.

I walked into the kitchen and started

making coffee when I noticed movement on the deck. Fate, with his feet kicked up on the railing was reading the paper in the afternoon sun. I'd felt a lot braver when I'd thought I was alone. I'd faced down pissed off juries, been one on one with murderers, and that had been easier than walking out there on that deck. But I wasn't a wimp. Never had been and I wasn't going to be cowed by him.

His head turned; he nodded a silent hello and resumed reading. I grabbed some coffee and went out onto the deck like it was just another normal day in Weirdoville.

Except for the whole blood ritual last night and the fact that even now I could see the universe swirling its power through the glass doors.

Oh, forget it. My life was a train wreck. Who was I kidding? Hooking up with some guy was probably the most normal thing I've done in the last couple weeks. I should probably be embracing it.

I balanced my cup and then kicked the door shut with my toe on the edge. Grabbed the seat that wasn't so far away to make it obvious I was trying to keep a distance, but not too close either. Seat choices can get very sticky in these circumstances. I decided to avoid eye contact. If I didn't make eye contact, it would be hard for him to read the awkwardness, embarrassment, rejection and slew of other negative emotions I felt this morning.

I kicked up my feet on the railing and settled part of the paper in front of me as I sipped my coffee.

And then spat it out all over myself as I looked down at the beach and remembered the other important thing that happened last night. Everyone I saw was changed in some way.

They ran the entire gamut. Some of them glowed brilliantly, some had a slight pleasant shimmer. Then there were the duller people who looked like they were in the shade, even under the bright afternoon sun. Some of them looked just dull. Occasionally, they had the same cracks running along their skin like I'd seen on Maxwell. Then, thankfully, some people looked normal. I tried to focus on them.

"I guess you forgot that part of the evening?" Fate asked, his eyebrow slightly raised.

I ignored the insinuation. It didn't matter; I wasn't a desperado. Actually, when I thought about it, if it hadn't been for Cupid, I probably wouldn't have even done anything. I'd bet it wouldn't have been very good either. I'd given Fate too much credit. He probably wasn't even that good without the added Cupid effect.

The packaging was nice and I'd been hopped up on Cupid curses.

"Why did you sleep in the guest room last night?" He was looking down at his paper when he asked.

"You take up too much of the bed and I wanted to spread out for one night."

I turned back to the people strolling along the beach.

The shadows, the pockets of the universal forces, they were everywhere, kicking up sand in someone's face, to catching a child's kite up into the wind.

"You can't stare like that in public, not around our kind. It's a dead giveaway."

"I told you I'd be careful and I will be."

"You'd better be," he said and laid down his paper, clearly in some sort of snit.

"Where's Lars?" He deserved that, even if I had decided I didn't care that much.

"He left." His tone let me know I'd hit a bull's-eye.

"What is your problem? Did you sleep poorly?" I'd always functioned best when I was working offense, why stop now?

"I've just been waiting for you to get your ass out of bed is all." He got out of his seat and headed inside. "Be ready in an hour. We've got an appointment."

Chapter Twenty-Seven

An hour later and I was hanging on to the last drop of civility I had. Fate was on edge for no reason I could fathom. It's not like I'd been the one making sure I was going to get rid of him.

Then there was the enhanced karma exposure. I felt a little like a ping pong ball, with alternating waves of good and bad karmic energy coming at me from every different direction, and *he* was of no help.

He yanked me into the stairwell of the office building, where we had appointment number two with Maxwell.

"Pull it together."

"Don't you think I want to?" Ever since we'd left the house, I'd been bombarded by the energy of the people we'd come in contact with. I felt like I was on contact overload, my nerves rubbed raw by what they were putting out. And the why was even worse. When I got too close, I could sense exactly why their auras looked like they did. I was proud I was holding it together at all.

"You can't act like a freak when we walk into that office."

"You know, I've had just about enough of you today. No one's asking you for hand holding through this process, but if you could tone down the attitude that would go a long way."

"This is who I am. Did you think last night was going to change anything?"

I was doing my best to forget last night and he just kept bringing it back up. What was his issue!

"Actually, I think it might have done the impossible and made you worse. Trust me, I will not be looking for a repeat."

Cupid better stay clear of me for the rest of the time I was here. He was lucky I didn't barge in and start breaking arrows the way I was feeling right now.

"You go in there, pick up on whatever you can and then get out before he starts picking up on how weird you're acting."

"Not a problem." I waved my hand toward the stairwell door. Quicker we got on with this the better. When he didn't budge for a second I tapped a nonexistent watch on my wrist and said, "Time's a-ticking." It was the last official sendoff of my southern manners, but it got him moving. It wasn't a huge loss. My manners were never really worthy of the south, anyway.

We headed to the office and it turned out I didn't even need to sit down. I walked into the office, said I needed to use the rest room and walked right out. I was in a cold sweat by time I made it out to the parking lot and it still didn't feel far enough from the impact Maxwell's karma had.

I sat in the boiling hot car and didn't care. I hadn't even had enough time to grab the keys off of him before I ran out of there and I didn't want to risk coming into contact with anyone else the way I was feeling.

I heard Fate get in the car just as I was getting the bile in my stomach under control.

"What did you get?"

"Too much. Way too much. He's evil to the core." I wiped my forehead as I started to breathe a little easier.

"Details."

"Embezzlement, beats his wife, contemplating killing his partner...need I go on?"

He leaned forward in silence as he started up the car. I looked at Fate and it didn't make any sense.

"You don't get anything off of him?" I asked.

"No. I can't see his future."

The AC came blasting on and I angled a car vent to shoot straight in my face while I pondered what he didn't say. "You went through the same ritual as I did, right?"

"Yes."

There hadn't been a single person I'd come within fifty feet of that I hadn't picked up something from.

He's Fate. How could he not have picked up

on his future? And then it hit.

"He has no future. He's going to die soon."

Fate nodded.

"So Suit is going to get to him."

"Yes."

"I don't know what he wants from him, but it's not because he's a wonderful individual. That's for certain. He's killing him because he's bad. But why would Suit care?"

"Either Maxwell has done something that would mess up his goal, or... Could he be looking to recruit him? The way Harold recruits? However he became one of us, maybe he can make others like us. But why would it be so hard to kill him?"

We sat there in the parking lot, AC blowing in my face as I bounced my head against the seat headrest.

We sat in silence for a while, just thinking, then he finally spoke.

"I think I know. He's trying to do it under the radar."

"How?"

"Certain types of deaths don't register as quickly and take longer to process."

I instantly knew the type he meant. "Like mine. Sudden, traumatic and mass casualty."

"Yes. It would buy him just enough time to get in there. We should stay local, because whatever Suit is planning is going to happen soon."

"I agree."

***

I'd seen movies where the couple approaches the front desk at a hotel and then do the silent debate as they gaze into each other's eyes. A private communication happens as they both acknowledge their desire for one another. A soft smile, a loving look, maybe a handhold right before they declare themselves by asking for one room.

This wasn't one of those moments.

"We'd like one—"

"Two—"

"No, just—"

"We'll be right back." I grabbed his arm and dragged him to the other side of the lobby to pound this out in private.

"I'm on *full blast* so to speak on the karma front so there is no need for the coziness of one bedroom. I want separate rooms." I crossed my arms, jutted a foot out and concentrated on beaming the message through his stubborn brain on every level that I was unmovable on this topic.

"But you won't pick up on Bad Guy. The only way I can is from the residual traces of the part he played in your past life. One room."

"Suit will show up for Maxwell, so no, two rooms."

He countered my foot jut with a forward leaning hover. Phew, if he thought that was going to work, he had no idea who I was. He'd reached a place in my psyche no man had ever gone before. The place where I'd cut off my nose—not once but repeatedly—just to spite him, and not regret it at all. Even as I was sucking air through two holes where I used to have nostrils.

"I'm not going to stand here arguing over something this stupid. I get that you feel awkward after the other night but we work together and you'll have to get past it."

"I'm awkward? What about how miserable you are? Think maybe I need a break? Even if it's while I sleep? This has nothing to do with being uncomfortable."

"Liar."

"I am not a liar. Don't call me that."

"Then don't lie."

"I'm sorry your humongous ego can't handle the rejection," I said in a tone that made it clear was anything of the sort. "But, I'm going to have to insist on having my own room. That's final."

"Last chance." He spoke softly as he closed the small distance between us and his hand reached up and cupped my cheek. Oh no, he was switching tactics. I didn't like this one little bit, but it wouldn't work. All I had to do was remember his words right after we'd had sex.

He'd still been inside of me, hadn't even rolled off, before he started worrying about entanglements.

"Bring it on, big guy, we'll see who folds on this."

His hand moved lower and right before he hit my pressure point, I realized what he was doing but it was too late. I passed out thinking about what a huge jerk I'd slept with.

***

I woke up in the bed of the hotel room. I could hear him in the bathroom, doing whatever it was he did.

"You knocked me out?" I knew he had, but I found it so appalling I needed to hear confirmation from his lips.

"Had to," he yelled out over the sound of running water.

"I can't believe you did that." No shock in my voice now, just verbal condemnation.

He walked out of the bathroom, towel slung around his hips. His torso covered in tattoos.

"People don't do that. Not normal ones anyway. Only psychos and criminals." When he looked at me, I nodded as if to confirm that he fell in one of those columns, perhaps both.

"First off, why do you assume I would have been human?"

In spite of myself, I gaped. "What else

would you be?"

"So closed minded."

So many things clicked with that statement. Even for someone that hadn't ever taken a human shape, he was still too rough around the edges. Murphy, Luck, and most of the others in the office hadn't either, but somehow he'd always been different.

He walked over to the closet where things looked like they'd already been hung and pulled out a shirt and pants.

"Seriously, what are you?"

"I'll tell you right before you retire." He pushed some hangers around. "I picked up some things for you as well."

The gesture of him picking clothes out for me seemed oddly personal. It's strange how sometimes those things were more intimate than anything else.

"That thing you did in the lobby? You will not do that again."

"You're human morality is becoming so tedious."

"Even if I was never human, isn't that what I am anyway? Karma? Good, bad, right and wrong?"

He leaned over, two hands on the bed, bringing himself eye level with me. "What I did wasn't wrong, it was necessary." The muscles in his arms tensed as he pushed himself back up.

"How is that?"

"You were digging in for a fight. I wanted to take a shower. Necessary."

"And what I want?" It was such an arrogant statement and I was more than ready to take up that fight...until he dropped his towel.

"What are you doing!" I turned my head quickly. "Go in the bathroom!"

"We've slept together. What's the difference?"

And we weren't going to again. I didn't argue, just grabbed an outfit from the closet and went to take a shower, hoping he'd be dressed when I got out.

***

"I hate airport food. Couldn't we have at least eaten at one of the restaurants? I never thought I would say this, but I think I miss our office caterer." We were sitting in Terminal A at Orlando Airport and I was debating which part of this was worse—the food or having to wait for a plane we weren't even taking. "The bread's soggy. Can't they figure out a way for the bread to not get soggy?"

"They?"

"Yes. The powers that be that control airport food. Everything else gets a little push in one direction or another. Did the universe really decide to draw the line here?" I waved my soggy bread at him.

"I told you to wait."

"I'm hungry. You ate, remember?" He'd had a fine little feast while I'd hid in the shower until my fingers pruned.

"Next time, don't take an hour long shower."

"Next time, don't be an animal. How about that? You couldn't even save me a tiny bite?"

"I ordered you something."

"And then ate it!"

"It was getting cold because you wouldn't leave the bathroom." Elbows on the table, he leaned forward, daring me to disagree.

I rolled my eyes and then looked at the flight board. The plane should be taking off in forty-five minutes, but I still wasn't sure Maxwell was even going to show. Fate had been doing some normal human type digging and found out he had travel plans this afternoon.

I'd been more impressed before I'd found out that his detective work had really been flirting with Maxwell's secretary while I was *sleeping*. Then I was just annoyed. I wondered if he had plans on having sex with her too, and then asking if any of her plans had changed.

"Are you watching for him?" he asked from across the table.

"Nope."

"Why?"

"Because this soggy mess is bad enough without having to look at cracked open faces oozing pus."

"That bad?" His face scrunched up as he asked.

"Yes. And your face doesn't make it any better. Why, what do you see?"

"The people look the same, but they have trails in front and behind them. Sometimes the trails are very strong and some are translucent."

I'd just taken a rather large bite when he nudged me. "There."

I turned to see Maxwell walking through the airport on the way to the terminal. He looked worse than ever and I had a hard time swallowing back the bite of half chewed food. I forced it down with a swig from my water bottle.

"You couldn't have given me one more minute?" I stood and tossed my sandwich in the trash. So much for food.

"He can't get on that plane," Fate said as I sat back down. "If we lose track of Maxwell, we might never find Suit again."

"Are we on our own?" I looked upward.

"Are you asking me or are you trying to talk to the universe again?"

"I'll settle for anyone that will answer me."

Fate put his hands out as he lifted an ear upward. "Yeah, I'd say it's just us."

"How do you know he can't get on that plane?"

He was already standing and motioning for

me to get up as well. "We don't have time to discuss it right now. Just keep him off the plane. The attendant looks like she's about to call for boarding."

"How am I supposed to do that?"

"Any way you can. I'll go up and try to stall the attendant."

"But how?"

"It doesn't matter how. Just don't let him get on that plane."

I watched as he literally swaggered over to the attendant, a young pretty thing in her twenties. Maybe he'd sleep with her and ask if she was still going to get on the plane. I cringed as the thought entered my head. I pushed the thoughts from my brain. Being the *used, bitter girl* wasn't a good look.

I sashayed over to Maxwell. Or tried to, anyway. I'd never really practiced sashaying, there's not much use for it in the courtroom, so I tried to emulate Luck.

Maxwell's eyes lit with recognition as soon as he saw me, while I tried to hold down the soggy sandwich.

"Maxwell? I thought that was you!"

"How are you?" He stood and took my hand in greeting. It was hard to keep the smile on my face with the bad karma. It actually looked like he had pus dripping onto his dress shirt. How was it that only I could see this?

"Good!"

"How's everything going?" His eyes darted to my stomach briefly as he asked, a reminder of the pregnancy ruse last time we'd met.

"I lost it." I said it in a soft voice as if it was hard to speak of.

"Oh, I'm so sorry!"

"My husband and I split and the stress of it all..." I added a dramatic shrug, the kind that said I was disappointed but accepting.

"I understand."

"Were you heading out?"

"I was about to catch a flight to New York."

"Oh..." I tried to weigh that comment down with as much disappointment as I possibly could. I'd never been a natural flirter, so I wasn't sure if it was coming across as intended, or more like I had a sudden stomachache.

His lips were pressed together and his eyebrows pulled close in confusion. But I'd seen the way he'd looked at me when he thought I was alone. I could pull this off. A soft gesture would push him off the cliff.

"I was hoping you'd come back to my hotel and have a drink?"

His face lit up and I belatedly realized I'd touched down an F5 instead of the gentle breeze I'd been going for. It didn't matter. It had worked.

"Let me just go up to the counter."

I grabbed his arm. "No. Just call them. It'll be easier."

"But the counter is right there?"

I tugged on his arm. "I hate airports. I need to get out of here, right now."

He looked at me, and the way I was now clinging to his arm, and acquiesced.

He dug out his phone as we walked away from the terminal. I looked back to make sure Fate saw, but instead of looking happy, or even relieved, he looked a little pissed. Another reason we didn't make good partners. He was way too angry. I did what he wanted and he still wasn't happy.

Our hotel was across the street from the airport. We walked into the lobby, arm in arm, and I started steering us toward the bar. Maxwell steered us to the elevator. Maxwell won, for now. He tugged me into the elevator after him.

"What floor?" His hand hovered near the keyboard.

"Eight."

The button lit and he came and stood beside me, arm snaking around my waist. Between the look of his face, skin cracking and oozing and the smell he gave off, it was almost impossible to not pull back, let alone keep the smile on my face.

I was trying to remember why we were keeping this guy alive. Oh yeah, Suit wanted him dead. As I was choking on the scent of rotten eggs, I wasn't confident in that choice.

Would it be so bad if we let Suit have his way with him?

"What were you doing at the airport, anyway?"

"I've got family here. I just dropped my sister off."

"They let you in the terminal?"

"My cousin works security."

He nodded, buying my story.

The doors slid open and I walked as slow as I could toward mine and Fate's hotel room. I fumbled around in my purse.

"Oh no. I can't find my key. I must have lost it! We're going to have to go to the front desk." I looked up at him. Was he buying this? It looked like he was. I thought I was actually quite a bad actress, but I guess he must have really wanted to believe.

"Hang on." He walked away and I saw a man with a nameplate on further down the hall. What the hell! I'd had decent luck my entire life. Everything had gone smoothly right up until I died. Now? Nothing went right.

"I'm really not supposed to do this," the man said as he walked back over with Maxwell, his skin glowing even brighter in comparison to Maxwell's oozing. "But okay."

A minute later he was opening the door and wishing us a pleasant evening. Thanks, bozo. Good job. Glowing karma or not, I wanted to trip him down the stairs, right now.

I walked in the room and looked at the clock. Fifteen minutes of stalling and his plane would be gone. Fifteen *very long* minutes, as he stared at me like I was a rump roast and it was dinnertime.

Fate's things were here and there, but Maxwell didn't seem to care enough to ask about them. Really? You don't notice a guy's shirts hanging in the open closet?

"Come here," he said, patting the bed next to where he'd just taken a seat.

"Let me make you a drink first." I opened the mini bar. Long Island Iced teas had a lot of stuff in them. That should kill a whole whopping minute or so as I opened up all the mini bar bottles. I could probably "freshen up" for another five.

"That's not what I want." His hand snaked around my waist from behind and he pulled me into him. Never should've turned my back on him.

"What the hell is this?" We both turned to see Fate standing in the doorway. I was glad I knew it was an act or I might have been nervous, because he looked pretty damn pissed. He appeared exactly like the angry husband about to be cuckolded. Now *Fate* would make a good actor if he ever went human.

"You said you split!" Maxwell said, turning on me.

And you had no problem ignoring all the

male items in the room, you sniveling jerk.

"I lied." I threw my hands up in a bewildered way. "I hate to tell you in this uncomfortable fashion, but I'm a bit of a loosey goosey." I had a hard time not laughing at my own words. No one else seemed to find me as funny as I did though.

Maxwell was putting as much space between us as he could now, as he tried to circle around where the seething Fate stood, toward the door.

"I had no idea. She lied to me," he said to Fate in what sounded like his best fake indignation.

Am I the only lousy actor here?

"Get. Out." Fate said, his jaw tense and his veins pulsing.

Maxwell scrambled from the room and I didn't blame him. Fate was really putting on a great show, maybe a little thick for my tastes, but good nonetheless.

He even slammed the door after him.

"What about the plane? Can he still make it?" I asked as soon as we were alone.

"It left early."

"Any sign of Suit?"

"I've got it covered."

"What's wrong with you?"

"You don't follow directions well."

"You said keep him off the plane. I kept him off the plane."

"You bring him here, alone?" I watched him walk out, slamming the door, again.

"Jerk!" I screamed at the door. I gave him a ten-minute lead and made my way back to the airport. Time was running out to find the murderer before I would move on and I didn't have patience for his games.

I looked down into my purse to make sure I had the knife I'd packed. I wasn't leaving here without handling this situation. Fate could figure out another way to prove his conspiracy theory. I'd never had an interest in finding alien burial grounds, JFK's killer or any other such plots. Taking out the direct hand in my murder would suffice for me.

Chapter Twenty-Eight

I didn't know where Fate had gone after his arbitrary order. Guy seriously needed to lighten up a little. Still couldn't figure out what had gotten him all in a puff. He complained when I didn't do what he wanted; now he was going to complain when I did.

I was standing across from the entrance of the airport, stewing over why he was so irritable, when I saw the cops arrive. Too many cops and all with a purpose.

He can't get on that plane, Fate had said. I'd been so pissed off about my food I hadn't even thought about what that meant at the time. Only one thought sprang to mind, and unfortunately, I was afraid it was the most likely.

I crossed the street quickly, not caring about Suit at that minute. I entered the main airport lobby. There were screens everywhere, all with the same picture of a fiery mess.

I edged in closer to one of the TVs, trying to hear the details.

"It went down soon after it took flight without any kind of warning or distress signal," the newscaster said, the camera never budging from the scene.

"I told you to stay in the room," Fate said from beside me.

"You tell me a lot of things I don't listen to." I turned on him. "You knew."

"Not here."

He turned and walked out of the airport. I left as well, not having the stomach to watch anymore and wanting answers.

He was crossing the street when I caught up to him and yelled, "Admit you knew!"

He turned and stopped. "I don't remember denying it." He shrugged like it was no big deal and then turned and kept walking.

I followed after him. "Why didn't you try and stop it?"

"I couldn't," he said, stopping in the middle of the parking lot.

"Would you have if you could?"

"No." He was straight faced without an ounce of regret.

"Why? Aren't we supposed to be making this place better?"

"You're still thinking like a human. We aren't here to make it better, we're here to keep everything in line. There's a significant difference between the two."

"But Harold said I could—"

"Harold was giving you the company line. He said you could get your murderer too, knowing you wouldn't be able to do it on your own."

"I can't wait to get the hell out of this and away from all of you."

I caught the movement out of the corner of my eye. We had an audience. Suit was standing in the shadow of a van, watching our every move.

Fate moved closer to me and whispered softly, "Don't look at him. Just follow me back to the hotel."

"But we'll lose him."

"No, we won't."

"Do you have other skills I'm unaware of?"

"Not skills. Resources."

"If I follow you and we lose him—"

"We won't. But I'd love to know why he seems so interested in you." He closed the gap even more, "If you're lying to me, I will kill you."

He turned on his heel and took off toward the hotel.

I could stay here with Suit, who'd already killed me once, or follow Fate, who only threatened death. Really, it was a no brainer.

***

Dinner came and went, as we sat in the hotel room and watched the clock strike midnight.

I was sitting by the window, calling myself every kind of name in the book for relinquishing control, again.

"You said you had '*resources*.' Where are

they and why aren't they calling? Did they lose him?"

"They'll call once he sets down somewhere." A knock at the door signaled the room service he'd called in and I went back to staring out the window.

I wanted to do something but I had no idea where to even begin to find Suit. Why did I listen to him? Why? I was mad at him and furious at myself.

"Here. I got you a tea." He placed a filled teacup on the table next to me.

I eyed the peace offering. It wasn't nearly enough to take the edge off the anger I had at him for blowing it. But I *was* in the mood for tea.

He went back to one of the queen beds and leaned against the headboard, watching TV. Strike that, feigning interest in the TV. He was actually watching me. Why? What was I not seeing, here?

I eyed the cup of tea on the table and then slowly brought it to my lips. I'm a tea drinker. There isn't a blend that exists I haven't tried and I'd never tasted one like this.

I wanted to spit out the tiny sip immediately but I couldn't. He drugged my tea. Why? I didn't think it was lethal. He could've taken me out countless times before now, if that was his objective. That only left him wanting to keep me away from Suit.

That wasn't happening.

But what do I do now? I could feel his eyes on me from across the room. I couldn't tell him I knew. It would force a confrontation I'd lose. If I didn't drink it, it might *still* force a confrontation I'd lose. If I drank it, no immediate confrontation, but I'd definitely lose.

I did the only option I could think of. I chugged it back as quickly as I could then got up. "I'm going to take a shower. I still feel disgusting from being so close to Maxwell."

He nodded but didn't budge or seem alarmed.

I shut the bathroom door and turned the water on full blast. Luckily, there was a radio system in there, too. I turned that on for good measure. Now, to throw up.

That wasn't going to be easy since I don't throw up. I've got a pretty tough stomach that only the worst of flus can take down. I grabbed the toothbrush Fate had picked up for me, then poked and prodded my tonsils like it was a full time job.

Every minute counted but I finally emptied my stomach while I thought about how I was going to make Fate pay for whatever he was up to. And that was alarming. What was he doing?

I jumped in the shower to put on a good show and then walked back in the bedroom with my hair dripping wet, adorned in a comfy white terry robe. I didn't say anything as I lay down on the other bed and pretended to pass out.

He didn't waste much time.

"Camilla?" he said about ten minutes later.

When I didn't answer, I heard him get up and move around the room. The door opened and shut shortly after.

I jumped off the bed, pulled the robe that hid my clothes underneath off and ran out the door after him.

The elevators were to the right but I took the stairs to the roof. As long as he was walking, I'd be able to figure out what direction and follow him. If he was driving, I was screwed.

I saw him walk out of the front of the building...and get into a white SUV. I slammed my fist down onto the roof I was squatting on. Now what?

I could try and take off after him on foot but I wasn't sure that was going to do me much good. Even if I tried to steal a car, by time I figured out *how* to steal it, he'd be gone.

And then, gently sailing down from the sky, came a bright neon green slip of paper. It fell neatly to where it lay just beside my foot. On it, an address, and the color and make of a car.

I looked upward. "Dude, I'm sorry for all the lousy things I might have said about you or your people...your office. You know, let's not drag this out. You get the point."

I shoved the paper in my back pocket and

headed toward the parking lot.

***

I pulled up to a two-story building about twenty minutes south of the hotel. There wasn't a house or other structure in sight. I hadn't even seen a light, other than my headlights, for miles.

He wasn't alone. There were five other cars besides the white SUV parked at the side of the building.

I parked a good distance away and then I slowly crept up next to a window by the door.

It was pitch black out here—so as long as I stayed out of the light, I was pretty sure they couldn't see me.

Suit was sitting in a chair in the center of the barren warehouse. I wanted to punch my fist on the wall next to the window. Double-crossing jerk!

Fate stood dead center in front of him, with Lars to his right, and three other large men to his left. And not a single one of them showed any kind of aura. Was it possible one of the other three were human? Yes, but not likely. What the hell was going on here?

Fate walked toward the man until he was inches away from his face. I knew he was talking to him, even though I couldn't see his face or hear the words. He straightened up and walked away, then turned back lightning fast and punched the guy in the face. The man and the chair flew backwards together, blood already dripping down his face.

I took a step back and then caught myself. I needed to hear what was being said.

"If I tell you, I'm dead anyway," the man screamed loud enough that I could hear him through the pane of glass.

Fate didn't bother looking at him when he said the next words. "You'll wish it was him killing you if you don't tell me."

Lars stepped forward, grabbed the front of the guy's shirt in one hand and the chair in the other and dragged them both upright.

"What are you doing with them?" Fate asked Suit.

"You've got the wrong guy. I'm not what you think."

"You're exactly what I think. Don't play stupid. You know what I am."

Lars stepped back. "You want to kill him?"

"No. I want answers and I'll keep him in chains until I get them, if need be."

He wasn't going to kill him. The only thing I'd wanted. But I wasn't moving on until this guy was dead.

"So what do we do?" Lars asked.

"Work him over but keep. Him. Alive. I'll be back shortly. I've got to go handle something."

When Fate headed toward the door to leave,

I scrambled to hide around the corner.

Pressed against the wall, I tried not to even breathe until I heard his footsteps receding. When I didn't hear any at all, I started to wonder if he'd stayed inside.

Until he was right in front of me. I turned to dodge to my right and his hand slammed into the wall. I changed direction and the other one came slamming down.

Without any other option, I looked right at him. "I take it you'd like to talk?"

He didn't smile. "How are you here?"

"You mean at this locale or alive?" Considering he'd slipped something into my tea, it was a valid question.

"If I wanted you dead, you would be. How did you get here?" He moved in closer.

"I got a memo."

His eyes squinted as he tried to stare me down. "Why do you keep getting memos?"

"I guess the universe likes me better." This was definitely one of those moments I should be playing nice—he had something I wanted. And yet I couldn't. Sometimes I'm amazed I've made it this far in life without ever being punched in the face. If that never tipped me off to some sort of universal intervention, I guess nothing would've.

He took a step back and then turned his back on me, looked upward, and shook his head.

Aha! I wasn't the only one that tried to talk to the universe!

He finally turned back. "I don't get it, but if it wants you here, I can't stop you." He started walking toward the door and looked back at me. "Are you coming?"

I pushed off the wall and followed before he decided to change his mind again.

We stopped right outside the threshold, where we still had a view of the man. Lars was now leaning over him and looked like he'd done more than that from the swelling over Suit's left eye.

"This group," he pointed inside, "what's going on here, goes a lot deeper than a few tattoos and a couple of secrets. You walk in, and you are in. Do you understand what I mean?"

"For what? The little time I have left?"

"And what if, for some reason, you decide to stay?"

"I told you. I'm not staying."

He looked at me and I could see the hesitation there.

"Do you know something I don't?"

"No. I told you, I can't see our kind's fate."

"Then trust me when I tell you, I don't want this gig."

He grabbed me by the shoulders and pressed me against the side of the building by the door. "This isn't a game that if you lose you just move on. You join and betray us, you die. Not move on, you're just gone. Are you prepared for that?"

The intensity I felt from him was overwhelming, but I didn't have that much time left, anyway. Did it really matter? And I wanted Suit. I didn't care if I wouldn't remember after I moved on. He needed to die.

"Yes." He said I couldn't repeat the secrets. He said nothing about taking out the mass murderer before I left.

"So be it." He took a step back and then paused by the door, waiting for me to follow. We walked back into the room together.

They all looked at Fate and then me.

"Put him below," Fate said. There was a pause and then two of the guys left with Suit in tow, leaving Fate, Lars, another guy I didn't know, and I alone.

Lars spoke first. "Why is she here?"

"She got a memo."

I saw from their faces, they found it as strange as Fate had, perhaps even alarming.

But neither of them asked what a memo was.

"If you bring her in, you're the one that has to kill her. I've got enough blood on my hands." The one left who I didn't know said to Fate.

"I'll handle it, Cutty," Fate said.

"It's too late, anyway," Lars added. "She's already seen us here together. It's all or nothing, now."

"I have to agree," one of the returning men said.

The two guys came back from downstairs, while I was pondering my latest decision and Cutty was eyeing me up.

"I think we should skip introductions," one of the returning pair said.

"It's little late for me." Lars stepped closer. "We've already been introduced."

Cutty, the larger one with a shaved head, spoke. "So how much we telling her, then?"

Fate answered, "She already knows about Suit, and I'm guessing she's figured out that no one here is human."

They all looked at me. Even if I'd had my doubts, he'd just confirmed it anyway.

"I'm the only one still on the inside." He looked at me again with a stare that said *I hope you realize what you agreed to*. "About twenty years ago, Lars disappeared. A week or so after he went missing, he reached out to me. He'd always been into tattoos and he accidentally stumbled onto a way to drop off the grid completely. To Harold and the universe, it just appeared like he died. But as you can see, he didn't. No one here did.

"That man downstairs is like us, and I suspect is working with others like us, but none of us ever met him at the agency. We don't know how he came to be, what he's up to or who else he is involved with. The only thing we do know is he's actively recruiting."

The ramifications of more of us out there, playing with the outcomes of people's lives with no upper authority, chilled me. It robbed me of words. I wasn't sure I liked how things were running but at least there were parameters. We didn't know what type of capabilities these people had but the idea was unsettling.

Lars walked over and sat in the metal folding seat Suit had occupied. "I don't think she understands."

"She gets it," Fate said.

"How do you know there's more?"

"That part is a hunch."

"I want to talk to him." No one spoke or said anything. "If I'm in, I'm in."

Chapter Twenty-Nine

There was a storage basement below the ground level of the factory where they had Suit handcuffed and locked in a metal cage.

"What are you?" I asked as I approached him.

"Like I told them, I'm just an average Joe. I have no idea what you people are talking about," is what he said, but his stare was saying something altogether different. With his eyes, he was greeting me as a long lost friend.

I needed to get this guy alone. If I didn't and he talked, I might be the one that ended up dead. The looming gang of bandits hovering at my back could be deadly for both of us.

I motioned Fate over to the far end of the very long room.

"I want to talk to him alone."

"Why?"

"Because he's more likely to talk to me without you guys hovering, looking like you're going to strike him dead at any moment. I'm a single woman, I might be able to get him to let his guard down."

"No." He crossed his arms and it didn't look good but I'd known it would be a fight.

"Do you want to get this guy or not?"

"I *saw* the way he looked at you."

I started to swallow but I forced myself to

keep a calm demeanor. I imagined that Fate was an angry judge and I was in the courtroom trying a losing case.

"If you can read Suit that well, you know he won't talk. He'll die first. But he'll talk to me." Calm, keep your calm.

"Five minutes. And you tell me everything."

"Fine."

"And he stays in the cage."

I nodded.

He turned and ushered everyone out. They were disgruntled but they followed him up the stairs.

As soon as I heard the door close, I turned back to Suit. I got too close to the cage but I didn't want to chance anybody overhearing our conversation.

"Who are you? And before you answer, know that I'm your only shot at living, because if you haven't figured it out, there isn't a single person upstairs that doesn't have blood on their hands and none of them seem to mind." It was all lies, except for the blood on their hands, which might have been true.

It didn't bother me a bit, though. This was the person who robbed me of my life, and left my parents childless. He was better off being fed to the guys who just left than with me.

"If you want to live, you'll let me out." His voice was so low I barely heard it.

"And why is that?" I couldn't wait to hear his explanation.

"Because you belong with us, Camilla." His lips turned up just slightly at the corners.

"Were you always a bullshitter? Or did you put a lot of practice into this?" My words didn't match the hitch I felt in my throat. I needed to find out why he'd been stalking me before anyone else did.

"That train wreck? That was all for you."

He clearly wanted to tell me everything so I'd let him, but I had a sinking horrible feeling I wasn't going to be happy once I knew.

"Go ahead, let's hear the rest." I wished my feelings matched my bravado. Inside I was a panicked mess. What was this guy talking about?

"I know all about you, but you already know that, don't you? You remember me. I can see it in your eyes, you know something's wrong. And if you don't get me out of here, so will they." He glanced at the door and then back at me to make sure I knew exactly who he meant.

"You're off your rocker, buddy, because there's nothing to know about me."

"What about Edgar Radbury?"

I grabbed the cage bar in front of me as I remembered Edgar. He'd been one of the first cases that I'd really made a name as an up and comer with.

Edgar had been charged with assault with a deadly weapon. The case had been a slam-dunk. Edgar had been guilty as sin.

"I didn't do anything. I just tried his case. I did my job." Even as I spoke, I wasn't sure I believed it myself, not with what I knew now. I remembered the jury selection for his trial. I'd always been able to sense the people that I could twist to my needs. I knew the buttons to push, and even if it walked the line a bit, I always did it.

I thought back to Charlie. I'd done it with him. Somehow, molding his will to mine. He would've married me, even though he was in love with that other woman, simply because I'd wanted it and I would've somehow dragged him down the path with me.

"Edgar was your first, but wasn't your last. I wasn't trying to murder you, I was trying to recruit you. I wonder what your friends will think about that? Do you imagine they'll still be so welcoming?"

I was trained to stand in front of a jury and be prepared for whatever was thrown at me from the prosecution. I wasn't just good on my feet, I was fantastic. And here I was, mouth too dry to speak and a cold sweat breaking out on my forehead.

I wanted this man in the cage dead. I didn't want to help him escape but I didn't think I had a choice. Not if I wanted to make sure I lived as well. They'd already said they'd kill me if I leaked their secrets. What would happen if they thought I was being recruited?

I couldn't see a way out of this. If Suit talked, and they believed him, they might kill me. He would eventually; I didn't doubt the lengths Fate would go to for answers.

But if I got him out, maybe I could buy myself enough time. They'd be suspicious but it would be better than him telling them I was playing for the wrong team.

Unless I killed him.

I wanted him dead. I didn't know if I could take him, one on one, but what if I stalled and came back with a gun? Could I shoot him like this? He couldn't run. It would be shooting fish in a tank.

But he was slime!

Even still, he wasn't killing anyone. There was no one here to defend or protect. It would be cold-blooded murder, and I just didn't have it in me. Maybe if I hung around here for another century I'd be the kind of person who could, but that changed nothing for me right now.

"If I get you out, I want you to swear you'll never approach me again, in any life, from this point forward."

"Done."

I knew the keys to open the cage were down here. I'd seen Lars leave them on the hook across the room. They dangled there, like a beacon to escape.

I grabbed them before I could second-guess myself and let him out, cursing my weakness the whole time. I scanned the cement walls for some exit but I knew I wasn't going to find one. I'd have to cause a distraction upstairs so he could slip out.

And in that space of two seconds, when I turned my back on him, his arms looped over my head and he had his forearm pressed against my neck.

"What are you doing?"

"I can't leave you behind."

I had only one choice left, or the only one I maybe truly wanted. I grabbed the metal pen I had in my pocket. I'd grabbed it on my way out of the hotel because I'd thought I might need to make notes of what I saw. I felt for the point and fisted it in my hand. With surprising ease, I violently jerked my arm back.

I knew I'd hit my target. I didn't need to see the blood spurting in my peripheral vision to tell me. My aim had been uncanny. And unlike in my mortal life, I knew it wasn't just luck, anymore. Without seeing what I was doing, I'd managed to stab him in the jugular.

His wrists still handcuffed together, I was pulled back with him, knocking over a chair and clattering some other things with us. We fell to the floor, me lying on top of him, facing the ceiling.

"What are you getting me into?" I murmured out loud, having a funny feeling that it would be heard by my intended target, not the dying man below me.

I heard the rush of people running through the door, Fate in the lead.

He was on me before I had a chance to extricate myself.

"Are you okay?"

I was covered in Suit's blood and I wished at that moment I could claim an injury.

"I'm fine. It's his blood."

I crawled out of Suit's embrace and got to my feet. My victim was lying on the ground with a pen sticking out of his neck. I didn't need to be a defense attorney to know that this looked bad, *really* bad.

He wasn't moving, and his blood was oozing out, not spurting to the rhythm of a heart. He was definitely dead.

"She killed him," Cutty yelled.

He lunged for me but Fate stepped quickly between us, making a human shield between me and the men.

"Back off," Fate said.

"She screwed us!" Cutty was pointing in my direction. "She knew we needed him alive. There's something wrong with her. She let him out!"

All four men that faced in my direction had

varying degrees of distrust written on their faces.

"That's a gigantic leap, Cutty. She's not with them," Fate argued.

"How do we know?"

"This is a problem," Lars said, staring at me in a very unsettling way. I would have put him at the lower end of the distrust scale a minute ago.

"Clean this up and get rid of him. I'll handle her," Fate said. He pushed me in front of him, always maintaining a buffer between me and the guys.

I hustled up the stairs quickly, happily putting distance between me and the men down there. I knew a lost cause when I saw one, and they all looked like they wanted to kill me, and not like "let's ponder the thought and get around to it next week," but "rip my limbs off and use my bones for some broth."

I didn't have a guarantee that Fate didn't want the same thing, but "handle her" didn't sound anything like "kill her." I could be grasping at semantics, but Fate was my best bet, right now.

He pushed me toward the door, another good sign. If he wanted to kill me, he'd probably do it here. And he'd defended me. I didn't know what to even think of that.

I took a shot and decided to head toward the car I'd stashed further back, but he grabbed my arm and pushed me toward his. I didn't argue or fight. It was time to do damage control. Keep everything calm until I was out of this situation.

He grabbed a towel from his trunk and laid it on the passenger seat, obviously looking to avoid the blood stains.

"I guess you have this problem regularly?" The words slipped out before I thought better of it.

"Get in."

I shut up. This wasn't about playing nice, I was in pure self preservation mode. I'd messed up badly and I knew it.

"What happened?" he asked after he started driving.

"I was trying to get answers. I wanted him to think I was on his side and I was going to get him out so he'd talk. Then he attacked me."

"You know that story is ridiculous." He shot me a look that dared me to deny it.

"It's what happened." I mean he did dare me, everyone has their limits. Plus, I certainly wasn't going to come clean. I couldn't. He had towels in the back of the car for sopping up blood and I wasn't sure how much the universe liked me. Was it I'm head over heels for you, or more of a passing fancy without any real commitment? Did I want to find out while Fate was choking the life from me that the universe had found a new favorite?

I could just imagine trying to explain to

Fate how I, someone whose position is supposed to handle karma, had saved criminals that would've been sent to jail so that I could build a name for myself. It seemed so much worse now but it hadn't then. I'd never really thought it was me. Yeah, I knew I could be convincing, but I didn't realize I'd been actually swaying them beyond what was natural. Hell, I still didn't know how I'd even done it, exactly.

I used to think as a judge, I would make a difference and it would all be worth it. I'd rationalized it away, right up until Suit had just tried to recruit me. What kind of monster was I that a mass murderer wanted me on his team? I was in the ranks of someone like Maxwell? If I were human, what would I have looked like? I lifted a hand to my skin, as if I could feel the pus already.

"Do you know how long I've been trying to get a lead on this guy?" He punched the dashboard of the SUV. I'd never seen him this upset.

I shivered and he probably thought it had something to do with him. It didn't. I shrugged off the image of my face covered in cracks, at least for now. I couldn't change or fix what I'd become if I didn't make it out of this predicament.

"From the moment you showed up, you've been nothing but a walking disaster. Cutty is right, there's something wrong here. And then

I'm forced to defend you when I know it too."

"I'm sorry but threatening to kill someone doesn't inspire confidence." But the more he talked, the more I realized he never would've done it.

"You take nothing seriously, but *that* you decide to listen to. How many times have you heard someone say that?"

"You said it with a very scary tone."

"You think this is funny? That it's a joke you thought I'd kill you?"

I could see how much it insulted him. I didn't know what to say and the way he was looking at me made me feel like a worm, squirming around. How could I explain that, for some reason I didn't get, I went stupid around him? I missed cues. That I knew it wasn't funny but I didn't know how to take it back?

He pulled up to the front of our hotel but didn't shut off the car.

"I don't get you. I don't understand why everything doesn't work right where you're concerned. I don't want to know. Just get your ass to Harold's office and leave when your date is up." He leaned over me and pushed the car door open. "Now get out." He sat back and looked away from me.

"I'm covered in blood? I can't walk through the hotel lobby like this."

"You'll get by, somehow, I'm sure."

I grabbed the towel with me and watched as

he sped off. Not the best way to leave things but I *would* be leaving. My murderer was dead. There wouldn't be any heartfelt goodbyes, but I wouldn't remember any of this. I was glad.

Chapter Thirty

At three P.M. today, I would walk into Harold's office and, as he had described it, reenter the system. I would remember nothing of this time after I was reborn.

There was no way I'd miss this meeting, so I was going to head in at one P.M. and sit there, waiting. I grabbed the keys to the Honda and headed out.

I walked out my front door and almost instantaneously, the guards appeared in front of me and a doorway to a cinder block room opened up.

I pulled back just in time to avoid stepping through it but wasn't prepared for the push at my back.

I stumbled through into a room with no doors.

And, for the first time since I'd entered this crazy new reality, no one needed to explain a thing. I knew with an undeniable clarity what had just happened.

Someone had just screwed me over.

I sat with my back against the cinder block wall as I stared at my phone that had service. I'd called the door guard number several times, even though I knew it was hopeless.

The only thing that didn't make sense was who. Harold wanted me gone. Fate had wanted me gone before I'd even joined. The guy trying to recruit me was dead but perhaps someone he worked with? No. I couldn't get the guards on the phone. It had to be someone directly involved with the agency, but why would they want to keep me? It just didn't make sense. Everyone with a say wanted me gone.

I looked down at my phone. Four o'clock. My window had officially closed. I'd be here for another thousand years, minus one moth served. I felt beaten down and defeated. It was an altogether new experience for me, and one I never wanted to feel again.

I wanted to cry. I should've, but the tears simply didn't come. Maybe I'd shed too many already. Was it possible to run out? That's how I felt. Hollow, like there was nothing left to give.

Finally, in the middle of my small cubicle, the door appeared. I grabbed my purse and my phone as I slowly stood. I looked at both the guards.

"Why?"

They hung their heads and then the one on the right uttered a single name. "Paddy."

I walked out to my condo, leaving the cinder block room and small chunk of the humanity I had left with it.

***

I walked into the office like I was now doomed to do for countless years to come. The sole purpose of my existence in the world was now to dole out death and pain.

I was hardly in a partying mood when I saw the cake with the words "Welcome to the Club" scrawled across it, but I tried to smile for the people who were at least trying to attempt to embrace me. It was a little late but I'd take hold of the olive branch with both hands.

Even Harold was there, not exactly smiling but I'd learned that was a rare occurrence.

"So you're officially one of us!" Murphy said handing me a slice of cake.

"We're going to be besties," Luck said, as she came to stand on my other side. "I'm so glad you're staying. Kitty just really wasn't very good female companionship. First thing we're doing Monday is going to Nordstrom's, my treat."

"Do you get raises?" I asked, knowing I'd never be able to shop there on what I was getting.

"No, Harold's a real cheapo. You just forgot who you're talking to. Couple trips to Vegas with me and we'll have you fixed up real good."

"Oh." At least I wouldn't have to live on hot dogs forever.

Somebody turned the radio on and jacked the volume all the way up on *One Headlight* by *The Wallflowers,* while Crow handed out glasses of heavily spiked punch.

And then Fate was there. All conversation stopped making the radio seem especially loud. Kitty tried to hand him a piece of cake, but he declined without saying a word. His eyes scanned the room until they settled on me.

He didn't come closer or say anything.

Just stared at me for a moment while I stared back. No one spoke.

Finally, after the moment stretched on past uncomfortable to almost unbearable, he shook his head and walked out.

"What's his problem? Who does that?" I heard one of the Jinxes say, after Fate was well out of hearing.

"Someone pour shots!" Luck called from behind my left shoulder. "We need to get this party going."

Everyone resumed eating but the mood had been lost. I stayed until the little party died out and then I walked out to my Honda and faced the reality of my future.

"Wait up!"

I turned to see Luck running out towards me. "Where you going?"

"The cond...home."

"No, not tonight." She hooked an arm in mine and pulled out her phone and called up a door. "So far you've only seen the bad side of this gig. You and Fate aren't the only ones that overlap. I think it's time to see some of the perks."

The doors sparkled in front of us, a casino visible on the other side. She tugged me through with her.

The minute we hit the floor, I heard the slot machines pick up their pace.

"Some of my favorites are here tonight, over by the craps table. When we get there, you focus on the people with good karma." She tugged me along with her. I realized that we had become visible to the crowd.

"I can help them win?"

"Oh darling, you have no idea what you can help them do, yet. But it's not all about them tonight."

She dug out a $1000 chip from her bra.

"What do I do with this?"

"Seed money. Don't worry, you can't lose today."

A little cheer went up from a group of three guys at the end of the table. "There's my lady luck!" one of the guys screamed.

"They don't know I'm actually her. They think I work in P.R.," she whispered as we walked over.

"How do you know who to help win?"

"Me? I just help whomever I like. And I really like them." She was staring at her little group of men. "Hi, boys! I want you to meet a friend of mine. She just loves to shoot dice."

An hour later, we were on our third bottle

of Crystal, I had a stack of chips in front of me that I couldn't even keep count of and the casino floor was on fire. Every time I touched the dice, I rolled the point of someone with good karma at the table. Every time Luck rolled, she hit one of my numbers. It got to the point that the table only had us two rolling the dice and the people were two deep trying to get bets in.

The laughter was loud, and the spirits were high. Annie, a single mother of two who'd been dragged here on her birthday by her sister, won enough to put both her kids through college. Al, newly retired and here with his wife, won enough to buy their dream house. It would go down as one of the best days of their lives.

And me? I realized that, just maybe, this wasn't the worst position in the world to be stuck in.

Chapter Thirty-One

I placed a fern in my carriage. A potted plant might not seem like much but it was a big step. It meant I was staying. It would be the first mark of me in the condo that had, up until now, been a short-term situation.

Kitty had offered me one of her kittens. Apparently, they weren't all naturally cut out for the work. I'd declined. I was having a hard enough time with a plant.

"You might be better off with a Jade. They don't need to be watered as much."

I turned to see Paddy holding out one to me in the middle of the garden center.

I turned, making it obvious I wasn't interested in conversing with him.

"The guards are normally so good about secrets. That whole non-talking thing usually makes them perfect co-conspirators but they like you. I get it. I like you, too." His face scrunched in thought for a second. "Or it might have been the compound. No one has ever given them a gift before."

I was torn between being too furious to speak to him and wanting to beat him in between the ferns and the hostas. As much as I hated the idea of even acknowledging his existence, I'd never been good about walking away from answers.

"If you like me so much, then why did you do that? Why get me stuck here when you knew I wanted to leave?"

"Because I might need you."

"With *recruiting*?"

"Okay, I'm not exactly a recruiter."

"After what you did, do you really think I'd help you? I don't even know who you are."

"If it helps, I didn't do it just for me."

"You certainly didn't do what I wanted."

"No, and you should be grateful for that. What you want usually turns into a mess, anyway."

"You don't know that."

"I've seen you do it enough. What you've got is a curse and a blessing."

"What do you mean?"

"You're immune to the forces more than anyone I've ever seen. Each life you've led it's gotten worse. We try and steer you left and you dig in and go right. Over and over again, fighting your path. Wrong career, *always* the wrong guy. I mean, I'm not saying you have to nail it exactly and get your soul mate in the first few go-arounds, but you pick the worst men for yourself. Then you screw them up too in the process, because even if they aren't supposed to be with you, your sheer force of will railroads over them until they agree with you."

"Maybe I botched my relationship but you can't say I wasn't a brilliant lawyer."

"Yes I can. Half the cases you won were supposed to lose. You only won them because this thing you have, this force.

"I used to curse you for it. It took a while, but I eventually started to admire it, a bit. Now it looks like I'm going to need it."

"If you wanted help, you should've asked. Not tried to force it from me."

"I couldn't take the chance. I need you where you are."

"I don't care what you need. You're on you're own."

"You'll come around. You're going to have to."

"Paddy, what the hell are you talking about?"

I turned around, ready to demand answers but he was gone. I didn't know who Paddy was, and I decided I didn't care. Not today. Today was about owning my situation and making the best of things. I checked out and didn't notice I had a Jade plant until I got home.

Chapter Thirty-Two

A week had gone by since I'd become official. To be honest, it wasn't that bad. I was starting to find my place in the building. The Jinxes were teaching me to skateboard in the parking lot, Murphy brought me a fresh newspaper in with him every day. Even Harold was giving me fewer dirty looks—or maybe I was just getting used to them. It didn't matter. I was realizing I could do this.

Luck had been the biggest help. Ever since the night in Vegas, I'd realized this job wasn't going to be all death and torture. I could make people happy.

I also realized quickly that whether or not I was ready for a new best friend wasn't going to matter. *She* was ready, and she was tenacious.

But ever since the party, we'd found common ground and I really did enjoy her company. She was out there, did what made her happy and didn't care what anyone else thought. In my opinion, she was fantastic.

So there I was, out with Luck that Thursday night. We'd just finished dinner, mostly filled with chats about her current boyfriends—she had quite a few—when her eyes shot to the door. "Uh oh," she said.

"What?"

"Fate is here and heading straight toward

our table."

"He's here?" I hadn't seen him since the party and I knew it wasn't an accident. The time before that had been when he'd dropped me off at the hotel covered in blood. At this point, Fate and I were like a tricky tray of unresolved issues.

"What are you doing?" I asked as I watched Luck grab her purse.

"Did you see his face? He's talking to you and there's nothing I can do."

"So you're just abandoning me?"

Fate was at our table before she could reply.

"I've got to head out to Vegas." She made her eyes big when she had her back to Fate, clearly sending a signal, *this should be fun.* "See you in a couple of days," she said and left.

He stood there for a minute and we both apprised the other. Fate still hadn't said a word and he took Luck's chair. He stared across the table at me and I matched it. I thought not seeing him would help me, but it seemed to have only increased my awareness of him.

"You said you were leaving. You lied."

"I didn't lie. I had every intention of doing so." I sipped from my half empty martini glass.

"It's not over."

"I got my killer. I wish you and your companions luck but, for me, it's over."

"It's too late. You know too much."

"Which I have no intention of repeating."

He smiled as he stood to leave and I thought the matter was settled. But instead of walking out, he came closer and leaned down next to my chair, his mouth near my ear. "You can't escape your fate."

He stood, turned and walked from the room.

Visit me on the web at
www.Donnaaugustine.com.

Sneak Peek at book two of *Karma Series*.

A glass of red wine was placed in front of me and I turned to the bartender.

"I didn't order this."

"It was sent by that gentleman." He pointed to a man sitting at the other end of bar.

"Please thank him." I wasn't going to drink it but sometimes a simple thank you was the easiest out.

My aversion to having to speak to anyone tonight spurred my energy and I grabbed my purse from the seat next me to leave. By time I looked back up, he was standing there next to me.

He was in his late forties and, in a Clooney kind of way, aged to perfection. Everything about him was well manicured, like he had all the time and money in the world. He was the type of guy that wouldn't have noticed me when I was human.

I still didn't want to talk to him.

"Just a moment?" he asked, not even waiting for my reply before sitting. His impeccable manners encouraged my own.

"Of course." I settled in my chair as I tried to get a read on him. I couldn't figure out if he was human or if his karma was in perfect balance.

He pulled out the stool and settled in with more elegance than should have been possible.

Who was this guy? I hadn't met anyone in the building who looked like him but I knew there were still others that I hadn't seen yet.

"I'd like to offer you a job."

Hands in front of him, fingers knit, he waited for my reply.

"I'm already employed but thank you." He didn't even know who I was. He could at least ask a few questions before using a line like that to make it a bit more believable.

"Yes, Camilla, I know you do. And you could be so much more."

KARMA

Made in the USA
Middletown, DE
08 March 2018